THE
SEVENTH SENSE

THE
SEVENTH SENSE

T.J. MacGregor

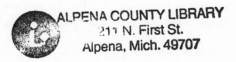

Kensington Books
http://www.kensingtonbooks.com

KENSINGTON BOOKS are published by

Kensington Publishing Corp.
850 Third Avenue
New York, NY 10022

Library of Congress Card Catalog Number: 98-067616
ISBN 1-57566-411-9

First Printing: May, 1999
10 9 8 7 6 5 4 3 2 1

Printed in the United States of America

For Rob & Megan, again & always;
and for Al Zuckerman & Kate Duffy,
for making all things possible.

THANKS TO:

Ambrose Soler, MD, for the zebra story;
Renie Wiley, for sharing the story of her NDE way back when;
and Mom and Dad, for being here.

PART ONE

•

Blood Whispers Miami

"I have been and still am a seeker,
but I have ceased to question stars and books;
I have begun to listen to the teachings
my blood whispers to me."
—Herman Hesse, *Demian*

I

Frank Benedict

Saturday, May 24
12:02 A.M.

(1)

The BMW's windshield had fogged up again, reducing the traffic on I-95 to a long, glistening red snake of taillights. Frank Benedict rubbed his palm in quick, angry circles against the glass, clearing a small area through which he could see the road.

Stupid drivers ought to be in bed, he thought, and tipped the flask to his mouth. The scotch burned a sapid path down his gullet and ignited in the pit of his stomach. But it didn't even touch his pounding headache. He reached into the glove compartment, helped himself to a couple of Tylenol, and washed them down with another swig from the flask.

He would need more than Tylenol by the time he got home. This headache had all the hallmarks of a killer migraine, one of those crippling suckers that would lay him up all day tomorrow, forcing him to cower in the darkness of the bedroom, the pain like the crushing force of excess gravity. He blamed that bastard MacLean.

He'd spent the last eight months courting Jerome MacLean—gourmet dinners, concerts, art exhibits, deep sea fishing, all of the old man's passions. He'd visited MacLean's hotels in the Caribbean, in South America, in the U.S. He and his family had attended MacLean family barbecues, weddings, and christenings. He'd endured more bullshit in the past eight months than he had in his entire eighteen years as an attorney.

Tonight it should have paid off. He should have been celebrating the six to eight million bucks of business a year that MacLean would bring to the firm and the new continent of contacts that would spell potential millions in additional business. Tonight he should have been celebrating the deal that would seal the partnership at Thacker and Tillis that he'd coveted for the last decade.

Instead, MacLean had told him he still hadn't made up his mind. *I need a few more weeks to decide, Frank.*

What the hell was there to decide, for Christ's sakes? No one, Benedict thought, could handle MacLean's affairs better than he could. No one.

I'm not entirely convinced that Thacker and Tillis is right for MacLean Enterprises.

Benedict could still hear MacLean's low, gruff voice as he said this, his sterling silver fork scraping against his antique China plate. They'd been sitting at the long oak table in the dining room of his Palm Beach home, where the east windows looked out over the ocean. Maids had appeared and vanished, part of the contingency of servants who kept his fifteen-thousand-square-foot home running as smoothly as his hotel empire. Now and then, ringing phones had echoed through the cavernous rooms, urgent messages that some well-paid assistant in another wing had taken.

In the moments after MacLean had made his pronouncement, every noise in the house had seemed grotesquely amplified, mocking the silence between them. Benedict had felt blood rush into his face, had felt rage shrieking inside him, and fought an impulse to tell the old man to go fuck himself.

Instead, his fingers had tightened around his wineglass, and he'd forced himself to raise it, to sip from it, as if he were mulling everything over. And when he had conquered his impulse, he asked MacLean what reservations he had. He tried not to sound desperate, tried not to let on that his entire legal career from that point onward rested on MacLean hiring Thacker and Tillis to represent his worldwide interests.

MacLean had replied that he needed a firm with more expertise in international law and admitted that he'd been talking to several other firms, but didn't name them. Benedict had started ticking off every statistic that had sprung into his mind about the firm's international division. But within sixty seconds, MacLean's eyes had glazed over and Benedict shut up.

Give me three weeks, Frank, four at the most.

Like he had a choice.

"Fucker." The word hissed out and he slammed his fist against the steering wheel.

His wife, home tonight with their sick six-year-old son, was expecting good news, the kind of news that would mean a private school for Joey, Christmas in the Greek isles, where MacLean had two hotels, a trip next spring to Peru and Brazil, updated cars. She wasn't prepared to hear about more late nights at work and more weekends sacrificed to MacLean's dangling carrots. She'd been living with that shit for the past eight months.

But she hadn't been living it the way he had, working his ass off seventy hours a week, his life jammed so far in fast-forward that he barely had time to brush his teeth in the morning or to kiss his son good-bye. For MacLean, this was just another potential deal; for Benedict, it had been a war that he was determined to win.

He dreaded going into work Monday morning and telling Colin Thacker that MacLean still hadn't made up his mind. Thacker would click his fat little tongue against his Pepsodent teeth and tell Benedict that one way or another he would just have to convince the old man otherwise. Then he would dangle the pending partnership, one more gold-plated carrot in a string of goddamn carrots. *Sign MacLean up or forget the partnership, Frankie.* Bottom line.

He slapped his palm against the windshield again, irritated that the defroster didn't work, that he hadn't had time to get it fixed. He hadn't had time to do anything. The garage needed cleaning, his sloop needed cleaning, his attic needed cleaning. The beast called chaos stood just around the next bend, waiting for him.

But MacLean didn't give a damn about that. He didn't care what these months had cost Benedict. He didn't care that Benedict would be forty-five in August, the same age his old man had been when he'd dropped dead of a heart attack. He didn't care what this deal would mean to Benedict.

He swerved into the right lane and sped down the interstate ramp, MacLean's voice whispering in his ear. *Give me three weeks, Frank. . . .* Ha. Three weeks, three months, what the hell difference did it make? Benedict knew a kiss-off when he heard it, and tonight had been a boot right out the door.

His headlights burned against the line of pines that embraced the curve. The front tires skidded on the wet pavement. *Thacker and Tillis is weak in international law, Frank.* What he'd meant was that Benedict himself was weak in that area. . . . *Not entirely convinced that Thacker and Tillis is right for MacLean International.* Translated: MacLean wasn't convinced that Benedict was right.

"Fucker," he spat out again, and leaned into the steering wheel as the Beamer sped into the steep downward slope to the main road.

The surreal glow of sodium vapor lights spread across the windshield like tinted varnish. He barely noticed. His head pounded fiercely now, pounded with MacLean's voice, his words, his *kiss-off,* pounded with all that he might have had, a future MacLean had jerked away from him.

You can't do this to me, cocksucker. No one does this to Frank Benedict. . . .

He ran the yellow light at the foot of the incline, hands gripping the wheel, teeth clenched against the seething rage that now filled him like some toxic gas. He shot out onto the deserted neighborhood road, his head hammering, MacLean's breath like August heat against his ear, his rage riding him, his mouth filling with a hot, metallic taste.

A dark car, a Cherokee or an Explorer, he couldn't tell which in this rain, suddenly appeared in his path, *in his way.* He brought his fist down hard against the horn. But the driver—*like MacLean*—didn't see him. He was invisible to MacLean. He was an ant the prick squashed under the heel of his shoe, he was nothing, no one, a fat zero.

Benedict jammed the accelerator to the floor and shot straight toward the car—an Explorer, he could see it now—and rammed it broadside. The impact threw him forward, his seat belt snapped him back. The Explorer spun in broad, erratic circles across the road and slammed up over the curb. The Beamer skidded, shuddering like an epileptic in the midst of a seizure. The engine rattled but didn't die on him.

"Get out of my way, asshole," Benedict shouted, and jerked the gearshift into reverse.

He sped backward through the rain, across the road, the rear end fishtailing on the wet asphalt, and rammed into the car again. Then he sped forward, whipped into a turn, and revved up the engine, rage pounding so loudly in his skull that he barely heard the Beamer's clatter and wheezes, its loose nuts and bolts.

"And stay out of my way," he hissed, hand tightening on the gearshift, ready to pop it into first.

Then the Explorer's passenger door swung open and a woman stumbled out, a large woman. She seemed to sway, a human tree in a high wind, her arms pinwheeling for balance as she fell back into the cushion of darkness. She crumpled to the ground and didn't get up.

Benedict blinked, rubbed his eyes, blinked again, and something happened inside him, he heard it, the noise a screen door makes when it slams open in the dead of night. "Jesus God," he whispered, and threw open his door and got out.

The wind blew rain in his face and flapped at the legs of his slacks. He saw a large dog scramble out of the Explorer, limp over to the woman, nudge her. The dog trotted around her body, then hobbled off, howling, into the rain. The blare of the Explorer's horn pierced his awareness, and he looked wildly about for other cars, for *witnesses*. He saw no one and leaped back into his car.

Get out of here now. Fast.

He slammed the Beamer into gear—first, second, third, fourth, and tore down the road, tires shrieking. As he passed the Explorer, his headlights exposed the shape slumped over the steering wheel. The body that lay against the horn. He didn't stop. He pressed the accelerator to the floor and sped away, his head roaring.

Sweet Christ. What have I done?

Instantly, habit rescued him, sealing off the strongest emotions and forcing him to view the situation like the attorney he was. An accident, right? Wasn't it an accident? Of course it was. The Explorer had charged out right in front of him and he . . .

. . . went after it . . .

No. He hadn't gone after it. He'd tried to swerve, hadn't he?

Calm down, it's okay, you've got it all under control.

Habit started to break down, emotion leaked through again. Benedict alternately rubbed at his face, at the windshield, at his face, the windshield. His breath kept exploding from his mouth, and when he tried to stop it, to shut it up, to suck it in, he got so dizzy, he thought he might pass out.

He glanced in the rearview mirror. Rain. Blackness. And way back there he spotted the celestial glow of a streetlight. He swung left at the first intersection he reached, then took a right, another left, turning haphazardly until he got lost in a maze of neighborhoods he didn't recognize.

Intoxication, leaving the scene . . . and vehicular homicide?

The charges added up in his head, his skull pounded, he needed to get home, to think it through, to figure it out.

What's there to figure? You killed two people.

Maybe they were only injured. Maybe . . .

Witnesses, were there witnesses?

He needed to focus on that, on whether anyone had seen the accident and might be able to identify his car.

You went after that car, Frankie. Rammed it intentionally.

MacLean's fault, this was all that bastard's fault.

He rubbed frantically at the windshield, trying to see, to pinpoint his location.

Home, get home.

If he were caught . . .

No, it wouldn't come to that. It couldn't. It was an accident, he wasn't a killer, he wasn't that kind of man, he wasn't . . .

You left the scene . . .

He panicked.

You went after that Explorer, Frankie. Road rage, that's what they call it.

Benedict swallowed hard and sped through the rainy darkness.

(2)

My baby.

Charlie Calloway lay on her side on the saturated ground, legs drawn up, arms wrapped around her huge belly, and squeezed her eyes shut against a tidal wave of pain. A contraction? *No, please . . .*

Rain poured over her, running into her eyes, her mouth, into her ear. She heard a horn blaring somewhere and knew that it had something to do with her, but couldn't remember what. A liquid warmth gushed between her legs, and she knew that her water had broken, that her son would die if she didn't get help, if she didn't . . .

The horn. Jess is in the car. Jess hurt, bleeding. Christ oh Christ, have to get up, go for help . . .

She tried to rise up on an elbow, but didn't have the strength, she weighed too much. Eight months pregnant and fifty pounds heavier, she was a forty-one-year-old bimbo, trapped against the ground.

Roll onto your back.

But when she rolled, pain swept through her again, and she lay there on her back, legs bent at the knees, arms clutched to her belly, the rain falling straight into her face. She sobbed and turned slowly onto her right side, and the pain subsided again.

Distantly, she heard howling and knew that it came from Paz, their dog. If she had something to grab on to, she might be able to pull herself up. She screamed for Paz, but the wind swallowed her voice.

The dog can't help you. Jess can't help you. Lift up now. Before the pain comes back . . .

Adrenaline poured through her, floodgates slammed open, and her meager resources seemed to rush into her right arm. *Up up up.* Her body felt as heavy as wet concrete, but she managed to lift her head from the ground. The horrible blaring kept on and on, reverberating inside her skull, making it pound.

Jess needs help. My baby needs help. Hurry, hurry.

Her fingers dug into the wet grass, and she pressed her left hand against the ground and rolled onto her knees. For seconds she remained like that, on all fours like a dog, the rain pounding her back. Her head spun.

Move, crawl forward, get to the sidewalk.

Darkness ate up her peripheral vision, the rain kept hammering at her, and another pain seized her. She gasped and her right hand flew to her stomach as if to stop the pain or hold it back. Then she simply collapsed.

2

Damage Control

Benedict somehow made his way out of the labyrinth of unfamiliar neighborhoods and across the intracoastal bridge to his own turf. The BMW continued to knock and clatter, the fender got looser, the engine coughed louder, the racket under the hood threatened to overpower the din of the storm. The tendons in his fingers ached from gripping the steering wheel so hard. His mouth tasted sour. The ache in his head had rolled between his eyes and pulsed like some giant mutant heart. But he was nearly home.

Here, the streets all seemed to turn in on themselves like hopelessly tangled pretzels. On blocks that still had electrical power, the streetlights merely blinked and flashed; reds and yellows eddied against the wet pavement. Wind blew off the ocean, swept across the intracoastal canal, and bent the trees like straws. Palm fronds, beaten and brown, lay on sidewalks and curbs. And the BMW never shut up. It burped and wheezed, knocked and protested down one block and up another.

Benedict slowed as he turned onto his street, grateful now that he'd conceded to his wife's wishes about not buying a home in a gated community, with a guardhouse out front and some old fart in a uniform checking people in and out. They had bought on a quiet cul-de-sac, a five-bedroom, two-story place that backed up to one of the deep-water canals.

Even if any of his neighbors were awake, he doubted they would hear his car rattling through the darkness. Air conditioners around here came on in late May and didn't go off until the first cold front swept through in late October or early November.

Just the same, he eyed the houses to either side of him, seeking a lit window, a blur of light. He saw nothing but blackness. And yet, some insomniac might be standing at a window, peering out into the rain. All it would take was one nosy neighbor who knew he'd driven home in a damaged car during the early morning hours of Saturday, May 24.

Only one streetlamp seemed to be working, a loner midway down the block. As he drove past it, he felt exposed and vulnerable, as obvious as a broken bone in an X ray. Every noise the car made seemed to vibrate through his body, humming like a tuning fork. Then he was past the light, hidden again in the rainy darkness.

He quickly reached up to the visor and pressed a button on the remote control device. The driveway gate yawned open. Through the rain he spotted the smear of the porch light Anita had left on. She would be asleep, of course she would. But if she woke . . .

She won't. She can't.

The BMW chugged through the gate, coughing and sputtering. He double-clicked the button and the gate shut behind him. He suddenly noticed that only one headlight worked, its ghostly beam illuminating the shape of the hibiscus hedges that lined the drive and the towering pines behind them.

He pressed the second button and the garage door rose soundlessly in front of him. He pulled in, the dim light illuminating his workbench, yard tools, sailing supplies, the familiar accoutrements of his personal life. To another person, these items would look to be well organized, perhaps obsessively organized. But to Benedict, whatever order he had once imposed on these items seemed to be breaking down, and this fueled his panic.

He put the car in park, turned off the engine, the headlights. He punched the button again, lowering the garage door. The light went off. As he sat there in the dark, tension rushed out of his hands and formed a hard, pulsing knot in the center of his chest. The click of the engine punctuated the silence.

Safe.

The attorney in him raced through a mental checklist. Possible witnesses. Time that he'd left Palm Beach. Time of accident. Time he got home. If the people in the Explorer were dead.

Damage to his car.

What the fuck have I done?

I rammed a car.

They deserved it.

Think, you need to think.

Benedict pressed a button under the dash and the garage light came on. Then he opened the door. It creaked, he heard something dripping. Something under the car. Oil, water, no telling. He swung his legs out, dropped his feet to the floor of the garage. He remained like that for a moment or two, one hand still gripping the steering wheel, the other clasped against his right thigh, sweat oozing into his eyes. His head spun.

Hurry, asshole. Get moving.

He pushed himself up, forced his body to step away from the car. He stood there blinking hard and fast, terrified to look at the BMW, to see the damage. Instead, he caught sight of himself in an old tarnished mirror that stood against the far wall. He looked demented, his trousers and shirt soiled by the rain, his dark eyes wild, primal, his black hair disheveled, his tie askew.

Benedict tore off his tie, removed his shoes. He stripped off his damp clothes and put on a pair of jeans and a work shirt that he kept in the garage. He felt better after that—not great, but better. The attorney in him had seized control again, left brain snapping orders. Logic. Reason. Order. Assess, plan, implement. The practice of law had taught him these things.

Benedict turned and stepped farther back, eyes darting across the left side of the car. Scratches in the paint, dents in the door, side mirror hanging by a jagged thread of metal. Okay, not too bad, this stuff could be repaired. But when he moved to the front of the car, he stopped dead.

The front fender on the left side looked like an accordion, the chrome squashed up against the shattered headlight. Flecks of maroon paint from the Explorer gleamed in the chrome. The left headlight had shattered and the grille between it and the cracked right headlight had been crushed inward, exposing part of the engine.

The fender on the right side hung by a silver thread. More maroon paint was buried in the chrome.

Another deep gouge ran the length of the right side of the car. The middle of the passenger door looked like a crushed aluminum can. When he tried to open the door, a bolt fell off, struck the floor, and rolled through the silence. The rear of the car looked worse, taillights shattered, the fender crushed inward, the trunk's lid squashed in at the edges.

Benedict squeezed the bridge of his nose and kneaded the spot between his eyes with his knuckles. The pain didn't go away, didn't diminish. It just hung where it was, pounding and screeching, a fact of life that he had to deal with, just like the car.

Shit happens.

He'd rammed the Explorer, that was the long and short of it. But he blamed MacLean. None of this would have happened if MacLean had closed the deal over dinner, just as he'd indicated that he would when he'd invited Benedict for dinner several days earlier. MacLean was at fault and he, Frank Benedict, would have to deal with the fallout.

He suddenly heard noises from inside the house, pipes clattering in the wall, a toilet flushing. Anita or Joey. *Don't come down here, please don't come down here.*

Benedict wrenched back from the car, grabbed a flashlight from his workbench, and lunged for the light switch, turning it off. The absence of light comforted him. Since he could see only the vague shape of the car and none of the damage, he could almost believe nothing had happened. Almost but not quite.

He pressed his back to the cool wall and willed his wife and his son to stay upstairs. But if Anita had awakened, then she probably had looked at the clock; his wife was always time conscious, even in the middle of the night. And once she noted the time, of course she would come downstairs to check the garage.

She'll see you cowering against the wall, she'll turn on the light . . .

He should go into the house so she wouldn't see the car. That would work best. Go in now, then get up after she fell asleep and decide what to do. How to deal with it. *Shit happens.*

An entire scene played out in his mind. He would be standing at the open fridge when Anita entered the kitchen. He would pretend he didn't hear or see her; he would be filling a glass with cold water.

She, eager for news about the dinner, would sidle up to him, slip an arm around his waist, and whisper, *Should I be planning our trip to Greece for December?*

A warm fragrance would emanate from her body, that sweet scent of recent sleep. He would want to bury his face in her short, pale hair. Instead, in the moment their eyes connected, she would see too much. She would recognize the *wrongness* in his face. And he wouldn't be able to hide it from her, not after sixteen years of marriage.

I had an accident . . .

Yes, she would believe that.

Are you hurt? Are you okay?

I'm fine, but . . .

But what? Someone might be badly injured or dead? He couldn't tell her that.

He had to tell her. If someone had been hurt or killed, it would be in the news. She would figure it out.

An accident, Anita. The car was suddenly just there and I couldn't stop, the rain, the wet streets . . .

He almost believed it himself.

Benedict listened for more noises but heard nothing. She or Joey had gone back to bed. He waited several moments just to be sure, then turned on the light again and went over to the car.

Calmer now, he moved slowly around the vehicle. Yes, a mechanic could repair the damage. Although it wouldn't be cheap or fast, it could be done. But once someone else knew about the car, the risk grew substantially.

Forget the mechanic, he decided. Forget repairs. He simply couldn't take that chance.

And you can't keep it here, Frankie. No way.

He had to get rid of the car.

The knot in his gut tightened another notch, his knees threatened to buckle, he felt suddenly dizzy. He quickly leaned against the car, the garage spun, and he took several deep breaths, forcing the air way down into his lungs.

Gradually, the dizziness faded away and left him staring into a

yawning abyss, a gulf of unknowns. Get . . . rid . . . of . . . the . . .
car. It sounded simple. But how the hell should he do it? He was
an attorney, for Christ's sakes, not a criminal. Should he torch the
sucker? Drop it at the junkyard? Find someone who could squash
it like a tin can and turn it into scrap metal?

Benedict went over to the storage shelves, grabbed an old gym
bag. This would do, he thought, and got into the car. He swept
everything out of the glove compartment—papers, matchbooks, cell
phone, a notebook, pens, a container of breath mints. Everything
would have to go, every last goddamn thing that could connect him
to this vehicle. He still didn't know how he would get rid of the
car, but he would think of something.

In the meantime, he had a goal, a definite goal that would take
him from A to B. Remove everything, vacuum the floor, the seats,
the ceiling, the inside of the glove compartment, then rub down the
steering wheel, the dash, the radio dials, any surface that held his
fingerprints.

Benedict worked rapidly and efficiently and fell into a rhythm
that dulled his thoughts. Clean, vacuum, rub, over and over again.
He kept going over what had happened. But he couldn't recall the
moments when he'd rammed the Explorer; he simply knew that he
had. He'd been thinking of MacLean, and his rage had seized him,
and now here he was.

Shit happens, Frankie. Deal with it and move on.

As he worked, He put everything he removed from the car into
a large tool chest next to his workbench. The stuff from the vacuum
cleaner went into the large trash can that would be hauled off
Monday morning.

By the time he started fiddling with the trunk, trying to open it,
an idea had begun to take shape in his mind. He didn't examine it
too closely yet, but sensed he was headed in the right direction.

He finally got the trunk lid open and proceeded to clean it out.
"Frank?"

He froze, his upper body hunched over inside the trunk, his ears
ringing with his wife's voice. If he didn't move, didn't speak, didn't
breathe, she would go away. She would vanish.

Footsteps, fast and urgent. "Frank, my God, the car . . . What . . ."
Shit.

He rose so quickly, he smacked his head on the edge of the trunk's lid. He left the vacuum cleaner on the floor of the trunk and stepped away from the car, rubbing his head. His wife's face swam into view.

Thirty-eight, but her translucent skin seemed to have stopped aging around twenty-five. Her large, expressive dark eyes, eaten up with anxiety, darted from the car to his face, searching for answers. Her hair, the color of summer wheat, framed her face in tight, impatient curls, and she kept running her fingers through these curls, as if to straighten them.

He knew she wore nothing under her short silk robe, that she'd gone to bed nude, waiting in her perfect sleep for his return. Two hours earlier, this would have aroused him. But his desire for her, for everything, had been swallowed by the urgency to cover his tracks, to avoid discovery.

"Frank?" She frowned and moved toward him.

"An accident," he managed to say. "I'm okay."

She reached out to touch him. He flinched, she saw it, and her arms dropped instantly to her sides, then folded like wings at her waist again. "What . . . what the hell did you hit?"

"A parked truck."

"From the front and the back?"

"I was parallel-parked."

"And it did *all* this damage?"

He didn't say anything.

"Was anyone hurt?"

"No."

"You're sure you're okay?"

"Just a sore neck." He rubbed the back of his neck as she walked around to the front of the car, her slippers clicking against the garage floor. He noted the slight sway to her narrow hips, the light shimmering against the blue silk of her robe. *She believes me.*

"It's a good thing we changed the deductible," she remarked, touching the hood. "This is going to cost eight or ten grand, Frank."

"At least that." He blinked as beads of sweat ran into his eyes.

"You'll need a copy of the police report for the insurance claim."

"I didn't call the police."

She raised her eyes, brows lifting. "Why not?"

"It's raining like crazy out there. I wasn't going to wait around in the storm for the cops to arrive."

"You'll have to call them in the morning."

He walked back to the trunk without replying. He unplugged the vacuum cleaner, rewound the cord. "How's Joey doing?"

"Okay. The antibiotics Dad prescribed kicked right in. His fever's down, the strep will be on its way out by tomorrow."

Her father, a pediatrician, practiced up the coast in Flagler Beach, a wealthy community where Anita had grown up. Her childhood had been leagues beyond his own, not quite Cinderella in reverse, but almost. Doctor's daughter versus school cop's son.

"Hey, how'd the dinner go?" she asked. "Should I plan that trip to Greece for Christmas?"

"MacLean hasn't made up his mind yet."

A frown thrust down between her eyes. "But I thought that was the purpose of tonight's dinner."

Benedict shrugged, attempting a nonchalance he sure as hell didn't feel. "He wants a few more weeks. I'm not worried. He'll come around."

"Of course he will, hon. Jerome trusts you."

Benedict flung his arm out, indicating the ruined BMW. "This mess . . ."

Her eyes darted toward the car, a brief acknowledgment that yes, it would be a pain in the ass to go through the whole police report and insurance thing. But to his imminently practical wife, it was simply something that had to be done and they would have to pay only the deductible.

For the eighteen years he'd known his wife, Anita had been a big believer in insurance. Even in college, where they'd met, she'd carried a shitload of insurance, all of it paid for by her father.

Benedict hadn't understood this predilection then, and he didn't understand it now. To him, it smacked of disaster preparation, like buying nursing home insurance in your twenties. And yet, at the moment, he desperately wished he had an insurance policy to protect him against a homicide charge.

"You didn't hear a thing I just said, Frank."

He blinked and her face came back into focus. "What?"

"I said that as soon as you've got the police report, we can call the insurance guy."

"I can't report it to the police." He blurted it out, the words popping out of him like a series of deep burps over which he had no control. They pinged against the silence, echoed, faded away.

Anita rolled her lower lip between her teeth. "You didn't hit any parked car."

She uttered this in the same astonished tone that she often used when speaking of the gifted children she taught, the kids with the huge IQs who would have to fix everything that previous generations had screwed up. He wanted, suddenly, to just walk away from her, to hurry into the sanctuary of his home, climb the stairs, and gobble down several of those codeine tablets her father had prescribed for his headaches. Instead, he shriveled beneath her scrutiny.

"What happened?" she asked.

"The rain, I couldn't see a foot in front of me and suddenly . . . suddenly the car was just *there*, Anita. I . . . I swerved, but I hit it . . ."

Such a facile lie. It sounded so good, even he could believe it.

"Jesus, Frank." She whispered it, her arms went around him. "Was . . . was anyone hurt?"

"I don't know." In his mind he saw that large woman stumbling from the van, collapsing. He saw the figure slumped over the steering wheel. He heard the blaring of the horn. "Yes. But I . . . I don't know how badly."

She stepped back. "You just *took off?*"

"I panicked. I . . . I was coming off I-95 . . ." And the rest of the lie rushed out, no longer embryonic, but fully formed, right down to the last detail. His explanation for the rear-end damage to the car was that when he'd hit the Explorer, the BMW had spun and crashed into something, he didn't know what. "I didn't have a choice," he finished.

Anita simply stood there, her expression locked in shock and disbelief. The constant *drip drip drip* from the car broke the silence between them. She bit her lip again, lowered her eyes briefly, then looked at him, tears glistening in all that blue.

"You have to go to the police, Frank. Explain what happened. Right now the only thing you're guilty of is bad judgment. You panicked. No one will hold that against you. Besides, the other guy might be at fault."

Benedict laughed, a sharp, caustic laugh that made her flinch. "You don't get it. I fled the scene of an accident, Anita. That makes me look guilty even if the accident wasn't my fault." How utterly convincing he sounded, Benedict the attorney. "If the driver was seriously injured"—*or if he or the woman dies,* Benedict thought, but didn't say it—"then I'll be charged regardless of whose fault the accident was. And if I'm charged, there won't be any partnership at Thacker and Tillis. I won't have a goddamn job, I'll be disbarred."

She paced now, her slippers clicking against the floor, her robe whispering against her legs. "You're making a lot of assumptions that—"

"For Christ's sakes, Anita. I'm a lawyer. I know how the system works. ABC. I'll be questioned, then charged. If the driver sustained serious injuries, it'll go to trial. If the driver sues my insurance company—or me—then there'll be a civil trial. By then it won't make much difference, because we'll be bankrupt."

She stopped pacing. Stared at him. Raked her fingers through her hair. Then her face seemed to crumble like a stale cookie. "But . . . but we're not criminals. We're not the bad guys, Frank."

"The law doesn't give a damn who or what we are or aren't. It's concerned only with what happened and who's at fault."

Anita glanced quickly at the car, then looked at him again, eyes clear now, the blue almost hard, like stone. "Were there witnesses?"

"I don't know."

"Jesus," she whispered, and shook her head as if to clear it. "I can't believe this has happened to us."

Us. She hadn't just bought into his lie, she'd become his accomplice.

Whispering again, she said, "What the hell are we going to do?"

"I'm not sure."

"We can't fix the car."

"We'll get rid of it. Then I'll report it as stolen or something. I'll figure it out."

"Where . . . how do you get rid of a car?"

"I don't know yet." The vague notion he had needed to be filled

in, worked out step by step. "I can't drive it very far. I'll have to rent a U-Haul or something and pull it."

"At night. It has to be at night. We can cover the car with a tarp."

"After Joey goes to your mother's tomorrow, I'll rent the U-Haul. Pull it into the garage. Hook up the car."

As he spoke, he nodded and looked around, seeing the U-Haul, the hitch, the tarp that would cover the BMW. And if he could already see these details, visualize them, then he was headed in the right direction.

"And then what?"

"I don't know."

"Frank?" Still whispering, tears rolled down her cheeks. "Hold me."

Anita pressed her face to his chest and his arms went around her. They stood like that for a long time, holding each other in the silence of their commiseration, his lie wrapped like wings around them.

3

Anita

In the dark silence of the house, the frantic beat of her heart sounded like mismatched drumrolls. *And now, ladies and gentlemen, we'll see how bad it really is . . .*

Anita Benedict threw off the sheet and pushed slowly up on her elbows, careful not to jar the bed and wake Frank. How the hell could he have fallen asleep after all that had happened? How? She'd lain there for hours now, going over every little detail, every word that he'd uttered, every horrible nuance. And her only hope was that the situation wasn't as bad as she'd thought.

The clock on the bedside table read 5:30. It would be light in another hour. Dawn, for Christ's sakes, and the only sleep she'd gotten had been a few hours before Frank had gotten home. She was beat, her eyes ached with dryness. But she couldn't sleep. Every time she shut her eyes, she saw the Beamer, damaged, ruined, kaput, and an electricity surged through her body.

She shrugged on her robe and hurried across the hall to Joey's room. She knew he had slept through everything that had happened in the garage, but just the same, she needed to see him, smell him, touch him.

In the glow of the night-light, she could see his stuffed animals piled high in the pet net strung up in the corner. A Pooh bear, perched on top of his TV, watched her as she entered the room. In contrast, his true passions crowded his toy shelf—a microscope, a chemistry set, dozens of books and games and intricate puzzles. And there, on his desk, sat his computer, a gift from her father. Her six-year-old son surfed the Web with the ease of a pro, as if he'd been born knowing all the particulars. Like the third-graders she taught, he was gifted, brighter than either her or Frank.

Joey slept on his side on the lower bunk, curled up with his gray bear tucked under his arm. Nemo, their orange tabby cat, lay on his back at the foot of the bed. Joey had kicked off his covers during the night and his little legs seemed pale and fragile against the dark blue sheet. She brushed her mouth against his forehead, relieved that his skin still felt cool. She wished, suddenly, that the solution to their other problem would be as simple as a prescription for an antibiotic.

Anita pulled the covers up over Joey, gave Nemo a quick pat, and slipped out of the room, feeling stronger now. Braver. Joey did that to her, gave her courage when she had none.

Maybe the car wouldn't look as bad as she'd thought at first. Maybe she'd been unduly influenced by Frank's agitated state. She started down the stairs, her hand sliding over the smooth wood of the railing. Pine. All the wood in the house was pine, one of the custom touches she'd insisted on. The builder, a long-time friend of her father's, had given them a break on the house, tossing in extras like this at cost.

They'd moved in when Joey was two weeks old, and for the most part the years here had been extraordinarily happy. Yes, Frank worked long hours and yes, it seemed that schoolwork often consumed her evenings and weekends, what with papers to grade and lesson plans to create. Other couples they knew, professionals with dual careers, faced the same time constraints. Most summers, though, they'd been able to get away for three or four weeks. They camped, went to Disney World, rented a cottage in the Smokies, took a train across Europe, never the same thing. But they hadn't been anywhere in a year. Frank had been too busy courting Mac-Lean, his ticket to a partnership at Thacker and Tillis.

But now everything had changed. Everything. The accident threatened the very core of the life they'd built for themselves and their son. The possible ramifications hit her suddenly, all at once. Anita gripped the railing to steady herself. A dull ache drummed behind her eyes. Her knees felt as if they'd been hollowed out and filled with sawdust.

She sat down hard on the bottom step, rubbed her hands over her face. Fear and grief built up from someplace deep inside her. She felt the pressure, a terrible physical throbbing. But she refused to let it overpower her. She shot to her feet and hastened through the living room and kitchen into the garage.

This won't destroy us. It can't. I won't let it.

The door shut behind her, she turned on the light. The BMWs stood side by side, hers white and polished, his black and damaged. They had bought both cars two Christmases before, when Frank had gotten a hefty bonus. She would have been content with a Honda, but Frank had insisted on Beamers.

Fear clawed at the walls of her chest as she circled Frank's car, circled it warily, as if a part of her believed it might spring to life and mow her down. When she had made one complete revolution, she backed up to the wall and just stood there, rolling her lower lip between her teeth and fighting back tears.

We get rid of it, report it stolen, do whatever we have to do to put it behind us. Then they would move forward. It had to be tackled like any other problem, one step at a time, with the larger picture always at the forefront.

But suppose someone in the other car had died? Could she live with that?

She didn't know. Nothing like this had ever happened to her. Until now her life had proceeded in a tidy, orderly fashion. No hidden tragedies, no ugly secrets, nothing in the family closets, just an ordinary American life. As far as she knew, no one in her family had ever been the victim or perpetrator of a crime. Hell, she'd never known anyone who had been arrested for anything.

Now there she stood, thirty-eight years into her life, contemplating an act that would put her squarely on the other side of the law, as an accessory to a hit-and-run and, possibly, a vehicular homicide.

She felt an overpowering need to talk to one of her parents, but what could she possibly say? *Hi, Dad, we've had some trouble and I need your advice. . . .*

She already knew what her father would say. Get an attorney, go to the police, follow the letter of the law. She didn't have to talk to him to know what she and Frank *should* do; they both knew what was *right*.

But would doing the *right* thing keep her husband out of jail? Would it preserve all that they'd built together? Would it mean the justice system would take into account the extenuating circumstances?

And what circumstances are those, Mrs. Benedict?

The storm . . .

And the booze . . .

Booze, Christ, she hadn't even noticed if he'd been drinking. But of course he had; MacLean always had wine with dinner and cognac after dinner and Frank always joined him. But if she hadn't noticed any effects, then he probably hadn't had much to drink.

Or he was scared sober.

Anita looked slowly around the garage but didn't really see it. In her mind she saw the house, their property, their boat tethered in the canal. She saw Joey's playhouse and jungle gym in the yard, his friends, his lovely sunlit room, his little world. She saw her job in the gifted program swirling down the tubes, saw the house foreclosed and herself and Joey living with her parents. She saw herself visiting Frank in prison, unable to sever the tie completely, unable to carve out a new life for herself.

In the moments she stood there, every terrible possibility flitted through her skull, each more horrifying than the one before it. She realized it wasn't enough to know what was *right* and to have lived according to that *rightness* in the past. What mattered was whether she could live with it now, and she knew that she couldn't. She couldn't live disgraced and humiliated, with her son as the object of other people's pity and gossip. She couldn't bear to contemplate a life with Frank in prison.

Leave him, then. Leave Frank tonight. Bail out. Now. This second.

The thought appalled her. She loved Frank. He was a good, kind man, a conscientious and loving father and husband. Yes, he had weaknesses. His temper could erupt without warning or provocation; he tended to be obsessively picky about petty things; he was driven. But hell, who didn't have faults? It didn't change his intrinsically good nature.

An intrinsically good man, Anita, doesn't hit and split.

She heard these words in the voice of her father, then realized her father had never used the word *split* in his life, at least not in that context. This was only the voice of her own conscience, which her parents had molded and shaped. It was the same voice that warned her, years earlier, not to marry Frank because he would mean trouble. But her parents belonged to a different generation, one with clearly defined gender roles. Her father, she knew, had never washed a dish, ironed a shirt, or done the laundry. Frank, on the other hand, shared equally . . . well, not exactly. He'd never done the laundry, his cooking was confined to grilling burgers or chicken on weekends, and they hired someone to do the lawn and clean the house.

He *did* help, she just couldn't think of the specifics right this second.

Stop it, stop it . . .

Deep breaths. There. Okay.

She opened the door to the storage cabinet along the wall. Somewhere in there she would find one of those fabric tarps she'd bought for the cars when they were having the garage remodeled and the breakfast room built on. She rummaged through boxes, then found them on an upper shelf, neatly labeled, categorized under CARS. She grabbed one, shook it out on her way over to the car, and proceeded to fit it over the Beamer.

Nothing but the tires showed. This would do.

She pulled the tarp off, started to open the door to check the inside of the car, but scenes from hundreds of movies coalesced into a single scene of a forensic specialist lifting fingerprints from some surface on the car that she'd touched. Anita wrenched her hand back and returned to the storage cabinet, looking for a clean towel and a cleanser.

She wiped down the fender and the roof with the towel, then fashioned a glove out of it to open the door. As soon as she slipped behind the wheel, she smelled whatever Frank had used to wipe down the inside. He already had removed everything from the glove compartment and from under the seats too. The car hadn't been cluttered to begin with, but he'd vacuumed the carpet so thoroughly that she didn't see even a crumb or a stray wrapper.

Just in case he'd overlooked a spot, she wiped down the inside, rubbing every surface vigorously. When she finished, she returned the cleaner to the storage cabinet and stuck the towel in the washing machine.

It struck her then that she'd made her choice, made it in the moment between one breath and the next. Now she would live with the consequences, whatever they might be. But she preferred it to ambivalence, with which she'd never gotten along. Decide, then act: This had been her code—and her greatest strength—as long as she remembered.

Satisfied that she'd done what was necessary in the garage, she retreated to the downstairs den. Her den. Her space. Shelves ran from floor to ceiling on two walls, every inch jammed with books. The third wall boasted a picture window that overlooked the canal, the Levelors still drawn. Paintings and drawings by kids she'd taught over the years covered the fourth wall.

At the moment, the room looked neat, organized, clean, but only because the cleaning woman had been there yesterday. Its usual appearance bordered on a chaos that redefined the laws of quantum physics, the kind of clutter that drove Frank nuts.

Maps, she thought, and jerked open one of the file cabinet drawers. She recalled stashing away maps of the area west of Miami that she'd intended to use for social studies but never had. She dug out a folder stuffed with maps, dropped it on her desk, and pawed through them until she found the one she needed.

Anita smoothed it open on the desk and turned the gooseneck lamp so that it shone directly on three rock quarries. At one time, the area had been targeted for commercial development. Environmentalists had protested because of the proximity to the Everglades, farmers decided to hold on to the land, and the development had been scrapped. The area had remained wild. No trespassing signs had been posted after a child had drowned in the deepest quarry. His body had never been recovered.

And that, she thought, made it the ideal spot for Frank's BMW.

Listen to yourself, the voice chided.

Anita slapped the map shut and backed away from the desk, her hands covering her mouth, tears stinging her eyes. *I can't . . .*

The most important decision you'll ever make is who you marry.

She stood very still, eyes glued to the framed photo on her desk of Frank and Joey. The camera had caught them in midair as they were jumping on the trampoline in the yard. They were holding hands, both of them laughing, Joey's head thrown back, the sunlight burning through his hair.

Have to.

She forced herself to move over to the desk. She smoothed open the map, plucked a red and a yellow marker from a holder. She circled the quarries in red, then studied the various routes and selected the one with the least traffic. She marked it in yellow.

There's still time to back out . . .

These words came to her in her mother's voice now, not accusing exactly, but laced with caution. She knew she could go to her parents, tell them what had happened, what Frank had done, and that they would protect her. Her father would call one of his powerful friends and that powerful friend would set legal proceedings in motion that would ensure her safety from there on in.

But her husband would be gone, her son would lose his father, her life would turn to shit. She would have to move away, move to someplace very distant, like Oregon or Tucson, someplace where no one knew her. At thirty-eight, she would have to begin all over again.

Why should that reality become hers? Frank had made a grievous mistake, but it wasn't premeditated, he wasn't a criminal, he didn't deserve prison. Politicians did worse than this daily and they never even went to trial. It was an unfortunate *accident* and he shouldn't have to pay with his life. Neither should she. Or Joey.

She folded the map carefully, slowly, and put it in her purse. Tonight, she thought. Tonight they would take the BMW to the quarry and sink it. Then they would get on with their lives.

4

Developments

(1)

In the silence of her own body, Charlie felt the emptiness of her womb, the absence of pressure, and a vague discomfort. She somehow knew she'd had a C-section, that Matthew had been lifted out of her and now lay sleeping in the nursery.

Got to see him.

She struggled to surface from the murky depths of the place that drugs had taken her. She tried to open her eyes, tried to speak. But her eyes felt too heavy, her lips too dry. So she simply lay there, a prisoner in her own body, and attempted something simple, to wiggle her fingers.

Little finger first. Good, very good. She felt it bending, felt the fingertip sliding over fabric, felt it rising. This seemed to act as a signal to her other senses, hearing first: hums, clicks, beeps, voices, distant strains of music. Then her sense of smell kicked in with a rush of sweetness, like flowers, and she caught the fragrance of something clean and sharp that reminded her of metal. And then . . .

A warm hand touched her finger. "Charlie."

That voice. She knew it. The voice belonged to Alex, her younger brother, and her finger tightened around the edge of his hand and she moved her mouth, trying to speak. Nothing came out. Her tongue felt thick and awkward, her throat was parched.

"No, don't try to talk. I'm here. You're going to be fine."

Baby. I want to see my baby. I want to see Jess.

Jess, something about Jess that she couldn't remember. Something urgent, something

Terrible . . .

Charlie clutched her brother's finger and forced her eyes open. Everything blurred, colors melted together like wax, and the world tilted, spun. Then, for a brief moment, the blur snapped into clarity and she stared into her brother's eyes, into blue pools of profound sorrow. And she knew. Just like that, she knew.

She groaned, her eyes snapped shut, and she dived back into the waiting blackness.

(2)

Doug Logan's cat heard it first. The black tom lifted his head from the bucket of bait he'd been sniffing and glanced out over the bay, then up into the sky. Logan set his fishing pole into the holder that protruded from the edge of the dock and picked up his binoculars.

As he raised them to his eyes, a blue heron swept into his vision, its long wings like pieces of silk floating in the summer sky. After three days of rain, the wildlife in the Florida Keys had come out in full force. But Buffet had heard something other than wildlife.

Logan looked to the north, through the branches of the mangrove that surrounded Minnow Key. He caught a glimmer of sunlight on metal, then saw the chopper coming in low over the bay that separated Minnow from the rest of the keys. He had the uneasy feeling it wasn't a tourist chopper and that it was headed his way.

He dropped the binoculars in his bag, reeled in his line, reached for his cane, and pushed to his feet. He limped up the dock, Buffet trotting alongside him. The constant rain over the last three days had triggered the old pain in his hip. You couldn't take a bullet to your hip and expect to come out of it as good as you were before. Or so his physician had told him repeatedly. But hell, it had been more than three goddamn years, Logan thought.

His hip consisted of a little bone and a lot of metal, enough to set off airport security detectors. It detested wet weather, but did just fine in Florida's subtropical heat. With any luck, it would be almost normal in a day or two. Right now, though, it hurt like hell.

The shooting three and a half years ago that had nearly shattered his hipbone had also ended a significant part of his life, twenty-two years with the FBI and a ten-year marriage. But he supposed you couldn't die and come back and expect that everything would be the same.

His death, during surgery on his hip, had lasted exactly eleven minutes and eleven seconds. He remembered none of it. As far as he knew, he'd seen no tunnels of light and hadn't conversed with the departed. But when he'd regained consciousness, he'd found that he picked up information from whatever he touched—inanimate objects, people, jewelry, plastic, metal, glass, it didn't seem to matter.

The ability had terrified him. He didn't know how to shut it off. Whatever he touched yielded emotions, secrets, intimate histories, the dark side of the heart. For a while he'd worn gloves, an effective barrier but hardly practical. When summer had rolled around, the gloves had come off and he'd been besieged again.

His marriage had fallen apart during this time, when he'd picked up that his wife was seeing someone else. She, naturally, blamed her extramarital activities on the long hours that he worked and the fact that dying had changed him. He was guilty as charged on both counts, but her affairs, he knew, had begun about a year after they'd married, long before his long hours or his death.

Two days after she'd driven out of his life for good, Logan's brother, a real estate developer, had offered him the use of his cabin on Minnow Key. Logan hadn't wanted charity from anyone, least of all his brother, but Rick had insisted he needed someone to keep an eye on the place and feed the cat.

So here he'd been for three years, isolated on a key so small, it appeared on maps as a punctuation point directly west of Big Pine Key. No roads connected him to the mainland, no surprise visitors showed up, no one bothered him.

He whiled away his days fishing from the dock, repairing the cabin, keeping the island cleared of fallen branches, and reading all the books he'd never had time for when he worked for the bureau. The ability that dying had given him and that he'd grown to detest wasn't much of an issue out here. His primary relationship was with a five-year-old tomcat that had no secrets, no dark pockets in his heart.

Every few days he took the boat into Big Pine or Key West for supplies or to pick up his mail. Once a month he collected a disability check that supplemented his pension from the bureau. Most of the locals, whose personal histories were more convoluted than his own, knew him only as a sunburned eccentric with a gray ponytail, the embittered brother of a real estate honcho. They probably figured him for a reclusive writer or an ex-con. They didn't ask questions and Logan didn't volunteer information.

On the rare occasions when he dropped in at one of the watering holes to shoot some pool or have a few beers, he enjoyed the human contact but never regretted leaving. There had been several women in the three years he'd lived there, brief affairs that temporarily sated his libido. These flings invariably ended when his detestable ability reared up and seized their secrets.

For the most part, he didn't mind his life on Minnow. He knew he was hiding, but it didn't matter, he didn't care. A couple of times his brother had suggested that he get professional help, and Logan had just laughed. Rick, Mr. Type A personified, didn't understand how Logan could simply drift through life. But Rick didn't have to worry about what truths he might see when he touched someone. He didn't hear voices, didn't see pictures in his head, didn't feel the burning heat rising through his fingers like a stream of lava. Rick, God bless him, hadn't been cursed.

And the bottom line, Logan thought, was that he had no desire to go anywhere or do anything other than what he was doing just then. But as the noise of the chopper's rotors got closer, he sensed all that was about to change.

Logan opened the screen door and limped into the cabin. His rifle, loaded and ready, stood upright in a corner near the windows that overlooked the south side of the key. He picked it up, then went over to the window, where he had an unobstructed view of the grass airstrip where his brother usually landed.

But Rick flew only twin engine planes.

The chopper came into view again as it circled the key, its occupants probably looking for a sign of habitation. Buffet leaped onto the windowsill and Logan stroked him absently. "What do you think, big guy? Are we under attack?"

Buffet just meowed and rubbed up against Logan's hand. He wished now that he'd brought his bag and reel up from the dock. He quickly picked up the cat and hobbled back toward the door, down the steps, and into the pines near the side of the house. He set Buffet on the ground and sat on a fallen tree trunk, the rifle across his knees.

The chopper descended like a giant bumblebee and touched down on the grass strip. The pilot remained in the chopper, but the passenger stepped out, a tall, lanky black man wearing MIB shades, khaki slacks, and a black T-shirt that accentuated his muscular arms and broad shoulders. "Shit," Logan muttered, and remained where he was.

The man strode up the grass strip with a canvas bag slung over his shoulder and followed the meandering, overgrown path toward the cabin. As he came around to the side, he called out, "Hey, man, you around, or what? It's Leo. Leo Wells. You don't answer your mail, you don't got a phone, how the hell is someone s'posed to get in touch, dude?"

Buffet meowed and plopped down at Logan's feet, obviously bored by the whole thing. Logan remained quiet, watching Wells walk up to the front door. He knocked, paused, knocked again, then tried the knob. The door hadn't been locked in three years, Logan thought, but Wells didn't open it. He didn't presume, didn't violate.

"C'mon, Doug," he called out again. "I saw your bag and reel down on the dock." He turned slowly in place, arms thrown out at his sides, as if to embrace the world. "Hey, *kemo sabe*, I come in peace, all right?"

Christ, Logan thought. He couldn't just sit there and wait for Wells to leave. He owed the man from their days together in the bureau's Jacksonville office, when Wells had been Logan's most dependable and valued source of information. He'd been present the day Logan had gotten shot too. He'd been the first fed into the building where the local cops had fucked up a surveillance and had gotten Logan out before the place had gone up in smoke.

He got up from the log and limped through the trees, leaning heavily on the cane, the rifle resting against his shoulder. "Keep shouting like that and you'll wake the dead, Leo."

Wells spun around, whipped off his shades, and hurried down the path toward Logan. He threw his long arms around him, nearly crushing him. "Goddamn, but it's good to see you, man."

Almost immediately, the contact triggered a flurry of images for Logan, vivid mental impressions about Wells's erratic emotional life—i.e., his various women. But beneath these impressions lay others less pleasant but no less intense, of his work as a forensic specialist with the Miami bureau. And connected to this lay a single burning image of a ruined car.

Logan broke the contact before he could see anything more. He didn't want to see anything else. He understood now why Wells was there. "Good to see you, too, Tonto."

Wells laughed and fitted his shades on top of his head. "You look like the gen-u-ine Key West conch, man. You meet any of the island legends yet?"

"Hell, most of the legends died before I got here." Logan gestured toward the cabin. "How about some coffee?"

"You have electricity out here?"

"A generator."

"What do you do for water?"

"A cistern."

"Got a phone yet?"

"Cell phone."

Wells shook his head, as if to say the vagaries of Logan's needs were beyond his comprehension. "Any women?"

"Nope."

"Animals?"

He stabbed his thumb behind them and Wells glanced back. "She's a witch, right? One of them shape-shifters."

Logan laughed. "He. And as far as I know, he's not a shape-shifter."

"Seen any good movies, Doug?"

Logan laughed. In Jacksonville, he and Wells had always been hitting the theaters. "Nope. The last movie I saw was that Grisham thriller with Susan Sarandon."

"*The Client.* Yeah, we caught it at the value cinema, remember that? That woman's something else. But you've missed her in *Dead Man Walking*, in—"

"Leo, you didn't come here to talk about the movies I've missed."

"True. Let's have coffee first."

They settled at the small wooden table in the kitchen, where the windows were thrown open to a breeze from the Gulf. Logan prepared espresso on the gas stove and brought two cups over to the table. "How does a guy in forensics rank a chopper, Leo?"

Wells shrugged. "Same way he ranks this." He reached into his shoulder bag and pulled out a bureau badge with Logan's name on it and a bulging envelope. "There's twenty grand in there, Doug. And another thirty when the job's done. You report to me, I report to the people who got the badge and the cash. I need you to look at the accident site, read the car, find the fucker who did it. You can stay at my place, at a hotel, whatever your pleasure. The bureau's paying all the way. The—"

"No." Logan pushed the envelope and the badge back across the table. "I'm retired. One hundred percent disabled."

"The fuck you are. You got a limp, that doesn't make you disabled."

"It's not the limp."

His dark eyes bored into Logan's. "That's the part of you I need, man."

"You're not hearing me." Logan leaned forward. "I'm here because I can't handle being around people, Leo." *Can't handle touching them. Or being touched by them.* "I can't make it any clearer than that."

"For Christ's sakes," Wells said hotly. "You've been hiding out here for three years. You can't do this the rest of your life."

"Sure I can. It's not a bad life. And frankly, I don't want to know why that vehicle is ruined, Leo. It's not my business."

Wells looked surprised. "You picked up something on it already? Just now?"

"When you nearly crushed me in that bear hug."

"What else did you see?"

"A white man and woman."

"That's it?"

"Yeah, that *is* it. Thanks for the offer, but the answer's no. End of discussion."

"She's one of us, Logan. Been in the bureau fifteen years. And her husband designed software for the bureau and—"

"I don't want to hear it."

But Wells didn't stop. "They met when he was setting up the bureau's new computer system. Married ten years. She was eight months pregnant with their first kid, Logan, and had just started a ten-week maternity leave. Some fucker barrels out of that storm, rams them, splits. Her husband died. She went into labor in ER, the kid lived half an hour. No witnesses yet and there probably won't be. She's still in ICU."

Logan rubbed his hands over his face to block out the naked pleading in Wells's eyes. "You'll have plenty of help from every fed in the Miami office, Leo."

Wells didn't say anything and Logan dropped his hands to the table. Looked at him.

"You don't need me for this," Logan said.

He knocked back the rest of his espresso, set the cup down, got up. "You're right, man. This woman is a close friend of mine and I'd be doing her a disservice asking a selfish, self-pitying, bitter coward for help. You're absolutely right, Logan. Have a nice life." With that, he strode across the room and out the door, slamming it behind him.

Wells's words echoed in the silent cabin and Logan just sat there for several moments, hating Wells, but hating himself even more. He shot to his feet, the pain in his hip forgotten, and hurled his coffee cup across the kitchen. It crashed against the far wall, shattering. Then he went over to the window, leaned out, and shouted, "Hey, Wells. Get your skinny ass back here."

Wells stopped on the path, turned with a wide grin, and loped back up the path.

5

Minotaur

(1)

Since the moment he'd opened his eyes early that morning, Benedict had felt an increasing urgency to set his plan in motion. But there had been things to do, ordinary household things like meals, showers, and packing Joey's overnight bag. Now Anita's parents were downstairs; now everything loomed so close, he could sense the shape and texture of his plan.

"What about this, sport?" Benedict held up his son's soccer ball. "You want to pack this?"

Joey eyed the ball, shook his head, and picked up a CD-ROM game called Ariadne's Thread. "I'll take this. I still haven't been able to get to the minotaur's labyrinth."

Six years old, Benedict thought, and his son knew more about Greek myths than he did. "Your grandfather is pretty good at those. I'm sure he'll help you figure it out."

Joey dropped the game in his suitcase, zipped it shut, and Benedict picked it up and held out his hand. "Let's go, sport. They're waiting downstairs for you."

"I wish you and Mommy could come."

"Oh, c'mon. You'll have a great time. You always do."

"But it's not the same. I have more fun with you and Mommy. Or at Aunt Bobbie's. I like going to her house."

Benedict smiled at that. His sister's chaotic household appealed to kids of all ages. "We'll go out and see her someday real soon."

Joey's hand felt cool and small in Benedict's. Most of all, though, it felt trusting. He had a nearly overpowering urge to sweep his son up in his arms and hold him hard and close, filling his lungs with the scent of his skin and hair. *For you,* he thought. Everything he did from this moment forward was for Joey.

And for me. A lapse of momentary rage: Why should he be held accountable for that? Nothing had been premeditated and he didn't deserve to suffer for something that hadn't been his fault.

So far, the only thing he'd heard on the news about the "incident," as he now thought of it, was that it had been a hit-and-run. No details had been released about the occupants of the 1996 Explorer.

They went outside, where Anita's parents waited. The early afternoon shadows spilled like India ink across the driveway, where puddles of water from the storm still stood. A breeze had kicked up out of the east, carrying with it the rich, almost sweet scent of the Atlantic. He breathed in the smell and drew a strange comfort from its familiarity. He'd grown up with this odor, of salt and fish, sun and heat and vastness.

On summer mornings in his childhood, that smell had drawn him to the sea, to the hot white beaches where the ocean stretched like a blue continent all the way to the horizon. Just the sight of it had filled him with hope that when he was grown, he would reinvent his life.

The summer he'd turned fourteen, his old man had dropped dead of a heart attack, leaving Benedict, his sister, and their mother to fend for themselves. Mom had started substitute-teaching and tutoring and Benedict had found odd jobs at the local marina. It was there he'd learned to sail, and a whole new world had opened up to him.

When he was at sea, he could forget that he often went to bed hungry at night because his mother's pride prevented her from asking for help from social services. Sailing, he could be whoever he wanted to be; he could reinvent himself.

He continued at the marina that fall, working for other sailors who docked their boats. They paid in cash, which he shared with his mother, and also took him sailing. Sloops, ketches, boats both small and grand. By the time he turned fifteen, he'd saved enough money to buy a little Sunfish and spent countless hours sailing out on the bay.

Sailing had remained his passion in all the years since. It hadn't just kept him sane; it had taught him the discipline he needed to make something of his life. It had brought him to the doorway of a partnership at Thacker and Tillis. The incident threatened all that.

"We're going to the beach tomorrow morning," his father-in-law, Chad Randall, was saying. "And then to a carnival in the afternoon." He glanced over at Benedict. "How about if we bring him back Monday evening?"

"That'd be fine," Benedict replied.

"So I miss school on Monday?" Joey asked, brightening at the prospect.

"You do, indeed," said Randall.

And at the moment when he laughed, his resemblance to Anita showed most clearly in his eyes, the same dancing dark pools of light. Benedict envied Randall's breeding, his aging good looks, his sophisticated presence. He also resented his father-in-law's opinion of him—that he somehow had never been good enough for his youngest daughter. The incident, he knew, wouldn't come as any big surprise to Chad Randall. It would be right in line with his perceptions of Benedict.

Benedict hugged his son good-bye, then Joey bounded over to Anita and threw his arms around her waist. A few minutes later, Benedict stared after his father-in-law's white Cadillac as it sped down the driveway. Joey's face was squashed up against the rear window, lips pressed to the glass in an exaggerated kiss. He had an arm flung around his teddy, its black button eyes staring back accusingly. As if it knew about last night.

"I've got to get my purse," Anita said, sweeping past him.

"I'll wait out here."

Earlier today she'd told him about the quarries and shown him the maps. He'd noticed the absence of emotion in her voice this time, the matter-of-fact tone she used whenever she tackled any problem. He'd agreed the spot seemed ideal, but while they talked, a pall of unreality had clamped down over him. It was as if he were watching a movie about some other man's life.

Minutes ticked by. The texture of the air changed again, a brief stillness, a tropical heat. Benedict consulted his watch once more. "C'mon, Anita," he called.

She replied, but her voice reached him as if from some distant place, underwater, perhaps, every word unintelligible. It unnerved him, made him feel that he was vanishing from his own life.

He moved quickly down the steps and punched in the numbers on the security system outside the garage. The door started upward, making a racket. The ruined BMW sat next to its undamaged twin, the penultimate reminder that *shit happens*.

While he reprogrammed the security code, his wife appeared, purse slung over one shoulder, her car keys in her other hand. Again she swept past him. Again she said nothing.

Benedict followed her into the garage. "I'll drive." He held out his hand for the keys.

"It's my car. I'll drive." She opened the door and slid behind the wheel.

Benedict bristled, but said nothing.

She drove out of the cul-de-sac, following the same route he'd taken last night, the only route in or out, except for the canal.

"Are you okay with this, Anita? With what we've decided?"

She shrugged.

"Is that a yes or a no?"

"I just have one question. Were you drinking last night?"

Benedict's insides tightened. "I wasn't drunk, if that's what you're implying."

"I'm not *implying* anything. I'm just asking you a question."

"And I just answered it."

"Actually, you didn't answer it at all. Were you drinking at dinner?"

"Wine."

"That's it?"

"A drop of cognac afterward."

"Anything else?"

"Christ, I don't know. You talk, sip, eat, and talk some more. I can't even remember what the hell we had for dinner."

"Don't get so agitated."

"I'm not agitated," he snapped.

More silence.

The road unrolled in front of them, shadows lengthened, his head ached. He needed his wife's compliance then, but he suddenly realized that the very thing he needed had become his weakest, most vulnerable point.

They drove on, neither of them speaking.

Anita pulled into a visitors' spot and turned off the engine. "Should I wait?"

"You don't have to. I'll be home in a little while."

"Don't forget the hitch." Her voice dropped to a whisper. "For the car."

Benedict nodded and got out, his legs stiff, his knees popping. He had his checkbook, his credit cards, cash. He knew he would have to put down a deposit, and the least conspicuous option seemed to be a check. They wouldn't cash it unless he returned a damaged U-Haul, and he could simply tear it up. Cash would be fine, too, but might prompt one of the employees to remember him. A credit card deposit might be okay if the card wasn't checked and the deposit wasn't posted. But the credit card remained the least attractive option.

Inside, he waited his turn in line. His eyes burned from lack of sleep, his stomach knotted, sweat seeped from his palms. He kept reminding himself that once they got rid of the car, he would be in the clear. His life would return to normal, whatever the hell that was.

Meanwhile, MacLean was probably up there in his Palm Beach mansion, yukking it up with other attorneys he'd been considering to handle his affairs, and this whole goddamn thing was *his* fault. If he'd signed with Thacker and Tillis Friday night, Benedict wouldn't have gotten mad, he wouldn't have rammed the Explorer, and he wouldn't have had to lie to his wife, to juggle the truth and the lie, and he wouldn't be standing there now.

Forget all that, Frankie. Forget it and pay attention.

As he neared the counter, the horror of what he'd overlooked struck him. Computers. Of course the company was computerized. His name would be on one of these computers. His name, the date, the amount and number of his check, his driver's license number, a goddamn electronic trail.

How long did the information remain in their computers? Three months? Six? A year?

The clerk flashed a perfectly white smile. "May I help you, sir?"

Back out.

No, he couldn't afford to do anything now that would call attention to him, that might prompt her to remember him. "Uh, yes. I have a reservation on a U-Haul with a hitch. Frank Benedict."

Her brilliant red nails clicked over the keys. "Yes, here it is. We'll need a five-hundred-dollar deposit, sir. Will that be a check or credit card?"

"If I write a check, do I have to wait for a refund when I return the U-Haul?"

"No, sir. We don't cash the checks unless there's damage to the vehicle."

"The deposit will be by check."

"I'll also need to see your license and insurance card."

Shit. "Sure."

When he'd given her everything she'd asked for, she entered the information in the computer, then handed him a key and a receipt. To his utter relief, she didn't run his check through any machine. "Go through those double doors." She pointed off to the right. "Show the attendant your receipt and he'll bring the vehicle around. And thank you for doing business with Miami Lakes U-Haul, sir."

She flashed another big smile, and he stepped out of line, his stomach tied up in so many knots, he felt like puking. Computer records: How the hell could he have overlooked that? Even more to the point, how could he delete the entry? He didn't have the expertise himself, but maybe he could pay someone to do it, someone who would just take the money and not ask questions.

Maybe this, maybe that, if, but. He suddenly felt as if he'd gotten trapped in his son's CD-ROM game, in the minotaur's lair.

The dull ache in his temple slid down behind his eye and throbbed. The longer he waited for the attendant to bring the U-Haul around, the harder his eye throbbed and the more he obsessed about the computer. He still hadn't found a solution when the U-Haul pulled up in front and the attendant jumped down.

"She's all yours, sir. Just put her in drive and take off. You know how to use the hitch on the back?"

Benedict nodded. He just wanted to get out of there, away, back to the relative safety of his garage. "Yes, thanks."

His knees popped as he climbed into the U-Haul. His head raced, his sweaty hands slid all over the steering wheel. *All problems have solutions,* his mother had said.

And it was true, he thought. But what she'd never told him was that the best solution might also be the most dangerous.

(2)

Logan stood on the curb at the accident site, hands thrust deeply into the pockets of his shorts. The sun warmed the back of his neck and the top of his head, reminding him that he would rather be fishing from his dock, with Buffet stretched out beside him.

Horns blared around him and cars sped past the barricades the local cops had erected around the area where the Explorer had been found. The car had been hauled off hours before, but the skid marks remained, various sets of them that obviously belonged to two different cars.

Logan didn't know what the hell Wells expected him to do there. He couldn't read the skid marks psychically. He wasn't even sure that he could consciously summon the ability. Most of the time, it was just a whisper in his blood. He might be able to make a reasonable deduction about the accident based on the patterns the skid marks made, but that would be due to his decades of bureau training. Left brain all the way.

He sat down on the curb because he didn't know what else to do, and watched Wells fishing around in the glove compartment of his car. Minutes later he hurried over to Logan, fiddling with a miniature cassette recorder.

"Here, put it in your shirt pocket. It's voice activated. I want to get whatever you say on tape."

Logan looked up at him and gazed at miniature twin images of himself in the lenses of the MIB shades that Wells wore. He looked— what? Demented? Wasted? No, not quite that bad. He looked like some crusty conch fisherman who had spent too much time in the sun, sipping margaritas, as out of place in Miami as an alien would be at the Pentagon. "I'm probably not going to have much to say, Leo. I can't read skid marks."

Wells fell into an easy crouch beside Logan. "Just try it. I bet you've never tried it."

"Leo, a skid mark doesn't hold any emotional residue. And that's what I read. Emotions, not lines on a goddamn road."

But Wells, whose relentlessness in the forensics lab was legendary, never gave up. He put his long index finger and thumb around Logan's wrist and moved his hand to the skid mark. Then he let go. "Just try, okay?"

So Logan tried. He pressed his palm to the skid marks and splayed his fingers and willed the marks to yield something. Anything. But this was like trying to coax water from a goddamn Frito.

He scooted back farther on the curb so that he could place both hands over the skid marks. His left palm touched the grass between the curb and the sidewalk and he felt a sudden, unexpected surge of heat.

"Weird," he said softly.

"What's weird?" Wells asked, coming closer.

"I felt something right here."

He pressed both palms to the grass again, grass still damp from all the rain, and suddenly everything vanished—Wells, the noise, the sunlight. Pain filled him, an ocean of pain and a terrible urgency. He had to move, to get help . . .

. . . *Can't move. Need to move. Have to move. Jess needs help. He's hurt. Lights. Headlights. An engine. Got to lift my arm. Can't. Move move move, please . . . Paz. Help me, boy. Help me up. Help . . .*

Logan jerked his hand away from the grass and rubbed it hard and fast against his shorts, his leg, his shirt. "Christ," he whispered. "What the hell was *that?*"

Wells reached for the recorder in Logan's pocket and pressed the rewind button. Logan heard his own voice, naming names, giving details.

"I didn't tell you names, *kemo sabe*. I didn't tell you squat except that she was a friend of mine and her husband and baby were killed. I didn't tell you she was found right about here, lying on the ground. I didn't tell you their dog was with them. Paz. That's the dog's name. Jesus, man, you sit there tellin' me you can't read skid marks and then you read *grass?*"

Shaken, Logan rocked back onto his heels, pressed his hands against his thighs, and stood. "I got lucky."

Wells cranked up the volume on the recorder and held it out so Logan could hear it. *"Jess needs help . . . headlights . . . Paz."*

Logan heard the words, the voice, but couldn't connect it to himself. He felt an irrational urge to slap his hands over his ears. He wanted to go home, back to Minnow Key, to his dock. He wanted to go back into hiding. "This isn't going to work, Leo."

But Wells didn't seem to hear him. He stared at something over Logan's right shoulder. "Shit," he muttered, and quickly slipped the recorder in the pocket of his slacks. "Trouble."

Before Logan could reply, a dark sedan with two men inside pulled up to the barricades, stopped. The passenger got out, a skinny guy sporting a thin Boston Blackie mustache. He wore a dark suit that was as inappropriate for May in South Florida as sandals and shorts would be in Canada in December. He puffed quickly on a cigarette as he approached Logan and Wells. Just before he reached them, he gave the cigarette an angry little flick that sent it flying away from him, arching through the air.

"Wells," he said, smiling thinly, not even glancing at Logan.

"Mitchell," replied Wells with the same supercilious tone in his voice.

"What're you doing here?" Mitchell asked.

"Probably the same thing you are."

"My understanding is that your people have already gathered all the forensic evidence they need."

"That's a stretch, Mitch. We haven't even seen the car yet because the locals hauled it away."

"I'm working on that."

"Yeah? In what way?"

"It's complicated."

"I need to get into the car, Mitch. Or their forensics people have got to share what they find with us."

"Like I said, Wells, I'm working on it." Now his dark, predatory eyes flitted to Logan, then back to Wells. "Who's he?"

Logan didn't like being treated like a nonentity. "Doug Logan," he said, and stuck out his hand.

He glanced at Logan but didn't offer his own hand. "Steve Mitchell, Bureau Field Director. You're not permitted in this area, Mr. Logan. Special Agent Wells shouldn't have allowed it."

It wouldn't take much to dislike this guy, Logan thought, and brought his badge out of his pocket. "I've got as much right here as you do."

Mitchell scrutinized the badge as though it were a bug under a microscope, then passed it back to Logan and looked accusingly at Wells. "I'm not aware that a special consultant was called in on this investigation, Agent Wells."

"Then I suggest you speak to Assistant Director Feldman. He'll fill you in."

Just then the sedan's driver got out and strode over, a GQ type in an expensive suit, jacket slung over his shoulder, his curly dark hair cut just so. Young, Logan thought, no more than thirty. Or maybe he was just an aging preppie.

"Hey, Leo," he called to Wells.

"Hey yourself, Jay."

"Mitch, you just got a call from headquarters," the young man said.

Mitchell made an impatient gesture and lit a cigarette. "Special Agent Jay Harnson, this is Special Consultant Doug Logan."

"Nice to meet you." Harnson flashed a set of teeth that probably had cost his parents a small fortune: braces, fluoride treatments, caps, the whole nine yards. "Mitch, that call? You going to take it?"

"No." He kept looking at Logan with narrowed, suspicious eyes. "Jay Harnson is in charge of the hit-and-run investigation. You report anything you find directly to him."

Logan felt like punching this officious prick right in the mouth and refused to respond one way or another. Wells leaped right in. "The last I heard, no one had been assigned to the investigation."

"Then you heard wrong," Mitchell replied, puffing away on his smoke.

"So what have you found so far, Jay?" Wells asked.

"Not much. We've got half a dozen men canvassing the neighborhoods to find out if anyone saw or heard anything. But frankly, it doesn't look hopeful. Until Charlotte gets out of ICU, we're working in the dark."

"Her name's Charlie," Wells said irritably.

Harnson pretended he didn't hear that. "We're also looking for her dog. Her brother says the mutt was in the car with them."

"It's not a mutt," Wells snapped. "It's a Rhodesian Ridgeback that weighs more than you do."

"Whatever."

Harnson looked uncomfortable now, a sweating GQ who draped his jacket over his arm and glanced at his boss for guidance, support, something. Mitchell, still glaring at Wells, said, "We expect to hear from you, Mr. Logan."

"He reports to Assistant Director Feldman," Wells said.

Mitchell blew a cloud of smoke toward them, dropped his cigarette to the ground, crushed it under his shoe. "We'll see about that." He turned without another word, then marched back toward the sedan, with Harnson hurrying along behind him like an anxious puppy.

"Who the hell is he?" Logan asked.

"An asshole," Wells muttered. "And Charlie's boss. Harnson is the guy they picked to step into Charlie's shoes while she was on maternity leave. Now I figure Mitchell is going to put her on bereavement leave and shut her out of the investigation. He'll cite policy, but there've always been exceptions to policy. Personally, I think Mitchell wants someone in Charlie's job who won't challenge or cross him, like she does. It's all just political bullshit."

"It always was, Leo. The employees come and go, but the power games remain the same."

"On your end, maybe, but not on my end."

Logan gazed after the sedan as it sped away from the barricades. There was nothing he despised more than petty tyrants. "Count me in."

"You sure?"

"I need to pick up some clothes and the cat, but, yeah, I'm sure. Mitchell's more interested in ordering people around than he is in finding the perp, and that GQ turkey couldn't find his way out of the little boys' room. So, yeah, I'm sure."

Wells punched the air with glee.

It's bright and sunny outside her window. This seems wrong, but Lily doesn't know why. She likes the feel of the paper under her hands, how cool it is, how white. She has five pretty pens with different colors of ink in them, and if she wants to, she can write every line in her journal in a different color. Or maybe she'll sketch something with the nice number two pencil tucked in the journal's back pocket.

Doris tells her to be sure to write the date, but Lily doesn't know the date. She doesn't care about dates. She's afraid to tell Doris though. Doris is a big black woman with a man's arms and Lily sees something bulging in the pocket of her uniform. Meds. Lily can't remember dates, but she remembers meds and she knows she doesn't want any.

"How about some cookies, Lily? Cookies and a cup of coffee?" Doris asks.

"Okay. I need some for Henry too, Doris."

"I know, hon. I know."

"Doris, I used to be a runner, you know."

"Don't I know it, hon. A marathon runner. Gone in a flash." Doris laughs and shakes her head, then brushes her hand over Lily's hair. "I heard you hold a few records, Lily. Never believed it till last night."

"I need to go to the chamber of commerce, Doris. Henry is missing and I need to report it."

"Oh, hon. Christine will be back from vacation very soon."

"Who's Christine?"

"Your daughter."

"But where's Henry?"

"He's with Christine."

Doris shuffles off across the day room, through the sweet smell of baking cookies. Lily sees some of the others sitting around the table, mixing more cookie dough and putting the tiny balls on metal sheets. She doesn't feel like making cookies today. But she needs to take food to Henry.

Outside in the courtyard, the sun warms the top of Lily's head and makes her sleepy. But she doesn't want to sleep. Her pockets bulge with goodies for Henry. While the others play shuffleboard and toss a volleyball around, she scribbles in her notebook, sketches, and stares at the fence.

She hates the fence.

On the other side of the fence, life happens. On this side of the fence, life is stalled. She waits. She doesn't know what she's waiting for. She can't remember why her pockets are stuffed with food, not just cookies but other things too. She doesn't know why Henry isn't here. She's afraid he's missing.

Lily feels restless and walks out toward the garden. The fence is nearly invisible here. She likes the scent of the flowers, the grass, the sound of water bubbling in the fountain. Here in the garden, her thoughts seem to belong to her.

She wants to write this in her journal but doesn't know how to describe it. Maybe it's just that she can remember more out here. She remembers that she used to be a runner. It's why her legs are strong. She doesn't feel like running now, but when she was younger, much younger, she used to run all the time. She clearly remembers this. Remembers the wind against her face.

"Henry?" she whispers, approaching the fence. "Henry, you out there?"

It's the only place he can be, out there where life is. She crouches down at the fence and calls for him, calls softly. The dog's head pokes out through the bushes and he inches up to the fence, whimpering, his head bigger than a basketball. Lily clutches the squares in the fence and he licks her palms, her face, his long wet tongue thick with the smell of life out there.

"Got some stuff for you, Henry."

Lily digs the goodies out of her pockets, crumbled cookies and meat wrapped up in a paper napkin and part of a potato and some other meat and a container of Jell-O with the lid still on. She stuffs everything except the Jell-O through the squares in the fence and Henry sucks it all down before she even gets the lid off the Jell-O.

After he finishes the Jell-O, Lily strokes his ears, his head. He turns those big yellow eyes on her and she understands that he's thirsty. "I'll get you water from the fountain. Don't go away."

She hurries over to the fountain and dips the empty Jell-O container into the fountain. The water is so clean, it sparkles in the light. It reminds her of something, she feels a memory trying hard to surface, but she can't quite seize it. Henry whimpers and she hurries back over to the fence with the container filled with water. She squeezes her skinny hand through a square in the fence and sets it down on the ground.

He inches over to the container and laps it up. Lily suddenly sees herself with him, with this dog named Henry, her arm encircling his neck, the two of them hiding under something. They're wet, they're scared. Remembering it scares her too, and she slams a door shut on the memory.

6

The Quarry

(1)

No wind, no distant hum of traffic, no animal sounds. The night, Anita thought, seemed to be holding its breath, as if in anticipation of something. The utter silence disturbed her, made her feel that someone or something watched her and Frank.

Frank started the U-Haul and the noise smashed the silence. She was sure their neighbors heard it, and if they hadn't, they would certainly hear it as the U-Haul headed out of the cul-de-sac, towing the ruined BMW. Even though a fitted tarp now covered it, any observer could tell it was a car.

Anita ran over to the U-Haul, waving her arms, and Frank poked his head out the window. "What is it?"

In the backwash of the dimmed headlights, his usually proud and handsome face looked haggard, as if he were coming off a four-day drunk.

"It's too loud," she said. "It's going to wake someone."

"Everyone's got air conditioners on. They won't hear anything."

"We have to do this some other way."

"The only other way is by goddamn barge down the intracoastal."

"Then we can't come back here with the U-Haul. We'll just have to hang out somewhere and wait until the rental place opens so we can return it. I'll follow you in my car."

Before he could protest, she trotted back toward the garage.

Moments later, the U-Haul pulled out of the driveway, into the cul-de-sac. It trundled up the street, towing the BMW, its headlights on dim. She felt enormous relief that the streetlights still weren't working, that porch lights were off.

Please let us pull this off. Please.

She didn't know whom she was praying to. She never had been a religious person, not even as a child. But she prayed nonetheless and promised whoever was listening that if they could put all this behind them, she would get involved with charity work. Something with children. Something meaningful. Something that would make a difference in other people's lives.

She promised that she would spend more time with Joey, doing the things *he* liked—swimming, hide-and-seek, the beach, the zoo—rather than doing things *she* thought he should do. She promised to be more patient, more loving, more tolerant.

Many of the lights along the interstate had been knocked out during the storm and hadn't been fixed yet. Anita welcomed the darkness, felt protected by it. For one long stretch of road she even managed to think about something else, about the ending of school next week and the creative writing class she would teach in mid-June. A pilot program. Something to anticipate, she thought, to hold on to.

She had a sudden image of herself clinging to a lifeboat that was leaking air. The image was so vivid, it snapped her back to the moment, to the highway, to Frank just ahead of her. *Clinging. Leaking lifeboat.* Like images from a vaguely remembered dream. Ignore it, she thought.

They got off at the next exit and headed west. They passed one cop, headed in the opposite direction, and Anita watched him in the rearview mirror, certain that any second now he would swing into a U-turn and come after them, blue lights whirling. But his brake lights eventually vanished, sucked into the darkness.

The farther west they drove, the fewer cars she saw. The city sprawl had ended miles back, and now the land turned into fields.

To her right, stalks of sugar cane stood upright and tall in the starlight, like an army on the move. To her left she saw fields of beans, tomatoes, a grove of mango trees, strawberry patches. The boonies.

Once they passed the sugar cane fields, Anita turned on the inside light and glanced at the map on the seat beside her. Not much farther. She flashed her headlights and pulled out ahead of Frank.

Half a mile later, she saw a dilapidated sign that read DADE QUARRY, and turned down a dirt road pitted with holes. She flicked on her brights, illuminating scrubby Florida pines, melaleuca trees, and tangles of wild bougainvillea. The road twisted back and forth for half a mile or so, then ascended a shallow hill and emptied into a gravel parking area. Beyond it stood a wooden fence posted with no trespassing signs.

She stopped within several feet of the fence, turned off the engine, the headlights, and slung her pack over her shoulder. As her Nikes touched the ground, she felt a brief tightening in her chest, as if an invisible hand had snapped rubber bands around her heart. Her skin felt extraordinarily clammy. She wiped her hands against her jeans, dug a flashlight from her pack, and turned it on as she approached the fence.

Some fifty-odd feet below, the three quarries glinted in the starlight. The largest and deepest of the three lay closest to them. Thanks to the rain, the water level was high.

She paced along the fence, looking for a spot where the car could be driven off the rise and into the quarry. But the fence ran, unbroken, for at least a hundred yards to either side of her and ended in trees. The wood, however, had borne the brunt of many summers of tropical heat. Insects had feasted on it. Rain had weakened it. She found a spot where a vertical post surrendered to the pressure of her foot and toppled over.

Anita knocked down three more posts, clearing enough space for the car, and Frank helped her gather up the debris and toss it into the trees. They didn't speak until they stood side by side at the edge of the precipice, their flashlights aimed below.

The twin beams of light skipped down the slope of dirt and rocks to the rim of the quarry. "We can't risk just driving it over," Frank said. "It might get stuck on the way down."

"Not if it's going fast enough."

"Exactly."

"It'll gather momentum on the way down."

"It won't be enough."

He turned away from the fence and trotted back to the U-Haul, Anita hurrying along behind him. "Hey, talk to me, Frank. What do you have in mind?"

"I'm going to jam the accelerator to the floor." He climbed into the U-Haul, reached between the seats, then stepped back down with two bricks and a length of rope. "The gas tank is scraping empty," he said, heading toward the BMW. "So I don't think we have to worry about an explosion."

"Are you going to be in the car?"

"At first. I've got to steer it."

"And then you jump out?"

"Yes."

"It's too dangerous."

"Look," he said irritably. "The only other choice is for me to drive the goddamn car down the hill and into the water and swim out as it sinks. That seems a lot more dangerous than the other way."

She bit her lower lip and glanced off toward the quarry, trying to visualize the car soaring off the hill, then plunging into the water. A million things could go wrong. But she didn't have a better idea than the one Frank had suggested, so she nodded. "Let's get started."

He backed up the car so it would have enough room to gather speed, then he began to fiddle with the bricks and the rope. Anita held the flashlight as he worked and wished she were elsewhere. The heat and humidity pressed in on her; fatigue ate away at her.

At one point she seemed to see herself and Frank from a point outside her body, as if her essence had stepped aside. They looked scared, like a couple of kids who knew they were doing something wrong and believed that any second now they might be caught.

What the hell am I doing?

"I think I've got it," Frank said.

"Show me."

She moved into the open doorway, listening as Frank gestured and pointed, showing her how it would work. "The rope is tied around the bricks and wound around the gas pedal. While I'm in the car, steering, I'll be holding the end of the rope so the bricks aren't jammed against the accelerator. In other words, I'll be controlling the speed. Right before I jump out, I'll let go of the rope and drop the floor mat over the bricks to hold them in place in case the car veers."

"That's it?"

"Pretty much."

"How do you know it's going to work?"

"I don't."

"Let's be sure."

"We can't be sure, Anita."

"Just try it without turning the engine on."

"I've already tried it."

"Once more, Frank. We can't take the chance that something will go wrong."

"Okay, okay."

He slid behind the wheel again and went through it as she watched. The part that worried her most was Frank leaping from a car that would be racing for oblivion. "How do you know for sure that you'll be able to get out before it dives over the side, Frank?"

"I'm not sure about anything, okay? There aren't any guarantees here, Anita, so stop looking for them. This whole fucking thing may backfire."

"Don't you dare talk to me like that," she snapped.

Frank looked at her a moment longer, then rubbed his hands over his face and shook his head. "I'm sorry. Let's just get this over with. Could you step out of the way? I need to shut the door."

She leaned forward and kissed him. He hesitated, then his arms went around her waist. They remained in that awkward position for several seconds, Anita hunched over in the doorway, Frank wedged behind the steering wheel. "Love you," he whispered, and pulled back.

Anita touched two fingers to her mouth, an old gesture between them, a kiss blown into the wind, and moved out of the way.

(2)

Benedict felt odd, getting into his car for the last time. He'd enjoyed this car from the day he'd bought it and Anita's two years ago. Its sleekness, its easy speed, its luxuries, had symbolized a level of accomplishment that he'd attained through hard work and perseverance. Sealed up inside with the sweet scent of leather, hidden behind the tinted windows, he'd felt safe, protected.

Now it only reminded him of the incident. If he didn't get rid of it, it could prove to be his nemesis.

He opened and shut his door, testing it. He pumped the brake several times. He wound the rope around his hand and tugged on it so the bricks didn't lay against the accelerator. When he dropped the heavy rubber floor mat over the bricks, the additional weight forced him to keep a tighter grip on the rope.

Benedict figured he would leap out when the car was still a safe distance from the edge of the hill. He wanted to do it with just a swift kick to the door, but needed something to prop it open. He opened the door and shone his flashlight at the ground, looking for a rock, a stick, something. Anita hurried over.

"What's wrong?"

"I need something to keep the door open."

"Here." She scooped up a rock, handed it to him. "I'd better take your flashlight."

"Yeah. Good idea."

He passed it to her, then stuck the rock in the lower corner of the door frame and slowly shut the door. Perfect. The rock kept it open just enough. He went through the preparation routine once more, then turned the key in the ignition.

The engine sputtered to life and he made a U-turn and headed back the way they'd come. A quarter of a mile. Half a mile. He made another U-turn at the mile mark. That should do it. He had enough distance now to gather speed. He fixed both hands to the steering wheel, the rope still wound around his right one, and kept his eyes glued to the starlit space between him and the edge of the rise. Now, he thought, and brought his foot down hard over the gas pedal.

The BMW raced forward, engine roaring, air rushing through

the open windows, the tires spewing clumps of dirt and stone that pinged against the sides of the car. Everything clattered. The speedometer needle sprang past forty, fifty, fifty-five. The end of the rise drew closer, his eyes watered, his hands ached, a pulse hammered in his temple.

Get out now. Fast.

No, not yet. He needed more speed.

The needle leaped past sixty and a voice inside him screamed, *Now now now!*

He simultaneously jerked his foot to the side and released the rope. Then he kicked at the door—and nothing happened, the rock had fallen out, the door had clicked shut. Benedict grabbed the handle, but his hands were so sweaty, they slid over the metal. He finally gripped the handle with both hands and jerked up.

The door swung open, but the rushing air struck it, pushing it toward him again. Before it shut completely, Benedict caught the door with his foot, slammed his hands against it, and hurled himself from the car. The lower corner of the door scraped across his back as he fell, but he barely felt it. Fear obliterated everything except his need to put distance between himself and the car.

He hit the ground and rolled. His head spun, his stomach heaved. Anita grabbed his arm, helping him to his feet, and they ran to the fence.

The car had left the hill, it was airborne. For moments it seemed suspended in the darkness, its metal and chrome glinting in the starlight. Then gravity jerked it downward, the nose plunging toward the quarry.

When it struck, the windshield shattered. He could actually hear it, the soft explosion of glass. For seconds afterward the car simply drifted on the surface of the water, bobbed there like an abandoned vessel.

"Sink," he whispered. "Sink."

Then it began to sink, the front end tilting downward. Anita reached for his hand and they stood there for a long time, neither of them speaking, watching as the BMW disappeared completely from sight.

PART TWO

————•————

Come Like Shadows

"Come like shadows,
so depart."

—Shakespeare, *Macbeth*

7

Return

On the tenth day after the accident, Charlie surfaced from the black ocean that had held her captive. She found herself lying on an examining table in her OB's office, having the stitches from her C-section removed. She felt strange, disoriented, as if she'd just returned from an overseas trip and hadn't quite acclimated herself to life in the U.S. again.

She stared at the ceiling, braced for the gloom that she knew would crash over her once more, dragging her under. She could feel it waiting in the black ocean, waiting with its toothless grin and glowing red eyes. But it remained hidden, and after a few moments she allowed herself to believe she had turned a vital corner.

She was briefly distracted by her reflection in the mirror on the far wall, a tall woman flat on her back on an examining table. Her face had lost its pregnancy plumpness and the little wattle of flesh under her chin had vanished. She no longer bore a resemblance to the Gerber baby. Her breasts still leaked milk occasionally, but no longer looked ponderous and odd. She was no longer a forty-one-year-old fat lady.

Her blond hair, which had fallen to her shoulders in luxurious waves while she was pregnant, now seemed dull in comparison and had started coming out in alarming quantities whenever she brushed it. The salubrious glow that had infused her face during her pregnancy had gone the same route as the dodo bird; now she had a vampire's pallor. She didn't want to focus too much on her blue eyes. She already knew that her grief had pooled there in all that blue.

"Okay, that's it for the stitches." Her OB, Lorraine "Rain" Sneider, glanced at her chart. "You're almost back to your pre-pregnancy weight. That's quite a feat in just ten days. Aren't you eating?"

"Not like I was when I was pregnant. I've probably lost four pounds just in hair."

"That's normal. Let me just take your vitals."

"What for?" Charlie pushed herself to a sitting position on the table. "All you did was remove stitches."

Rain wrapped a blood pressure cuff around her upper arm and smiled. "It gives us an excuse to talk. I'm really sorry I wasn't in town when this whole thing happened, Charlie."

"I'm not blaming you."

"I know you're not. I just want you to know that the OB on call did exactly what I would've done. They had to get Matt out. At eight months, he should have been able to survive. But there was trauma from the accident."

Charlie nodded, unable to speak around the tremendous lump in her throat. She avoided Rain's eyes and glanced around, noting that the examining room lacked the usual mother and baby posters, paintings, and photos that the other rooms had. No coincidence, that. Rain had been a friend long before she'd become Charlie's OB.

"What possessed you and Jess to leave in the middle of that deluge anyway?" Rain asked.

"Memories of Hurricane Andrew. He was afraid the canal behind the house was going to overflow and insisted we go to my brother's." She had a sudden image of Jess loading their computer equipment into the Explorer, of their dog cowering between the seat as thunder roared across the sky, of the endless hammering of rain. "We . . . we should never have left the house."

Rain squeezed her arm and when she spoke again, her voice was softer, gentler. "So how're you really doing, Charlie?"

"Okay. For right this second, I'm doing okay."

"That's good to hear. Alex had me worried."

Her brother. Her kid brother. He meant well. But he and his family had hovered around her for the last week, since her release from the hospital, suffocating her with their good intentions, treating her as if she were made of glass and might shatter at any second. "Did you talk to him?"

"Several times, but yesterday he called to confirm your appointment and we had quite a long talk. He says you don't eat, that you've been avoiding everyone, that you haven't even told your mother yet."

She ignored the first part of it. "Why should Mom's dream trip to Greece be cut short, Rain? She's been saving for this trip ever since Dad died, and now she's retired, so why shouldn't she stay where she is? Can she bring Jess and the baby back?" Charlie's voice caught on that last part, and she knew that Rain heard it. "I'll tell her when she gets home."

"You think that's fair to her? She and Jess had a terrific relationship."

Fair to her mother, her brother, her sister-in-law, her niece and nephew, her friends, Jess's friends. Fair fair fair. Hell, was it fair that Jess had been killed? That her son had lived all of thirty minutes? That she couldn't remember anything about the accident or its aftermath? Was any of that *fair*?

"It's fair to me. I need to do this in my own way, without my family crowding me."

Rain frowned, but still didn't fit the stethoscope in her ears. "What do you mean? Just what do you plan on doing anyway?"

"I'm going to find the fucker, that's what I'm going to do."

Until that very moment, she hadn't consciously realized that she'd intended to do any such thing. But as soon as she had said it, she understood why her gloom had lifted so suddenly about ten minutes ago.

"I don't think that's such a good idea."

"Thanks to my fifteen years in the bureau, it's the one thing I do very well."

"That may be, Charlie, but revenge is never a good motive for doing anything."

"It's not about revenge."

"Okay, so it's about justice, about making sure justice is served. But when it's as personal as it is for you, kiddo, it's revenge."

"Put yourself in my shoes and tell me what you'd do."

Rain pulled a stool over to the table, fit the stethoscope in her ears, and began pumping up the cuff. Moments later she said, "Perfect. One twenty over sixty-eight."

"You didn't answer my question."

She set the stethoscope aside, ran her fingers through her short black hair. "If I had to, I'd hunt the bastard across the planet."

Alex, waiting for her in the lobby, looked anxious when she came out with Rain at her side. He kept rubbing his finger under his nose, throwing his thick mustache into disarray. He wore his usual jeans, cotton shirt, and tie, his engineer attire, and slapped his baseball cap repeatedly against his thigh. She remembered him doing that when they were kids, a nervous habit, the equivalent of a facial tic.

"Well? How is she?" He spoke to Rain as though Charlie weren't there at all.

"She's fine."

"I'm fine," Charlie echoed.

Alex glanced at her, his dark eyes bright with compassion and concern. But she, after all, was merely the patient; Rain was the doc, the expert, and he quickly looked back at her. "You're sure?"

Lorraine slipped her arm through his. "Excuse us a second, Charlie." Her eyes telegraphed that she intended to set Alex straight on a few things, then she walked him away from Charlie.

Pregnant women filled the waiting room, the youngest about eighteen, the oldest in her late thirties or early forties. She envied them, no two ways about it. She envied all that lay ahead of them, all that she herself might have had, a child, a family, the joy of a new life.

Her hand went to her stomach, empty now and nearly as flat as it had been before she'd gotten pregnant. She felt her sorrow buried inside of her, a cactus in a desert, a motionless thing, suspended in its isolation. Then she sensed the shape of her life without Jess in it, and her rage burned, a supernova that swept everything else, only to collapse into sorrow once again.

But she couldn't afford to grieve. She felt, in fact, a sense of urgency to move forward. Her bureau training had kicked in, and it held a single indisputable axiom: The colder the trail, the tougher the investigation.

Charlie felt a sudden panic about the time that had gotten away from her. *Ten days.* By now, the perp could be living it up in Mexico.

When Rain and her brother headed toward her, Alex moved quickly, steps ahead of her. Charlie didn't know whether that meant he was pissed off or whether he'd accepted whatever Lorraine had told him. As soon as they were on the road, though, Alex made it clear that he didn't agree with anything Lorraine had said.

"Rain thinks you should go back to work. But frankly, I just can't agree with that. I feel you should take whatever time the bureau allows for bereavement before you go back to work, Charlie."

"That's about three days, Alex. I've already exceeded that."

"No, Mitchell told me they want you to take off the next four weeks."

Steve Mitchell, her boss, had called and sent flowers from everyone in her department, but he hadn't mentioned work. "When did you talk to him?"

"I don't know exactly."

"But why would he call you and not me?"

Her brother glanced over at her, eyes hidden behind a pair of dark shades now. "Because you haven't returned his calls. Because he wanted to know about the memorial service. Because he wanted to know if Paz had come home. Because we spoke when you were in the hospital. Because the bureau's got a policy about this kind of crime."

Because because: The words rang in her ears. "I've put up posters all over the neighborhood about Paz. I've put an ad in the paper. And I didn't feel like talking to anyone and I don't want a memorial service until Mom gets home."

Alex swerved into a gas station, screeched into a parking space near the rest rooms, and slammed the car into park. "My God, Charlie, ever since you got out of the hospital, you've closed yourself off from everyone. You sit in that goddamn house with Jess's ashes and you don't talk to anyone, you don't take calls, not even the calls from the cops, for Christ's sakes. I don't know what the fuck you do in there."

The words exploded from his mouth, and for seconds she didn't recognize him as the kid who had married right out of college and gone on to produce two children and a construction empire. He'd become a stranger with a very red face, a man whose frustration had brought him to the brink of a major coronary. "Calm down, Alex." Charlie patted his hand, fingers flexed tensely around the steering wheel. "Just calm down."

He relaxed—not a lot, but enough for them to talk without shouting. Charlie blinked against the bright sunlight and fumbled in her bag for her sunglasses. She put them on, but the metaphor struck her immediately. She and her brother had to hide behind sunglasses before they could speak honestly to each other.

"I know what you're planning, Charlie. I think I've known it since you came to briefly in the hospital."

"What're you talking about?"

"You can't go after this guy. It's wrong. You're too involved, too close to it, too. . . ."

"*Wrong?* How the hell is it wrong? What *he* did was wrong. He hit us and took off, Alex. If he hadn't taken off, Jess might've lived. I wouldn't have lost my baby, I . . . we—"

And suddenly she began to sob, then to flat-out bawl, hands pressed to her face. Alex put his arms around her, drawing her to him. They sat there for what seemed like a long time before he finally pulled back. "You're going to come through this, Charlie. You're tough. You've always been tough."

At the moment she felt vulnerable and angry, not tough, not even particularly bright. She knew the facts about the accident, but only because her bureau buddy Leo Wells had e-mailed her the FBI report. It had been written by Jay Harnson, the young prick who had assumed her job while she was out on maternity leave. And Harnson had written it in Harvard English, perfect spelling and syntax, perfect sentence construction, exactly the sort of thing her boss would be looking for.

Her doctor hadn't offered any false hopes that her trauma-induced amnesia about the accident would reverse itself. Even if it did, she might not know any more than she did now because it was possible that she hadn't seen the car that had hit them. So there she sat, feeling like a ten-year-old kid in custody of her brother, her head racing with *what-ifs*.

What if Mitchell didn't allow her to come back to work? What if Harnson figured he would just slide right into the loop while she was on leave, trying to piece her life back together? Even more to the point, what if the trail was now so cold that the perp had gotten away for good?

Charlie expressed none of this to her brother. Nor did she tell him that tomorrow night she would be seeing her Explorer for the first time. It had become clear that she couldn't share certain things with him now. If she did something of which he disapproved, he would call their mother in Greece and tell her about the accident, about Jess and the baby.

Tattletale, she thought. It all smacked of childhood patterns, unresolved sibling issues. Even as kids, Alex—younger by eighteen months—had run to their parents with a list of her transgressions. But why should that old tape be running now?

She didn't know. And she didn't have the energy to figure it out just then. But she intended to keep her secrets to herself from there on in.

As they neared her house, Charlie saw the blue Ford sedan parked at the curb. Steve Mitchell's car. "What's he doing here?"

Alex squirmed. "He threatened to park his body on your porch until you talk to him."

"Shit, you should've warned me."

"I'll come in with you."

"I don't need protection, Alex. I just don't feel like talking to him." Then she thanked him for the ride, gave his hand a quick squeeze, and got out of the car.

Her boss and the young prick waited on her porch, had made themselves quite at home by the looks of it. Mitchell straddled the railing like a cowboy on a horse, and he was smoking, of course, his head enveloped in a permanent haze, his neatly shredded butts in a little pile next to him. Harnson had made himself comfortable in the wooden porch swing where she'd conceived Matthew, his arms thrown out, resting along the edge of the swing.

"Hey, Mitch," she said, climbing the porch steps.

"Hey yourself. I guess you haven't been picking up your phone messages."

"That's how it is when your husband gets killed, Mitch."

Her bluntness brought a certain slackness to the muscles in his jaw. A brief compassion flared in his eyes. "We were all fond of Jess, Charlie. You know that. And all of us would like to see the bastard responsible put away. But we can't do that without your help."

Harnson sat forward now in one of those ponderous poses that young pricks learned in their Ivy League schools, forearms resting on his thighs. "We're on your side. But we need to know what you remember about the accident, Charlotte."

Only Harnson called her by her full name, and she hated the way it sounded when he said it. She hated the way his chestnut hair remained so utterly untouched despite the breeze. She hated his Brooks Brothers suit, his squeaky new loafers. "This doesn't concern you, Jay. If you'll excuse us."

Harnson's eyes darted to Mitchell, who gave a barely perceptible nod that said: *Get lost.* Harnson rolled his eyes and headed down the porch steps.

"What the hell did you bring him for, Mitch?" she asked.

"He's heading the investigation."

"Harnson?" She burst out laughing. "My God. He should be writing traffic tickets."

"It wasn't my idea." He slipped another cigarette from his shirt pocket and lit it with a quick flourish of a Zippo lighter. "And just for the record, I wasn't the one who put him in when you went on maternity leave. He's apparently got friends that we don't."

"He barely knew Jess."

"You don't have to know a victim to head an investigation."

His bureaucratic bullshit infuriated her. "I'm coming back to work tomorrow. I've got clearance from my doctor."

Mitchell's gaze didn't waver from her face. "You can't take on this case, Charlie. You know bureau policy as well as I do. So help us out. Talk to me about the accident, about what you remember."

There. Bottom line. *You can't take on this case, Charlie.*

Ha. Watch me, Mitch. Just watch me.

She leaned against the railing, arms folded at her waist, and glanced out at Harnson, his prim and proper ass perched on the blue Ford's hood. "I don't remember anything." She looked back at Mitchell. "Where's my car?"

"The local cops are releasing it to us sometime today."

"What the hell have they been doing with it all this time? Refurbishing it?"

"It's been complicated. Technically, the accident and Jess's death make it a local investigation. But the fact that you're a federal agent makes it ours. We had to reach a compromise about the forensics information."

Politics, she thought, disgusted that the process was more concerned with who got what than finding the perp. "What do you have so far?"

He hesitated, as she'd expected. Fifteen years with this guy as her boss had taught her a few things about what made him tick. She suspected he would tell her what he knew simply because he hoped it would trigger a memory, some small fact that might bolster the investigation. "We're working up a computer model on the crash."

"Yeah, so?"

"The car that hit you was black. We're running the chips through various databases. There weren't any witnesses, at least none that we've been able to find so far. We've canvassed the neighborhood, asking about Paz, looking for witnesses. So far we haven't found anyone who even heard anything, but a lot of people have already left for the summer. That neighborhood is mostly seasonal rentals. And no one has seen Paz."

"That's it?"

"Right now we're estimating that the perp was doing sixty or sixty-five when he hit you. Damn fast for exiting I-95. We'll know for sure when we've got the computer model finished. We think the perp was male, but only because statistics tell us that women don't ordinarily drive around at late hours in raging storms. Also, it doesn't look like it was a hit-and-run."

"Of course it was a hit-and-run."

"Your car was hit twice, Charlie. Once on the driver's side, once from the rear. Black paint was found in both spots. We're factoring that into the computer crash model, which will tell us more. But right now the indications are that it may have been deliberate, and that opens up a whole kettle of fish. Possible motive. Jess designed software for us. You're an agent. There may be a motive hidden within those facts."

"This guy *fled*, Mitch." But as soon as she said it, she doubted it and didn't know why.

"I thought you didn't remember anything."

"I remember being hit." But she didn't, not really, not in the sense that Mitch meant it. She remembered the impact, the bone-jarring shock of it, and the sudden pain. "It was storming. The roads were slick. It was a hit-and-run."

"And you're the only witness, Charlie. It's possible this guy may come looking for you."

"I doubt it. He's probably bright enough to know his best bet is to just go on about his life."

"You don't know that for sure."

Wrong, she thought. She knew it with a certainty that frightened her. "I think you're way off base with that line of thinking."

"We have to consider all the possibilities."

"What else?"

"That's it."

"You don't have shit, Mitch," she exclaimed. "Ten days and you don't have enough to shake a goddamn stick at."

His spine straightened, he looked indignant. "If you'd returned my calls, Charlie, we might be a lot further along."

"I don't see how, since I can't remember anything."

Mitchell jammed his hands in his pockets and looked down at his shoes. "You've got four weeks of bereavement leave, Charlie. You also have to go through bereavement counseling with a psychiatrist of your choice. It's not an option; it's a requirement. There have to be at least six ninety-minute sessions, then a recommendation is made for either more sessions or that you can return to work. The bureau maintains a list of psychiatrists who . . ."

The rest of what he said got lost in the rush of blood through her skull, the drumming, screaming current of her rage. "Harnson isn't qualified to tackle any of this. And I am."

In a low, threatening voice, he said, "Leave it alone, Charlie."

"What would you do in my shoes, Mitch? Leave it alone? I doubt it."

"I'm not in your shoes. My three ex-wives would cheer for the perp. I need your badge and weapon, Charlie."

She glared at him, appalled at his lousy timing, then opened her purse and withdrew her badge. "My gun's in the house."

"I'll wait."

She swept past him, unlocked the door, and headed into the bedroom. Her weapon lay in the nightstand drawer, where she put it every evening. She had another gun if she needed it—and Mitchell probably suspected as much—but that wasn't the point. By requesting her badge and her weapon, the dual symbols of her profession, he essentially stripped her of power. Without the bureau behind her, how could she hunt the man who had turned her life inside out?

A step at a time, same as you've always done.

Charlie returned to the porch, tossed her gun and badge on the porch swing, then went back inside the house without another word. She slammed the door behind her, ran down the hall to the den, and swept past the computer equipment. She yanked open the closet door, shoved things aside, and patted around frantically for the automatic.

She grabbed it and the extra clips, half a dozen of them, and carried them into her bedroom. She sat down, dropped the clips on the bed, and slammed one of them into the gun. "Fuck you, Mitch." She leaped up and aimed at her reflection in the mirror.

The gun felt good in her hands, familiar and sturdy. Her stance was perfect. Her body remembered. Then, suddenly, in the mirror she saw the faceless driver who had killed her husband and son, and rage crashed into her, a tide so violent, so raw and primal, she screamed and screamed and pulled the trigger.

The mirror shattered, glass flew everywhere. Still screaming, she raced down the hall, kicked open the door to the nursery. The room tilted and butterflies flew out of the wallpaper, unicorns galloped through the trembling light, the mobiles over the crib swayed and tinkled, the animals in the pet net seemed to rear up in greeting.

Sorrow spilled out of her. Sobbing, she turned in a very small circle and fired again and again and again. The shots nearly deafened her, but she didn't care. She welcomed the pain, the relentless echoes, she welcomed the destruction of what might have been.

8

Thacker

(1)

Frank Benedict felt like the generic slob in the aspirin commercials, the miserable guy who grimaced and held his head in his hands while an aspirin tablet danced circles around him. The two scotches he'd downed with lunch had pooled like acid in the pit of his stomach and left him with a dull, throbbing headache.

The meeting already had droned on for ninety minutes and showed no sign of winding down. He just wanted to get the hell out of there and go home. But at the rate things moved in the conference room, he doubted that would happen before dinnertime.

He'd been in this very room on that Monday after the accident when he'd read the first newspaper account of what had allegedly happened. Hit-and-run, that was what the cops called it. Very few details about the "accident" were given. But he'd learned more than he'd ever wanted to know about the people whose lives he had altered forever: a female fed, her genius computer-whiz husband, and her baby, which had lived half an hour after a cesarean. Two deaths on his head.

The woman, Charlotte Calloway, had been in the FBI for fifteen years and her experience spanned the criminal spectrum, from cracking drug rings to tracking serial killers. The article noted that she recently had been promoted to assistant field supervisor for the

Miami office. At the time of the accident she'd been on maternity leave for all of a week.

The article noted that the FBI had gotten involved because the hit-and-run was considered an assault on a federal officer. At that point he had stopped reading.

"Frank?"

The rolling southern voice snapped him back. Colin Thacker stared at him. "We need the figures on the number of cafés and restaurants in Europe that presently have plug-in ports for laptops."

"Got it right here."

As Benedict paged through his file, he felt a dozen pairs of eyes watching him, boring holes through him. And Thacker, the elder of the firm's two founders and the one who supported his being brought in as a partner, said, "Let's hurry it up here, Frank. We're all eager to get home."

He didn't remember compiling any figures about plug-in ports for Europe. For France, yes, but not for Europe. Thacker hadn't told him to get figures for the entire goddamn European continent.

Of course not, fool. It's a test. It made it clear to Benedict that Thacker's support might be waning because he hadn't snared MacLean. It pissed him off, being put on the spot like this. So he took the number he had for the plug-in ports in France and multiplied it by the number of countries in Western Europe. He spat it out and Greg Tillis, the other founding partner, sat forward now, a frown jutting down between his reptilian eyes and bushy brows.

"Are you absolutely sure about those figures, Frank?" Tillis's bald head glistened in the glare of the fluorescent lights. "They sound mighty low to me."

Benedict glanced over at him, hating him and trying not to let it show in his eyes. "There are no *exact* figures, sir, and until there are, I'd rather keep our estimate on the conservative side." He dredged up bits of information that he recalled from a news article he'd read several weeks ago. "We do know that plug-in ports are on the rise in Eastern Europe too, as more generation Xers head over there with laptops and their marketable skills. So even if you're in a city like Istanbul, you can stroll on down to the local beer joint and keep in touch with Mom in Des Moines."

Everyone laughed, even Tillis. Benedict knew he had just saved his ass.

"We'll be making a recommendation to our client in another day or two," Thacker said. "But I know that if I had this client's capital, I'd invest in a chain of cafés through Eastern and Western Europe with laptop ports at every table. Let's call it a day, shall we?"

With that, the meeting adjourned. Benedict didn't want to seem too eager to get away, so he took his time gathering up papers, stacking them, returning the files to his briefcase. Thacker came over to him before he left. "You have a few minutes, Frank?"

"Sure, I've got a few minutes." *Actually, I'm in a big fat hurry, Colin.* "What's up?"

"Let's step out into the hall."

Christ. A little chat in the hall. That didn't sound too promising. *I want to get home, Colin. Where I feel safe.*

Safety had become a major issue in his life since the incident. Safety from discovery. Safety from the pressure of work. At home, he could take the sloop out for a run on the open sea, the only place he was ever free of his rage. At sea, he didn't have to think about how, a week ago, Anita had reported his BMW as stolen and a cop had come out to the house and asked them all the standard questions. He wanted to do it sooner, but Anita had cautioned against it. *Too soon,* she'd said, and he knew exactly what she meant. He needed a time lag, just in case.

But in the grander scheme of things, yesterday or today remained immaterial. The report would go into a national database and not a goddamn thing would come of it. This was Miami, after all, where car theft was big business, particularly if you were in the exportation end of it—stolen cars bound for special orders in South America.

The police report had allowed him to file a claim with his insurance company. The insurance investigator had come out to the house several days later, and the questions he'd asked hadn't been standard. They couldn't be standard with a pending payment estimated at about forty grand. But Benedict knew that he and Anita didn't fit the investigator's profile for insurance fraud. They didn't fit the police profile for bad guys either.

Their credit cards got paid off monthly.

The mortgage on their home was high, but not so high compared to income that it raised red flags.

Their cars were paid for.

They paid their taxes regularly. They'd never been audited. They had considerable savings. They were well-to-do professionals who had never been arrested.

The cops had better things to do.

The insurance company would pay.

And no one will know.

Except Anita.

Out in the hall, Thacker shuffled along in his six-hundred-dollar suit and the fifty pounds he needed to shed. He was pushing sixty and looked every day of it. The sun had baked his face the color of pumpernickel bread, and deep creases twisted across his forehead and burst from the corners of his eyes. His arms and hands felt like leather.

His physical appearance and his southern drawl, however, deceived people into believing he was over the hill, a figurehead, nothing more. But Thacker's massive intellect fueled the firm and pushed it toward the future; in comparison, Tillis was window dressing, the firm's public persona.

"You nearly blew it in there, boy," Thacker said quietly, pausing near the water fountain.

"I gave you the information you asked for."

He nodded. "Got no argument with that, Frank. And if you were just another newbie in the firm, I'd be saying you did a fine job. But a partner has to think on his toes. A client asks you a question and you've got to be able to answer like *that*." He snapped his fingers an inch from Benedict's nose.

Benedict barely stifled the urge to bite off the end of Thacker's index finger.

"Take someone like Jerome MacLean, for instance. Let's say he wants to open a hotel in Caracas and you're going to be handling the legal end of it here in the States. What's that going to entail, Frank?"

He resented this little lecture, resented how Thacker patronized him, but he managed to laugh. "C'mon, Colin. What the hell is this, corporate law one-oh-one?"

Thacker's hazel eyes latched on to Benedict's, and for ten, maybe fifteen seconds, he said nothing at all. Then he seemed to bring himself to his full height, so that his eyes were even with Benedict's chin. And he sank his pudgy index finger into Benedict's chest.

"Fuck the textbooks. You fly to Caracas. You check out the competitors. You check out sites and prices, all the specs. Then you meet with the competitors. Listen to them. Drink espressos and Venezuelan beer with them. Convince them your client is a business-man, just like them, and he wants to play fairly, just like them. You consult with your client. And if he still wants to go through with it, you seek out the proper Venezuelan officials and you grease the appropriate palms." Then he dug his fat index finger into Benedict's chest and leaned into his face. "Are we getting the picture here, Frank?"

Rage surged up from that deep place inside him, a hot liquid rage that crashed over him so quickly, he didn't have a chance to control it. He knocked Thacker's fleshy arm away from him, and the old man wrenched back, his face seized up with shock. "What . . . what the hell," he stammered.

"Don't poke me in the goddamn chest, Colin. And, yes, I get the picture. You want me on an Air France flight tomorrow morning, right?"

Blood rushed into Thacker's face. "I want you to get the hell out of here and go home and relax, Frank. Have a drink. Take your wife to dinner. Go sailing. Just chill out."

He walked off, still rubbing his arm. Benedict leaned into the wall, knuckling his eyes.

Shape up, boy.

Get into the loop, son.

Get with the agenda, fuckup.

Yeah, he got the picture all right. *And don't ever poke me again, fat man.*

(2)

Jesus, those eyes, Thacker thought, rubbing absently at his arm. *Wild. Primal. Spooky shit.*

He swiveled his chair around and stared out the second-story window of his office. For moments he continued to see Benedict's eyes, floating like phantoms in the glass. Then he blinked, the image vanished, and he drank in the beauty below: the ficus trees that embraced the firm's half-acre, the lush courtyard with the fountain, the puffy cushions of colorful impatiens.

During the winter, while snow blew up north, he always opened his windows to a miraculous sky and temperatures in the sixties and seventies. Today, of course, his windows were shut; the air outside, even now, hovered above ninety.

Thacker and Tillis had bought this old Spanish-style house in Coral Gables more than twenty-five years earlier. Its twenty rooms had been refurbished several times over the years, modernizing everything. But the innate beauty of the structure remained untouched: walls paneled in Florida pine, Mexican tile throughout, and the marvelous courtyard around which the house had been built. He considered it home.

He had hoped that Benedict might also consider it home someday. But MacLean's failure to sign with the firm Friday bothered him, and so did Benedict's show of temper out there in the hall.

Thacker had known he had a short fuse; a lot of attorneys did, especially those who had the kind of passion for the law that Benedict did. He'd seen Benedict blow up at secretaries and other attorneys, usually under justifiable circumstances. Maybe he was imagining it, but it seemed Benedict's fuse had gotten shorter since a severe concussion had laid him up for nearly a month about four years before. Until today, though, Benedict had never turned his temper on Thacker.

In all fairness to the man, however, he had probably provoked it with his patronizing speech and poking him in the chest. It was something he used to do to his youngest son when he wanted to drive home a point. Benedict, of course, wasn't his son, and he had no business doing it. But the sentiment behind it had been the same. He'd been trying to impress on Benedict that he wouldn't be made a partner until he did something extraordinary. If he couldn't nab MacLean—and that remained to be seen—then he had to do something else that would be equally impressive.

"Colin?"

He turned in his chair again as Greg Tillis strode into the office, tugging at his tie. "I was just about to buzz you, Greg."

Tillis claimed one of the chairs in front of Thacker's desk and got right to the point. "I understand that MacLean still hasn't made a decision."

Translated, this meant: *Your golden boy must've fucked* up. "MacLean was never an easy catch, Greg. You have personal experience with that."

The slight didn't seem to bother Tillis. He wasn't the sort of man who dwelled on his failures, and his failure twenty years ago to sign MacLean was history. "MacLean's net worth's considerably higher now than it was when I courted him. That would naturally make him more cautious. But, Christ, it's been eight or nine months already, Colin. That's long enough. And quite honestly, even if Frank brings in MacLean at this point, I'm still not convinced he's right for the partnership."

If Thacker mentioned his own reservations or made reference to what had happened in the hall, Tillis would get one of those smug I-told-you-so smiles on his face. "Why not?"

Tillis rolled his eyes and ran his hand over his slick pate. "We've been over this a thousand times, Colin. And I still don't have an answer. It's a feeling, that's all. There's something not quite right about him."

Thacker laughed. "Hell, people say that every day about lawyers. We're bottom feeders, Colin, that's how they see us."

He shrugged. "I'm not here for clever repartee, okay? If you're still convinced he's right for a partnership, then I'm going to offer him the use of one of the firm's Mercedes until he gets his transportation problem squared away." His mouth twitched into a slow smile. "I had Mendez over in computers install a bug. Let's get to the core of who Frank Benedict is before this goes any farther."

"Whatever doubts I've got aren't going to be resolved by bugging the goddamn car, Greg. Not to mention that it breaks a few laws. I just don't see the point."

As soon as he'd said this, Tillis's expression changed and Thacker immediately knew where he would take the conversation. "With Lee Nichols it saved us considerable money and aggravation, Colin. You can't dispute that."

No, he couldn't. Seven years ago, when Tillis had suggested Lee Nichols, one of their most promising attorneys, as a possible partner, Thacker had balked. No question that the man had been a brilliant attorney, but something about him had disturbed Thacker. Maybe the same something that bothered Tillis about Benedict.

With Nichols, Thacker had resisted just as strenuously as Tillis was now. Tillis had suggested the bug and Thacker had gone along with it. They'd subsequently discovered that Nichols's brilliance had been directed to pursuits other than the law—namely, a money-laundering operation for Cuban drug runners. They had fired him, but hadn't tipped off the police because that would raise questions they didn't want to answer. Several years later, though, circumstances had caught up to Nichols. He'd been found dead in his home from a shotgun blast to the back of his head.

So, yes, the bug had paid off in the long run with Nichols. But Thacker didn't think Benedict was involved in drugs or anything comparably shady. He was too honest for that.

Benedict's old man, like Thacker's, had died when he was relatively young, which had plunged the family into financial straits. Benedict had risen above it, just as Thacker had, and had gone to college and law school on scholarships and grants and had graduated at the top of his class. Like Thacker, he'd married well, into a family with money.

None of that guaranteed character or morality, of course, but Thacker felt sure that Benedict had nothing to hide. His only problem was a short fuse, but so what? Every single one of the thirty-seven attorneys they employed had problems of one kind or another.

So if he had no reservations about Benedict, why was he nodding, agreeing with Tillis, commiserating? *Because I have to be absolutely certain.*

"I'll go along with this, Greg, because you went along with me on Nichols. But after this we're going to have to find some other way to determine if a prospective partner has anything in his background that might harm the firm."

"There is no better way than eavesdropping on a man's life, Colin." He smiled with his teeth gritted again, rapped his knuckles twice on the desk, and left.

9

Rain

Her brother had been wrong. Charlie hadn't been locked in her house night after night. She'd been walking the neighborhood where the accident had happened, looking for her dog. Paz was all that remained of her former life. She harbored a small superstition that when she found him, she also would find the bastard responsible for this.

She walked quickly through the twilight, her running shoes whispering against the sidewalk, and whistled for Paz. The special whistle, high, then low, was how Jess had trained him to come when he was just a pup. But no dog came bounding out at her from the shadows.

She tacked up more lost-dog posters to trees and phone poles and left several outside the Alzheimer's center catercorner to the accident site. She considered going inside and leaving posters at the front desk, but the signs out front about "no solicitation" discouraged her from doing so. When the posters were gone, her anger crested quickly, thickly, like a force of nature.

Within moments, it swept through her in huge, terrible waves, and she broke into a sprint. Her shoes slapped the sidewalk. Her breath exploded from her mouth. But she couldn't outrun her anger. It ignited into rage and the rage crashed over her and the next thing she knew, she was on her knees, face pressed into her thighs, as she rocked and sobbed, rocked and sobbed.

She finally pushed to her feet, wiped her eyes, and hurried up the block toward the van. How stupid, losing control like that. It wouldn't bring Jess or her son back. It wouldn't bring her dog home. It wouldn't return her other life to her. But she realized she felt better, lighter, as if her rage had purged her of something. Or given her something. She didn't know which.

As she neared her van, she saw Rain, her OB, leaning back against the van's side door, a cigar in her mouth. "You shouldn't be training for the Olympics for at least another month, Charlie." She uttered this in a dry, hard tone that belied the soft kindness in her face. "Your body needs a break. Trust me on that one."

"And you shouldn't be smoking," Charlie replied. "I thought you gave up that shit last year."

"I did. I don't inhale."

Charlie leaned against the van next to her. "Then what fun is it?"

Rain ran her index finger the length of the cigar. "Hell, I lied. I do inhale."

They looked at each other and laughed. "How'd you know where I was, Rain?" The nickname dated back to their days as college roommates.

"After twenty-two years, I ought to be able to figure it out." Lorraine lifted her left foot and carefully twisted the burning end of the cigar against the sole. Then she dropped the remains in the bulging bag that hung over her left shoulder. "I drove up just around the time you were having a slug fest with that ficus tree down the block."

"I was?"

"That's what it looked like to me."

"A lapse, that's all it was."

"You're going to have plenty of lapses, Charlie."

"Thanks for the vote of confidence."

"That's not what I meant."

"Then what did you mean? Am I going to lose it before this is resolved? Am I already in the middle of a breakdown? What?"

A car sped past, its headlights illuminating one side of Rain's head and face. She wore her dark hair very short, a stylish, perfect cut that set off her long neck, her green eyes, her enviable complexion. Except for a few laugh lines at the corners of her eyes and about five extra pounds, Rain looked pretty much as she had the day they'd met.

Nineteen years old, roommates by default at the University of Florida in Gainesville, they had hit it off within the first five minutes. They became the sisters neither of them had and had been present for every landmark in the other's life—weddings, graduations, celebrations, funerals. When Charlie had graduated from Quantico, Rain and her husband had flown in for the weekend. When Rain had her first child, Charlie had been in the labor and delivery room, spelling Rain's husband. They were blood the way blood was supposed to be.

"When I was doing my residency in Tampa, I used to volunteer one day a month at a hospice center. I watched a lot of people die, Charlie. In the beginning, it depressed me. I felt devastated that they slipped away despite my best efforts. Then I realized I wasn't there to save them. I was there to make their passage easier. And that's what it is. A *passage*. It's like going from a liquid state to gas, water to steam."

"Jess isn't steam, Rain. And he's not going to turn into condensation in my yard tomorrow morning. He's dead, okay? He's fucking dead and I'm not."

She just nodded, like she'd heard this before. "You think death is the end of it all, Charlie? Zap, you're gone, you're nothing, you're just shit in the wind? Is that what you really believe?"

Did she? She didn't know. For the first sixteen years of her life, she'd been raised Catholic. She'd gone through the various rituals—first confession, first communion, confirmation, catechism. She'd learned about the layered afterlife of heaven, limbo, purgatory, and hell. And because none of it had made any sense to her, when she'd turned sixteen she'd told her parents she wouldn't be going to church anymore. To their credit, they hadn't tried to argue her out of it.

In the years since, she'd had Jess, crimes, investigations, but no spiritual life whatsoever. "I don't know what I believe," Charlie said finally. "I wake up sometimes at night feeling him nearby. I dream about him. I dream about Matthew. They seem real when I open my eyes, but as soon as I sit up, it all fades away and what I find is an empty house. Silence. No husband, no baby, no dog, just some fucker out there who did it and split."

"Revenge, just like I said before." She shook her head. "It won't change anything."

"It'll make me feel better. Doesn't that count?"

"Yeah, it counts. Vent your rage and you probably won't get cancer."

"Well, gee, I guess that's something to be thankful for."

"If you have a few more minutes, let's sit in the van, okay?"

Charlie glanced at her watch, making sure she would have time to talk to Rain and get a bite to eat before she met Leo Wells at the bureau warehouse later that night. But even if she'd been short on time, which she wasn't, she wouldn't have said anything. She sensed Rain was working toward something important, something Charlie desperately needed to know.

Once they were inside the van, the windows open to the night air, Rain brought a folder out of her bag and set it on her lap. "Since the accident, have you noticed anything unusual about yourself, Charlie?"

Charlie, irritable now, snapped, "Shit, Rain, my life turned inside out. Of course I've noticed differences."

"An internal difference. Habits, thought patterns, hunches, dreams . . ."

"Dreams. My dreams are incredibly vivid. I can't stand the sight of meat anymore. And my hunches seem stronger."

"Stronger how?"

"I'm not sure." Charlie raked her fingers back through her hair and tried to find the right words. "For years my hunches were right here." She pressed her hands to her abdomen. "In my gut. Now they seem to move around. They're in my hands, my feet, my nose, my toes and eyes, and my goddamn ass. It's all screwed up."

Rain removed papers from the folder. "Did anyone in the hospital inform you that you died, Charlie?"

"Died?"

"Yes."

"C'mon. I had surgery. Jess died. Matt died. I was just out of it."

"Actually, your heart stopped for about two minutes, Charlie."

She handed Charlie a sheet of paper. "It's right here. In your medical records."

She glanced at the piece of paper, stumbled over the medical jargon, then saw words that even a moron could understand: *No vital signs for two minutes and twelve seconds.*

Charlie tossed the sheet of paper on the dashboard. Her head hurt. Her stomach growled. "I died and *no one told me?* How the hell can they do that?"

"The ER physician told Alex. I guess he left it up to Alex to tell you."

"Alex has been treating me like I'm made out of crystal. How'd you get my records?"

"I called in a favor. One doc to another. When you were in my office yesterday, I realized you exhibited some of the same behavioral patterns I'd seen in some of my hospice patients who died and were resuscitated. Two of them actually underwent such dramatic transformations, they went into remission and left the center."

"They had to die to be cured?"

"In a sense, yes. Both had classic NDEs—near death experiences. The tunnel. The white light. Talking to dead relatives, angels, the whole nine yards."

"I didn't talk to angels, Rain. I didn't—" A memory bumped up against her, something about Chiloé.

"What?" Rain asked. "What is it?"

"I don't know. I have this vague memory about the island off the coast of Chile where Jess and I went on our honeymoon. The memory seems connected to the hospital somehow."

"Maybe that will be a place to start."

"Start what?"

"Remembering. Quite a few people who go through NDEs are changed in profound ways. It's as if dying wakes up their spiritual selves. Some find that they're psychic."

"I occasionally watch *Oprah,* you know."

"Okay, sorry. It's just that we've never talked about this stuff, not really. I didn't know how much you were aware of."

"I'm a trivia expert. Go on."

"In one dramatic case, a woman died for about a minute during routine surgery. When she came out of it, she was able to describe everything that had gone on in the ER while she was dead. She even described the hairstyle of the head scrub nurse. None of this is uncommon with NDEs, but what makes this case unusual is that the woman had been blind since birth."

"In other words, consciousness isn't centered in your brain."

"Exactly."

"But nothing like that happened to me."

"Not that you remember. But you've changed, Charlie, and it's not just because your husband and son died. You've changed because you died."

"You saw all this during the fifteen minutes I was in your office?"

"You were in there for nearly an hour, not fifteen minutes."

"Impossible."

"What do you remember about the office visit?"

"You removed my stitches. Took my blood pressure. We talked. You had a chat with Alex. I don't know, routine stuff."

Rain nodded, but didn't say anything.

"That isn't how it went?" Charlie asked.

"It went like that. But there was more. At one point you seemed to zone out or something, and then you started telling me stuff about Nick that you couldn't possibly know."

Nick was Rain's twelve-year-old son. "I did? Like what?"

"Trouble he's having at school with some boys who used to be his friends. I didn't even know about it. I went home last night and confronted him, and he broke down and told me what's been going on."

"Why don't I remember any of that?"

"I don't know, but I have a few theories. You want to hear them?"

"Do I have a choice?"

Rain smiled sheepishly. "No."

"Yeah, that's what I thought. Okay, what're your theories?"

"It may be that you can't accept intuitive information on a conscious level yet. For years you've had hunches connected with work, but the hunches just came through and you acted on them. You didn't think about them. Now, suddenly, you're giving voice to that information and your conscious mind doesn't know how to deal with it, so it shuts you out."

"You're making me sound schizoid, Rain."

"Hey, honey, this is what happened to the most documented seer of the twentieth century. Edgar Cayce had to go to sleep before he could give psychic information. He wasn't schizoid, and neither are you. Consider yourself an explorer. Approach it with that kind of openness."

Charlie didn't feel like an explorer. She felt like a small kid who had gotten lost in a department store and wanted her mommy. She suddenly leaned toward Rain and hugged her. "Thanks for being there for me, Rain."

"This is what we are, you and me. We missed getting born into the same family, so this is the next best thing." She sat back, her hands still on Charlie's arms. "Your hunches? Those fall into the realm of the sixth sense. We agree on that?"

"Yeah, I guess so. I just never thought of them as a sixth sense. I mean, there was nothing weird or strange about them. I'd get them, act on them, and that was it."

"Clairvoyance, clairsentience, clairaudience, medical intuition . . . they're all part of the sixth sense." She touched her index finger to a spot between her eyes. "They come from here. The sixth energy center. But I think that what dying awakes in people is a seventh sense." She touched her hand to the top of her skull. "Your seventh energy center is blown wide open."

"I don't understand."

Rain hesitated before she spoke. "It's not just a psychic faculty. It's almost like your entire being opens up to the invisible world that runs just beneath the surface of consciousness. You open to the collective mind, to a new sense of space and time. The seventh sense is about learning to use your consciousness in new ways, and synchronicities play a part in all of it." She paused. "You know what synchronicities are, right?"

"Carl Jung. Psych one-oh-one."

Rain laughed. "Right. Meaningful coincidences. Be alert for them, Charlie." Then she glanced at her watch. "I've got to scoot. Nick needs help with his math homework. Stay in touch, okay?" She winked. "And follow your hunches."

Charlie watched her cross the street to her car and drive off. *Follow your hunches.* The sixth sense. *Learn to use your conscious-*

ness in new ways. The seventh sense. Great advice, except that at the moment she had no hunches, no insights, no sixth sense, and definitely no seventh sense, and maybe no sense at all. The only thing she felt right then was a burning unease that nothing at all was what it appeared to be.

Christine holds Lily's hand while they walk. Lily likes the way it feels in her own. She likes Christine's face too, a perfect oval framed by hair the same color as Henry's fur, not brown, but brown shot through with red. Her eyes are the color of honey and seem very kind.

The problem is that Lily can't remember how she knows this young woman. "Doris tells me you've been spending a lot of time in the garden, Mom."

Mom. There it is, Lily thinks. Mom. This is her Chrissy, her daughter, her only child. When did she get so big? Lily still remembers her as a little pink bundle of skin and hair. Now she's a grown woman.

"What garden?"

"This garden. Out here in the courtyard."

"Henry is missing. I have to look for Henry, Chrissy."

Her eyes go all funny and she looks away from Lily, toward the fence. "Oh, Mom," she says softly. "Dad's been dead awhile."

And the memory slides into place, her husband of fifty-two years lying in a coffin. A door slams on that picture.

"I hate that fence. I wish they would take it down."

Chrissy squeezes her hand. "Mom, you have to promise me that you won't run again."

"You run with me." Lily giggles, but her daughter doesn't even smile and she suddenly feels like crying. "Stay with me."

"I'm here, Mom. I only went on vacation, but I'm back now."

They pass Doris, who calls Chrissy over. "Be right back, Mom."

Lily watches them. They whisper. She knows they're talking about her. She slides her hand into the pocket of her slacks and feels food.

Food wrapped in napkins.

Her heart jumps and she hurries off, away from Doris and Christine and their whispers. The food, something about the food and the garden pushes her forward. Lily feels whatever it is, feels it on the other side of the fence that surrounds her mind. She just can't push through that fence yet and grasp whatever it is.

When she's deep in the bushes, where the shade from the trees is thickest, she crouches down at the fence and whispers, "Henry."

Lily isn't sure why she does this. She knows only that she must because Henry is missing and she has to call him home. Leaves rustle, a snout appears. The dog crawls on his stomach across the ground, remaining hidden. He greets her at the fence with licks, whimpers, a soft bark. Lily tells him not to bark, she's afraid that if someone hears him he won't be here next time. That happened to her when she was a little girl, that stray pup she found that her daddy took away. She won't let anyone take Henry away.

"Food, plenty of food." She empties her pockets on the ground and stuffs food through the fence. She scratches Henry behind the ears as he gobbles everything in sight. Such a big dog, so soft, he's her dog.

His ribs show. One ear folds over at the top. One of his front legs is injured, swollen, encrusted with blood. She wants to help him and starts digging at the bottom of the fence, trying to make a hole big enough for him to squeeze through. Then someone calls her name and she's afraid and the dog crawls back into the thick bushes on the other side of the fence.

"Lily honey, what're you doing down there on your knees? And what's all over your slacks?" Doris again. Doris.

Hands help Lily to her feet. She throws her arms around Chrissy's neck and holds her close and whispers, "Henry ate everything in my pockets."

"What?" She steps back, looking at Lily like she's crazy. "What're you talking about, Mom? Dad didn't eat anything in your pockets." She pats Lily's pockets. "Are you stealing food again, Mom? Don't they feed you enough in this place?"

Henry is thirsty. Lily needs to put water in his dish, but already he is slipping back into the brush, making himself invisible. Run, Henry, she thinks. Run before they find you. Run.

10

Explorers

(1)

Doug Logan hated the smell in the warehouse, a cold, metallic odor mixed with the stink of cleansers and grease and the past. The cavernous building, filled with cars and boats and planes that the FBI had impounded, reminded him of his years in the bureau. He had loved his work, loved that part of his life. But that door had slammed shut three and a half years before and now he felt like an impostor.

He waited near the front of the building while Wells walked off to find out where the Explorer was in this massive ensemble of vehicles. He didn't expect to pick up much of anything from the car. The local cops had held on to it too long. Any emotional residue from the accident probably had been obliterated by the dozens of people who had touched the car, turned it inside out for evidence. He felt like telling Wells to forget it.

But he couldn't. He had committed to this case that day at the accident site and had rearranged his life to accommodate it. Last week, he and Buffet had moved into a campsite near Hollywood Beach and set up temporary quarters in a camper provided by the bureau. They had also provided a car, a cell phone, an expense account, more perks than he'd known in his twenty-two years as a bureau employee. Then there was the money, which would pad his sorry bank account.

His perks, in fact, seemed excessive for this case. Even though it gratified him to see so much effort going into the investigation, he sensed it had little to do with the Calloways. This had all the earmarks of bureau politics, the same old power games, with Wells, Mitchell, and Harnson at the center of it all.

Wells hurried back over. "It's supposed to be way at the back, and if it's not there, it's in the garage. Crap shoot either way."

They stopped at the far end of the warehouse, where half a dozen cars in various states of ruin stood in the glare of the overhead lights, testimony to the perils of interstate driving. "It's the maroon Explorer," Wells said.

Logan walked slowly around the car, amazed that anyone had come out of it alive. The worst damage was to the driver's side, where the door had caved in, the window had shattered, and the windshield had so many cracks and fissures, it resembled a map of intersecting highways. The remains of the air bag stuck to the steering wheel, the seat, the dashboard, like pieces of some huge condom that had burst.

The story didn't improve much on the passenger side. The sliding door looked like a crushed aluminum can, the passenger door hung by a couple of threads and screws, and the seat rested at an odd angle.

"Pretty bad, huh," Wells said, following Logan. "You need to sit inside to read it?"

"I don't know. I've never done this before."

Wells glanced anxiously at his watch. "Charlie's going to be here soon. I think it'd be better if you read it before then."

"Why didn't you tell me she was coming, Leo? We could've scheduled it for another night."

"I forgot. It got sandwiched in between a lot of stuff that's going on at work, Doug. If it's a problem, we can—"

"Forget it. We're here."

Logan approached the Explorer as though it were a slumbering beast that might wake up any second now and bite off his head. He suddenly grew short of breath and started to sweat. Panic gnawed at his insides. He stopped and shook his head. "I can't do this, Leo."

"Don't give me that crap, man. Of course you can do it. Just slide your ass in there and start touching stuff."

"But even if I get impressions, it doesn't mean they're right."

"Let me worry about what's right. I've worked up some computer models on the crash and I've got a few ideas about what happened. You just get in there and tell me what you feel." He brought out that mini cassette recorder and slipped it in Logan's shirt pocket. "Go to it, *kemo sabe.*"

Logan felt that terrible tightness in the center of his chest again. He rubbed at it and moved closer to the car. He squeezed through the opening, scooted into the driver's seat, took a deep breath, and placed his hands against the steering wheel.

"Fuck," he whispered, and was gone.

Rain hammers the car, smears across the windshield, he can't see a foot in front of him. Lightning tears open the sky, thunder roars, the dog starts howling, Charlie shouts at him to slow down, to slow the hell down, the roads are wet, they might skid, it was stupid to leave the house, she shouldn't have listened to him . . .

Yes, yes, and yes. He's going to pull over to the curb, get his bearings. But when he switches lanes, a tide of water splashes over the windshield, plunging them into darkness. The engine sputters, coughs. He pumps the accelerator and the car lurches forward, kicking up more water. As it runs off, an explosion of light fills the car.

For some reason, it reminds him of the lights he and Charlie saw that night on the hillside in cheelowaye, waiting for a glimpse of the ghost ship, a local legend that had fascinated him then and still does. He starts to mention this to her, but the light swallows them and something slams into his side of the car.

His window shatters. Tiny missiles of glass pierce his neck, his cheek, his left eye. He shrieks and his hands fly to his face, the car spinning wildly, Charlie screaming, Paz howling, the unbearable pain eating him alive. His foot pumps frantically at the brakes, but they don't work, they're too wet. The air bag presses painfully against his chest, pushing him back against his seat, holding him there so he can't reach the key, can't yank it out.

The car crashes, the screams and howls continue, and outside, tires squeal. He tries to turn his head to look out the window, but it's already too late. A car rams them from behind and he feels something snap in his neck. No pain, just the snapping sensation.

Then silence. Charlie is no longer screaming. Paz no longer barks. He shouts her name, tries to lift his arm to touch her. His arm refuses to move. The air bag, his arm is trapped under the air bag. No, not trapped. It's dead. He can't feel it. Can't feel his legs either. But he feels the warmth of the blood pouring from his injured eye and the corners of his mouth, feels it streaming over his chin. He feels rain and wind stinging his cheeks.

And, distantly, he hears an engine revving.

"Charlie." He whispers her name again and again and finally she groans, she whimpers, she screams.

"Help, get help, I can't move," he gasps.

She struggles against the air bag, her fingertips graze his cheek. "Oh God, I . . . Christ, Jess . . . I'll . . . I'll get help," she sobs.

Her door creaks open, the storm rushes in, wind and rain, the roar of thunder. She stumbles out and Paz, barking, scrambles out behind her. Darkness encroaches at the corner of his good eye, an unforgiving darkness that he knows has nothing to do with the storm, the night. This darkness approaches swiftly, a headless horseman that gallops across the unknown continent beyond the night, beyond the storm, beyond his ability to imagine.

A heartbeat before this terrible darkness reaches him, he hears the car that hit them, hears its tires squealing as it peels away.

He turns his head—he can still do that, his head still swivels on his shoulders—and he glimpses it as it speeds past them. A dark sedan, moving like a bat outta hell.

Then everything goes black, utterly and silently black.

Logan pried his hands off the steering wheel and scrambled toward the passenger door as fast as he could move. His body screamed with pain, his eye ached, he could hardly breathe. Wells grabbed his arm and pulled him the rest of the way out, and Logan stumbled forward, away from Wells, away from the Explorer, away from the horror that lay inside it.

His knees gave out and he sank to the warehouse floor, his head spinning, his stomach heaving. He was dimly aware of a high-pitched keening sound that rose in the air around him and suddenly realized it was coming from him.

"Drink this, man." Wells thrust a tall cup in front of him.

Logan somehow managed to get it to his mouth and drank. Water, clear, cold water. He poured the rest of it over his head, and it sobered him instantly. He dropped the cup and rocked back on his heels and rubbed his hands against his thighs. He inhaled deeply, exhaled forcefully, and after a few moments he felt strong enough to raise his head.

Wells was no longer alone. A tall, slender woman stood next to him, her face so pale, she might have just risen from the grave. Her blond hair fell almost to her shoulders in erratic, frizzy waves. Piercing blue eyes. Compelling eyes. Charlie Calloway. Jesus. Had he said anything? How much had she heard?

Logan grasped Wells's extended hand and Wells pulled him to his feet. "You okay, amigo?"

"Better."

"Charlie Calloway, Doug Logan."

"Hi," she said.

"Hi."

Logan wanted to get the hell out of there, but couldn't think of a graceful way to do it. Even Wells looked awkward and uncertain, glancing between Logan and the woman, as if hoping for a cue from one or the other. "Logan's the guy I told you about that I worked with at the Jax office, Charlie."

"Right. I remember. But what was he doing in my car?"

"He was, uh, doing me a favor," Wells replied.

"A favor," she repeated, obviously not getting it.

"We hired him to work the case," Wells went on. "On our side, not Mitch's," he added quickly.

"I don't understand."

Logan knew he should leap in at this point and give it to her straight, but that wasn't his job. Let Wells do it, he thought.

"Tell her what you do, Doug."

"I don't know what I do," he replied, and walked off.

(2)

"Where the hell did you dig *him* up, Leo? The guy's whacked."

"He's eccentric."

"Eccentric. Yeah, he's definitely that." The long salt-and-pepper hair, the sagging mustache, the lean face deeply lined from years of tropical sun. He looked like one of their street sources, a goddamn space cadet. "He has the social skills of a hamster, for Christ's sakes. And what the hell was he doing in my car?"

Wells suddenly lost his patience. "He's psychic, okay, Charlie? The guy died nearly four years ago and came out of it with this ability to see shit that we can't. I was hoping he'd be gone by the time you got here because I know what you think of psychics."

Charlie suddenly felt ashamed of herself and quickly squeezed Wells's arm. "I'm sorry. I'm being an asshole."

"Naw, I am."

An awkward moment passed. "So what did he, uh, get? I'd like to hear his impressions."

Wells made a face and shook his head. "He just confirmed what we already knew from the paint chips: a black car. He said a sedan. Other than that, let him and me work this end of things."

Here it was again, she thought. The kid-glove treatment. Didn't anyone understand that work would be her redemption? "I appreciate that you want to protect me, Leo. But right now everyone's trying to protect me, and what I need the most are leads."

Wells rubbed his jaw, lowered his gaze to the floor, and glanced quickly at Logan, hunched over the water fountain. "I'll play the tape for you." He brought the recorder out of his pocket, rewound it, hit play. Nothing happened. "Shit. The voice activation gizmo didn't work."

Charlie took the recorder from him and murmured "Testing, testing," until the light came on. She put it in the pocket of her short-sleeved blouse and went over to Logan. "Excuse me. I'd like to hear what impressions you picked up from my car, Mr. Logan."

He raised up from the water fountain. His dark eyes reminded her of bottomless lakes; they merely reflected her face and revealed nothing of what lay in their depths. "It's not very pretty," he said.

"I don't give a shit about pretty. I just want to know."

"Right before you were hit, your husband was thinking of *cheelo-waye*. I don't have any idea what that is, but maybe you do. There was something about a ghost ship."

He can't possibly know that. No one knows about the ghost ship.

"This wasn't an accident, Ms. Calloway. The driver rammed you intentionally. I think he hit the driver's side first. Then he backed up and rammed you again. I believe that's when one of your husband's vertebrae snapped, leaving him paralyzed from the waist down. A piece of glass penetrated his brain through his left eye. The air bag hit him with such force that he could barely breathe. It felt like the air bag ruptured something in his chest."

His words pushed her to the edge of an abyss so steep, she saw only blackness below. She felt light-headed and dizzy and backed up to the wall to steady herself. *The driver rammed you intentionally.* Jesus God. This made it a first-degree homicide, not a vehicular homicide. This changed everything.

Logan paused. "Do you want me to go on?"

"Yes." She barely got the word out.

"No," Wells said. "That's enough, Logan."

"Leo, I need to hear this." Logan's words squashed out whatever doubt she might have still harbored about hunting the bastard to the end of the universe. "I want to know everything."

"I'm describing my impressions to you," Logan said. "And they may not be factual."

"The injuries are consistent with the autopsy," Wells said, glancing uneasily at Charlie. "We don't know about the rest."

"Go on, Mr. Logan," she said. "Please."

"You came to at some point, stumbled out of the car, and your dog went after you. When he couldn't rouse you, he took off. Just before your husband lost consciousness, he saw the dark sedan that had hit you. The driver fled."

A sedan, a dark sedan, and some maniac who rammed them *intentionally*. Her mind raced now, habit kicked in, and a dozen questions leaped to mind. "Can you describe the driver of the sedan?"

Logan shook his head. "Your husband didn't see the driver, only the car."

"Describe the car."

"A sedan, a dark sedan, that's all he saw."

No, she refused to accept that. "Did it have two doors or four?"

"I don't know."

"Was it expensive?"

"I don't know."

"What about the make or model?"

Logan squeezed the bridge of his nose and shut his eyes, as if trying to find the image that had come to him in the car. "I think it was a recent model. With four doors. Yeah, I'm pretty sure there were four doors."

"American? Foreign?"

"I don't know. What I do know is that the sedan was bashed up too, and I don't think the driver would've been able to drive more than twenty-five miles."

"The computer models say he couldn't drive that car more than fifteen miles from the accident site, twenty max," Wells said. "That'd be the equivalent of north Miami to south Lauderdale."

Charlie's brain instantly threw out a map of the city with a circle drawn around the accident site that extended fifteen miles in every direction. *Fifteen or twenty square miles.* She would have more luck finding a lost earring in a pile of cow shit.

"Is there anything else you can tell me?"

His eyes were open again, bottomless lakes that tossed her own image back to her. "What do you remember about what happened?" Logan asked.

"Nothing."

He nodded. Glanced down. She had the distinct impression that he was considering something. She looked over at Wells, hoping for a hint. But he shrugged and rolled his eyes toward the warehouse ceiling, as if to say he didn't have a clue what the hell was going through Logan's mind just then. Logan was silent so long, she thought he'd dozed off or something. Then he raised his head. "Give me your hand, Ms. Calloway."

No *please,* no *may I,* just a simple demand. Go pound sand, she thought, but didn't say it. She held out her hand. He hesitated, eyeing her hand with the same wariness she'd seen in Paz when some stranger with a soft voice approached him. Then he gently pressed her hand between both of his and shut his eyes.

Large hands. Warm, dry palms with calluses. Strands of his hair had come loose from his ponytail and curled against the sides of his neck. She could see the veins in his translucent eyelids. Then she felt a sudden flash of heat against her palm, and Logan winced, his fingers twitched against her hand, and she felt herself sliding, shrieking, toward the edge of the abyss.

Seconds before she reached the edge, before she jerked her hand away from Logan's, tears squeezed from the corners of his eyes. Charlie saw them in a weird slow motion, saw them falling and rolling down the sides of his face like beads of sweat, glistening in the warehouse lights.

At that moment she saw with utter certainty that Logan, this stranger whom she'd met about twenty minutes ago, felt what she felt, her loss and confusion, her sorrow and guilt, perhaps even her rage and, deeper still, her unexpressed grief. It shocked her so deeply that she abruptly broke the connection between them by jerking around and leaning over the water fountain.

The chill of the water became a chill in her bones. She straightened and rubbed her hands over her bare arms and wanted nothing more than to go home and fall into her bed, to feel sorry for herself, to rant and rave and mourn. She made a beeline toward the ladies' room, the insides of her eyes throbbing.

She felt, suddenly, like she was coming down with a cold or the flu or worse, something that would lay her up for days. A part of her welcomed the thought, welcomed the prospect of lying in bed and doing nothing, the TV droning in the background, her energy consumed by sniffles, fever, congestion, aching limbs.

But another part of her knew that if she got sick now, this investigation would come to a screeching halt because Mitch didn't give a shit, Harnson wasn't bright enough, Wells couldn't do it alone, and Logan would just wander back to his aimless life in the Keys. If she got sick, the bastard who had killed Jess and Matt would never be found.

Deliberate. *The driver rammed you deliberately.*

But why?

In the ladies' room she grabbed a handful of towels from the dispenser and soaked them under the faucet. She pressed the whole soggy mess to her face and rubbed and rubbed until her skin felt used up, raw. When she finally looked at herself in the mirror, it seemed that she could see Jess's face hovering in the glass next to her head, a mirage, a phantom, wishful thinking.

The ghost ship. Logan knew that.

On their honeymoon, she and Jess had taken a ferry from Puerto Montt, the end of land transportation in Chile, to the island of Chiloé. They'd stayed in the town of Ancud, a fishing village where the locals believed in mermaids and a ghost ship that supposedly sailed into the harbor from time to time. One night Jess had convinced her to climb a hill above the harbor and wait for the ghost ship.

Logan saw that.

She swept the mess of towels off the edge of the sink and tossed it into the trash can on her way out the door. She intended to suck whatever she could from Logan. The man could see things, no doubt about it. That meant he could provide her with leads. It meant the trail might not be as cold as she'd thought.

When she walked out of the rest room, she saw only Wells, moving slowly around the ruined Explorer, a video camera held to his eye. "Where's Logan?" she asked.

Wells lowered the camera. "He split. I need some additional footage of the car for the computer model."

"Split where? I need to talk to him some more."

"I don't know where he went, girl. I never know. That's the whole thing with Logan, okay? If he doesn't want to be found, you can't find him. You have to wait for him to come to you."

Wells looked over at her then, his naked compassion not only in his eyes, but in every part of him. Like her hunches. Then he opened his arms and Charlie walked into them, and after a time she couldn't tell which of them gave comfort and which of them took it.

"We'll find the fucker, Charlie. One way or another, we'll find him."

(3)

Logan screeched to a halt in his campsite, killed the headlights, and sat back, still gripping the wheel, his eyes squeezed shut. No more. He was outta there. He just couldn't do this kind of shit. He had his own fucking problems. He didn't want to know about the woman's pain. He didn't want to know the depth of what she'd suffered, the depth of her loss, the depth of her rage.

He scrambled from the car and stormed into the camper, slamming the door so hard, the windows shook. He flicked on a light, yanked the curtains shut. "Hey, Buffet!" he shouted. "Rise and shine, we're going home, back to fishing from the dock."

The cat poked his head out from under a pile of Logan's clothes and meowed. Then he curled up and went back to sleep. Logan hurried through the camper, scooping up his belongings, stuffing them into the pair of duffel bags he'd brought with him. Already, he could smell the windswept air on Minnow Key and feel the heat of the dock against his bare feet.

But then he thought of the dark sedan slamming into the Explorer, glass flying everywhere, metal collapsing inward, rain pouring down. He thought of its tires squealing against the wet street as it raced in reverse and crashed into the Explorer again. He thought of that petty tyrant Mitchell, of the endless bureaucratic bureau cogs who would generate mounds of paperwork, and no answers.

You're a selfish prick, Logan.

But it's not my problem.

You're a selfish prick coward.

I'm not up to this. I can't do this. I don't want to do it.

Then go hide in the Keys again. Go hide on the little island with your cat.

I'm not hiding. I'm—

"Shit," Logan murmured, and sank to the edge of the bunk next to his cat.

Who the fuck was he kidding? He wasn't going anywhere. He owed Wells, the debt had come due. He covered his face with his hands and sat there, feeling miserable and alone.

II

At Sea

(1)

They went out right after breakfast Saturday morning, the three of them on the sloop, putting up the canal, into the extraordinary light. Anita loved this time of day. The tropical light deepened the color of everything, gulls pinwheeled overhead, the air seemed steeped in promise.

The faint breeze would hardly fill a thimble, much less the sails, so Frank used the engine. She enjoyed the rhythmic, predictable sound of it, like a heartbeat.

She and Joey sat on a bench at the stern of the forty-foot sloop, shoulders touching, Nemo the cat rubbing up against them. Her son's orange life jacket nearly swallowed his body, but he didn't seem to notice.

"Mommy, look."

He pointed off to his right at a blue heron that lifted suddenly from the trees along the shore, its long wings beating at the amber light. Anita shielded her eyes with her hands and watched the bird fly toward the sun.

"Daddy, get a picture," Joey shouted.

"Got it already." Frank, steering the boat, held up the camera. "Come back here with me, sport. We'll take more pictures."

But Joey shook his head and pressed up against Anita. "Is it okay if I stay here with you, Mommy?"

"Of course it is." She slipped an arm around his shoulders and planted a kiss on the top of his head. How much longer would it be before this display of affection embarrassed him? But more to the point, why did he choose to stay here with her than to sit with his father?

"Hey, Nita," Frank called. "Can you take the wheel a second? I've got to use the head."

"Sure." She got up. "Be right back, Joey."

She noticed how good Frank looked out on the water, sunlight threading through his hair, his body tanned and compact from a spring of sailing with Jerome MacLean. The thought of MacLean brought back the accident and its immediate aftermath, and her mood plummeted.

It had been fifteen days since the accident, and she'd thought of little else. The details drifted through her constantly, flotsam from a nightmare she couldn't shake. The accident was the first thing she thought about in the morning and the thought that followed her into sleep at night.

But that morning when she'd rolled out of bed, her first thought had been that it would be a good day for the three of them to go sailing. A picnic lunch, snorkeling, basking in the sun, Florida stuff that would mark the end of the first week of June and the end of school.

Her reprieve had lasted only a few hours.

And what about Frank? What did he think about any of it? For the first time in all their years together, she didn't have a clue.

Neither of them had mentioned the accident since they'd returned the U-Haul. Not a word. Yet, it sat between them at meals and lay between them in bed at night. It metastasized beneath the surface of their marriage, infecting everything.

"Thanks," he said as she took the wheel. "Keep it on this heading. How about if we go to that island in the bay where we had a picnic last spring?"

"Sounds fine."

"You all right?"

No. "Sure. You?"

"Yeah, I'm okay."

He touched her hair, her shoulders, a touch that hesitated against her damp skin, asking to explore farther: His thumb slipped under the strap of her two-piece, nudging it down over the curve of her shoulder. "Did we remember to bring sun block?"

We. Whenever it involved a domestic situation, Frank spoke in the plural, even though he rarely thought of things like sun block or child care or how dinner would get to the table or how the cat would get to the vet. *And not so long ago, you were extolling the equality in your marriage. Ha.*

What equality? Yes, she worked in a professional capacity, but she wasn't *the breadwinner,* which meant she wasn't entitled to any of the perks of a breadwinner. Which meant she was still mom and housekeeper, laundress and chauffeur and cook. Which meant she still did all the grunt work in addition to her employment.

For Frank, however, everything was more clear cut. Domestic was her domain; finances were his. Whenever his work and their finances were involved, he spoke in the singular, the ubiquitous "I," as if she and Joey were no longer connected to his life.

"*We* didn't remember sun block," she replied. "*I* did."

His hands dropped away from her arms and he drew back, his expression utterly cold. "Someone got up on the wrong side of the bed."

"It would help if we talked about . . . about everything that happened."

Frank's eyes darted toward Joey, then back to her. "Don't talk so loud," he ordered.

"Loud*ly.*" It came out automatically, the result of her years of teaching. She started to apologize, just as she always had in the past for one thing or another. But the words refused to come out, and after a moment or two of his stony silence, she felt grateful that she hadn't said anything.

Frank, obviously irritated and doing nothing to hide it, drew his fingers back through his hair, fixed his hands to his hips, and gazed out over the water, offering her a view of his profile. "What's there to talk about? It's over. You're the one who said we need to put it behind us and move forward."

"It's not that easy."

His gaze met hers, eyes hard now, intractable, as cold as Pluto. "Of course it's not *easy*. None of it is *easy*, Anita. But what the hell's the alternative? You want me to go to the police? Is that it?"

"Of course not. It's just . . ."

"What?" He gripped her shoulders.

"That hurts." She wrenched away from him and he looked— what? Surprised? Stunned? "Forget it, just forget it."

She turned her back on him and a moment later heard him descend into the cabin. She steered the sloop out of the canal and into the intracoastal, but no longer noticed the light, the trees, the blue dome of the sky. She stared at her son's back, remembering the joy she'd felt the day he was born. She wondered if she would ever experience that kind of joy again.

A memory surfaced, one of those silly memories that seemed to have no connection whatsoever with her life now. She recalled standing in front of a class of gifted first-graders when she was a teaching intern and showing them a mixed-up drawing. *What's wrong with this picture?*

She glanced out at the homes they passed, green yards sloping down to the seawall, where boats were docked. Now and then she caught sight of parents playing basketball or swimming with their children. Peals of laughter drifted through the summer air. She looked at her son, heard Frank banging around in the cabin, felt the terrible tightness in her chest.

Yeah, Anita. What's wrong with this picture?

(2)

In the first few moments after Benedict entered the spacious cabin, the cabin that smelled faintly of salt and fish and mold, he felt as if he'd stumbled into the cellar of his own mind.

Dark shapes clung to the walls like sucker fish, like bottom feeders. Ugly stains the color of dried blood dotted the floor. The huge water keg in the far corner looked like a Pillsbury Dough Boy gone bad. His ears buzzed, a white noise of voices, all of them clambering to be heard. He pressed his hands over his ears and squeezed his eyes shut, willing everything to stop, to just fucking stop for five seconds.

But with his eyes closed, images from the incident rose up randomly, each one brilliantly and painfully detailed. The emotions he'd felt at the moment of impact, the unmitigated satisfaction. The shape of the gearshift under his hand as he'd slammed the Beamer into reverse and hit the car again. The squeal of his tires on the road as he'd spun into a turn to head toward them again. In his memories, everything seemed vivid, colorful, like a glass mosaic struck through with sunlight.

He saw an instant replay in his head of a newspaper photo of the man he'd killed. *He got in my way. Shit happens.*

Then the images collapsed into an amorphous lake, primal matter that bubbled up and spewed into a new shape, that of Colin Thacker, his fat cheeks puffed out. *Are we getting the picture here, Frank?*

Benedict's arms, fists clenched, swung to his sides. The driver, MacLean, Thacker, Tillis, and now Anita. Next it would be Joey giving him a hard time, he thought, and walked back to the head and threw open the door.

The stench inside made him gag. He lifted the toilet seat with the toe of his sandal and saw toilet paper jammed inside with enough shit to kill an elephant. His rage swelled and he slammed the door and shouted, "Joey, get your butt down here now!"

Joey didn't appear. But the engine died and a moment later Anita hurried down the stairs. "What the hell are you shouting about?"

Benedict stabbed his thumb toward the head. "Joey didn't flush the goddamn toilet, and now it reeks in there, that's what." He threw open the door. "One flush and it's going to overflow. Tell him to get down here."

Red crept up Anita's neck, then exploded across her face. "I've got news for you, Frank. Joey hasn't stepped foot on the boat in over a month. The only people who've been on board are those guys who were repairing the shower. Two weeks ago, I told you it reeked down here. You either didn't hear me or forgot about it."

"Why didn't you mention it this morning?"

"I have other things to think about."

"You must've smelled something when you brought the cooler on board."

Livid now, she let loose. "This boat isn't my responsibility, so stop acting like it is. I made the picnic lunch, packed towels and extra clothes, filled the gas tank, canceled Joey's karate lesson, and that was after I'd made breakfast and straightened the house. The only goddamn thing you did was wake up, pour yourself a cup of coffee, and stroll out to the dock. Stop blaming other people, Frank."

"Mommy?"

Benedict and his wife spun simultaneously to see Joey perched on the top step, his fists pressed into his cheeks, his eyes brimming with tears. "Don't fight," he said. "Please don't fight."

Anita rushed up the stairs. "We're not fighting, honey." She swept Joey up in her arms and vanished topside.

Benedict, fists clenched, winced when the cabin door slammed shut. In his head he saw his wife picking up her cell phone and calling her father, telling him everything, *confessing* to him. And good ol' Chad Randall, of course, would bring his considerable fortune and all it could buy between his daughter and her no-good husband. Benedict knew that he would be left holding the goddamn bag because she would turn state's evidence against him to save herself.

He made a beeline into the galley, hurled open one of the cabinet doors, and reached behind a box of supplies. His fingers closed around a bottle of scotch.

Just one. I need it. I deserve it. And fuck Anita and her righteous feminist bullshit.

With that, he spun the top on the bottle and tipped it to his mouth.

And when he dropped his head back, he saw it, a spiderweb strung up in a corner near the ceiling. The spider hung in the center, torturing a fly that writhed against the sticky threads. A *Laxoceles reclusa,* otherwise known as a brown recluse, or violin spider.

The bite, a nerve poison that destroyed cells as it traveled through tissue, rarely caused immediate pain. But within an hour or so, pain developed in the area of the bite, which became bruised, red, and swollen. The pain, he knew, could be excruciating. The destruction of red blood cells often caused kidney or liver failure in children, the elderly, and anyone with a compromised immune system. Death happened rarely from the bite, but if the person was left untreated or was bitten in the face or head, near the brain, death was a given.

Benedict set the flask down, dug out his keys, and unlocked a cabinet where he kept his private marine belongings and his portable spider gear. Anita couldn't even stand to look at this stuff. But over the years he'd collected some incredible specimens out on these islands, so fuck Anita and her squeamishness.

He picked up a small glass cage with tiny air holes in it. He unlatched the lid on top, swung it to one side, and snapped it shut, testing it. It worked on the same principle as a jaw.

Benedict spun the tiny circular glass top that covered a thick wire-mesh screen, testing it as well. Through this screen he could squeeze drops of water. Even though the inside of the cage was bare now, his spider cages at home contained a habitat, a little spider world replete with stones and moss and bark, leaves and humidity and other insects on which the spiders could sustain themselves.

Benedict worked a pair of thick gloves onto his hands. Metal braces fortified the fingertips. He supposed they weren't really necessary, because the fangs of most spiders simply weren't long enough to penetrate the fabric. But hell, the law had taught him caution in all things.

He pulled a chair over to a spot under the web, picked up the cage, the jaw hanging open, and stepped onto the chair. The spider, sensing his presence, scurried to the far side of its web. Benedict plucked a thread lightly with his finger, teasing the little fucker, trying to lure it back toward him.

His fascination with spiders had begun in childhood, after his old man's death. He used to spend hours in their attic, watching spiders being spiders. He'd learned how they spun their webs, how they caught and bit their prey, paralyzing them, then digesting them while their tiny hearts still throbbed. At some point during those years, he'd built the prototype for this little glass cage, a much cruder version to be sure, but effective nonetheless.

He plucked the silken thread again; this time the spider moved. It would take this fellow one more attempt; stubborn spiders usually succumbed on the third temptation. He had about two dozen habitats in the attic at home that held various species of spiders. Anita had seen his collection, expressed her unmitigated revulsion, and had never mentioned them again.

To Benedict, though, they represented the unmerciful beauty of nature—and a single vestige of peace that he'd known as a boy. In some ways, spiders had taught him more about the law than law school or his clients.

He plucked a thread of the web a third time, and the recluse took the bait. It darted forward and he brought the cage up under it and snapped the jaw of the lid over the spider, part of the web, and the pathetic, writhing fly.

He stepped down from the chair, latched the lid, and set the cage down. Inside, the spider scampered about furiously, aware that something had happened, but not entirely sure yet what that something entailed. Benedict fetched water from the sink and sprinkled it through the screen. Then he put the cage inside the cabinet, removed the gloves, and returned them to the shelf.

He had a sudden image of a miniature Anita inside one of the spider cages, her tiny fists banging against the glass walls, her tiny mouth open in a scream he couldn't hear. The perfect solution for a nagging wife: Shrink her somehow, then put her into a glass cage.

Would the recluse eat her?

He mulled this over as he stood at the open porthole, breathing in the humid sea air. It brought a perfect clarity to his thoughts, and he didn't like what he saw: that he remained vulnerable to discovery through the computer at the U-Haul company and through his wife.

If he sealed both of those leaks . . .

She loves you, Frankie. She's on your side.

Benedict heard the cabin door creak open and glanced back to see Joey coming down the steps. "Daddy, can I come see you?"

"Sure, sport."

And for the moments that he bounded down the stairs, in the sunlight that streamed through the open door, Benedict saw himself at six. The same body, the same hair, the same unquenchable thirst to make amends with his old man. Benedict moved toward his son, his smile widening, and swept Joey up into his arms and hugged him close. His son represented his genetic lineage; Joey was his eternal flame.

"I'm sorry, Daddy. I'm sorry I made you mad."

"You didn't, sport. I made myself mad. That clogged toilet is my fault, not yours." *I'll never hurt you, Joey. Never.*

He suddenly realized that he couldn't say the same for anyone else in his life, not even his wife.

12

Chico

(1)

Charlie, Charlie . . .

The voice snapped her out of a sound sleep and her eyes opened to light as pale as pus. She heard rain tapping the windows, but that was all. No voice. No one calling her name.

You imagined it, she thought, and rolled onto her side and shut her eyes once more. When it happened again moments later, she understood that the voice was internal. She didn't have a clue what to do, so she simply lay there, open and receptive despite the niggling fear that she was losing her mind.

A vivid image filled her, a mental postcard of a person and a place she hadn't seen for at least four months, maybe more. Charlie bolted upright, threw off the sheet, and tore into the bathroom to shower. Twenty minutes later, she backed out of her garage and headed east through the rain toward Miami Beach.

The Sunday-morning streets seemed blissfully free of traffic. The sun played hide-and-seek with the clouds, and the air that rushed through the van's windows smelled clean and rich, the way only summer air in South Florida could smell. She felt that she'd turned a critical corner, but toward what? Insanity? Or redemption?

She sped onto the MacArthur Causeway and shortly before she reached Miami Beach turned onto Star Island. She'd forgotten about the gate out front and dug through her wallet for the card that Chico had given her that would get her in. She couldn't find it. She called his number on the cell phone, his private number, the number that only his friends had.

The machine took her call, Chico's bouncy voice announcing in four languages that he wasn't available and all that. At the beep she said, "It's Calloway. If you're there, Chico, please pi—"

"Carlita?" The breathless, accented voice on the other end sounded half drugged with sleep or sex or some other excess. "It is really you?"

"I forgot my card, Chico. Can you open the gate?"

"The gate? *Dios mío,* you're at the *gate?* It's not even eight in the morning. Juan, Carlita, she is here. Hit the button for the gate. *Necesitamos café, con los pasteles que . . . Carlita, un minuto,* Juan has gone downstairs to open the gate. I meet you at the door."

Charlie started laughing. She could almost see Chico and Juan scrambling out of their canopy bed with the blue silk sheets, running in opposite directions and getting nowhere fast. *"Prontito,* Chico," she said, and hung up.

Moments later, the heavy iron gate slid to the right, and she drove on through, into the rarefied air of Star Island. Over the years, the island had been home to Don Johnson, Stallone, Gloria Estefan, and Madonna. She'd been out of that loop for so long, she didn't know which celebrities lived here now. Chico was the only one who mattered.

He'd dabbled in just about everything in his fifty years, but had started out as an actor on Spanish novelas—the Latino equivalent of soap operas. In those days, no one had known he was gay. Maybe even Chico hadn't known. For the last fifteen years he'd had his own talk radio show, which had grown from a one-man home business to a forty-man operation.

Chico Ruiz's show was now syndicated on every major Latino radio station in the country and more than three hundred American stations. He was the Cuban answer to Art Bell, a man who tackled every conceivable topic that might fall under "the weird and the strange," but who hadn't forgotten his Cuban roots. Talk radio hadn't made him rich—real estate investments had done that—but had nearly done him in.

A year into his career on talk radio, his lover at the time had been brutally murdered. And because the lover was a federal employee, Charlie had gotten the case. It was her third case out of Quantico and it had taken her twenty days to crack. The perp had gotten eight to fifteen and Chico had decided Charlie would be his friend for life.

He'd made good on his promise. When she'd been assigned to cover Little Havana, Chico had been her primary source. Because of leads he'd given her, she had been promoted after thirteen months and left Little Havana. Their friendship had endured in fits and starts after that, but he'd sent her a tremendous bouquet of roses when she was in the hospital and had left half a dozen messages on her answering machine.

He met her at the door, a short guy with dyed black hair and a Ricky Ricardo smile, who wore a black silk robe over blue cotton pajamas. He regarded her with dark, soulful eyes that saw everything, all at once, then he threw his arms around her and began to weep with loud, noisy sobs.

After a few minutes Juan appeared, a younger, taller man with the face of a hawk and the heart of a goddamn saint. He pried Chico away from Charlie and took him off into a corner for a few minutes. Charlie remained just inside the door, at the beginning of the long, marble hallway lined with the works of Cuban painters.

Chico returned in a more somber mood, with Juan forging on into the kitchen to create his usual epicurean wonders. "You never returned my calls," Chico said, hooking his arm through hers and leading her deeper into the house. The mansion. The cavernous palace that real estate had bought him.

The main room looked like something out of the late sixties, with posters on the walls of the Beatles, the Stones, the Grateful Dead. Alongside these were movie posters of Peter Fonda riding into the sunset in *Easy Rider,* of *2001: A Space Odyssey,* of *Woodstock.* The couch where they finally settled had come straight out of a Volkswagen Beetle, refurbished in red velvet and chrome. The house existed in a permanent sixties time warp.

"On May twenty-fourth, when I heard the news, I was in Nassau. Juan, he comes running in to tell me. I call Alex, eh? He says you cannot talk to anyone. I call the next morning, same story. I call that afternoon, same story. That night, the next morning, I decide your brother has one big problem. I get mad, he hangs up on me. I send flowers. I leave messages on your machine, I . . ."

"I woke up this morning thinking of you, that I hadn't returned your calls or thanked you for the roses."

His eyes misted and he looked down at the sapphire on his little finger, the ring that Juan had given him, a ring he twisted this way and that. "Name it, *mí amor. Anything.*"

Charlie pulled a city map from her shoulder bag and spread it out on the stone coffee table. A fifteen-mile radius around the accident site had been circled in bright red. "I need to know if any garage within this radius worked on a sedan around May twenty-fourth. A dark, recent model sedan with four doors."

Chico glanced at the map, at her, and said, "Leo called me a week ago. I'm already working on this. So far, it doesn't look good, Carlita."

Wells, always one step ahead of her. "Why not?"

He flipped open the lid of a small cedar box on the coffee table and withdrew a hand-rolled cigarette with a gold dollar sign inscribed on it. This blatant tribute to Ayn Rand's John Galt and *Atlas Shrugged* marked the true conservatism of his Cuban soul. He held out the box to her, she shook her head, and he helped himself to a cigarette. He fitted it precisely between his lips and lit it with a lighter that had probably cost as much as her monthly mortgage.

"There are eighty-three car garages in this fifteen-mile radius. Sixty-nine of them report no dark sedans with the kind of damage that Leo describes to me. Oh, we have flat tires and radiators and overhauls. But no structural damage like what he says, *mí amor.* But I have put out the word and if such a car appears in any garage in that radius, I will know about it."

"There's some evidence that it was deliberate, Chico, not a hit-and-run."

"*Maricón,*" he muttered. "But Jess had no enemies."

"I've made a few."

He sat forward, his pudgy face intent now. "Leo told me everything he knew. And Juan and I, well, you know how much we care for you and Jess, no? So we have decided to offer a million-dollar reward for any information that leads to the arrest of the driver. I announce it on my show tonight."

Everything went utterly still for her. When she finally opened her mouth, she nearly choked on the words. "A *million dollars?*"

Chico grinned. "It's a statement, no? It says we are serious about this." His smile vanished. "It tells the driver that he is not going to be like all the other *criminales* out there who get off." He dug his fist into the palm of his left hand and hissed through clenched teeth. "It says that justice now has a chance."

It would also bring every brain-dead weirdo out of the woodwork. It would create a dog and pony show. Charlie shook her head. "No, Chico. First of all, I can't let you throw away your money like that. Second, I—"

"No no no no." He held up his pudgy hands and moved them from side to side, like a line of dancers. "We have more money, Juan and I, than we can spend in two lifetimes. We want to do this."

"It'll be a zoo."

"We have thought of that," Juan said, hurrying into the living room with a tray. "We have thought of everything. You must not worry, Carlita. We know what we're doing. We're also putting a ten-day limit on the reward. The offer expires at midnight on June nineteenth. We'll extend it, of course, but no one else needs to know that now. This turns up the pressure, *me entiendes?*"

"You haven't thought about CNN, *Oprah, The New York Times,* Dan Rather, *60 Minutes* . . ."

"Yes, we have." Juan set out a platter of beautiful pastries, three *corditos* of Cuban coffee, and a plate heaped high with fruit. "It's precisely what we want. *Exposure.* The more exposure we have, the more pressure it puts on the driver, no? At night, in the silence of his room, he lies awake sweating. Anxiety eats through him. Maybe he pukes. Maybe he drinks too much. Maybe he's married and his wife knows what happened and she comes forward. A million *dólares,* Carlita, is enough to tempt. It makes the risk of coming forward much easier to deal with."

"You're going to have more nut calls than you can handle."

"We have hired people who will deal only with the phones," Chico said. "They will take calls tonight during the show and will continue to take calls for the next ten days. The reward will also be announced on *Television Mundial News* three times a day. We have hired public relations people. We will forward everything we get to Leo and to you, if you want to be involved."

If? These two men were the only people besides Logan who had given it to her straight, without trying to protect her, without treating her like she might break. "Of course I want to be involved. I'll man phones, follow up leads, whatever."

Chico sat forward and touched her arm. "Will you let me interview you on tonight's show? About what happened?"

Would she? Absolutely. But *should* she? "I don't remember much of what happened."

"No problem. The important thing is your loss. That's what our listeners will connect with. There will be other people on the show who have also lost loved ones through highway accidents, hit-and-runs, drunken drivers, impatience, rage. But your loss is the most recent and the only one for which we're offering a reward."

"My Spanish is pretty rusty, Chico."

"If you stumble, I will translate."

"Will you do it?" Juan asked, holding out her tiny cup of Cuban coffee.

"I suppose if I say no, you won't give me that cup of coffee, will you."

"If you say no, Chico and I, we will understand. But we hope you will not say no."

"What time do you want me here?"

Chico leaped up and threw his arms around Charlie. "You have made the right decision, *cariña*. You will see."

(2)

The silence felt like a luxury to Anita, a slice of time cut away from the time. She actually caught herself humming as she sat down at the kitchen table with a cup of coffee and the morning newspaper. Frank had already left for the day, Joey was still asleep, and she didn't have to be anywhere or do anything until the spirit moved her.

Then she opened *The Miami Herald* and the silence exploded with the wild, frantic pounding of her heart. Her world shrank until only the words in bold black type existed: **CUBAN TALK SHOW HOST OFFERS $1,000,000 REWARD IN HIT & RUN.**

Anita forced herself to read the entire article, and with every sentence, every paragraph, dread seeped deeper into her tissues and bones. Certain words and phrases leaped out at her, as if to mock her: *last night's show* . . . Chico's World, *Cuban icon . . . Special Agent Calloway . . . ten million listeners . . . 350 radio stations . . . broadcast in both English and Spanish . . sedan . . . southeast Miami neighborhood . . . early morning hours of Saturday, May 24 . . .*

When she finished the article, she shot to her feet so fast, the chair toppled back and crashed to the floor. Anita ran over to the TV set, turned it on, and flipped through the channels until she found CNN. Financial news. Weather. A commercial. Foreign news. And then, at the top of the hour, at eight A.M. on the nose, the newscaster said: "Remember when Robert Redford offered a million dollars to Demi Moore's husband for spending just one night with her? Well, a Cuban talk show host in Miami has matched that offer, but not to spend the night with Demi Moore.

"Last night on his weekly show, *Chico's World,* Miami radio talk show host Chico Ruiz offered one million dollars to anyone with information that would lead to the arrest of the driver of the hit-and-run that killed . . ."

Blood drummed in Anita's ears, drowning out the rest of what the broadcaster said. She spun around and ran to the phone. She picked up the receiver and started to dial, but couldn't remember Frank's cell phone number. She knew that the Mercedes he now drove, on loan from the firm, had a cell phone in it, but she couldn't recall that number either. She slammed down the receiver, hurried back over to the TV.

Jess Calloway's photo filled the screen. Next to it stood a photo of a pudgy guy with intense dark eyes and slicked-back hair. Beneath these photos was a phone number to call if you had information. Anita ran back to the phone, grabbed the receiver, and called Frank's number at the firm. His secretary answered. "Mr. Benedict's office."

She struggled to calm herself. "Uh, Lauren, it's Anita. Is Frank in yet?"

"No, Mrs. Benedict, he's not. He just called from the car." She ticked off the two cell phone numbers, then did the usual chitchat routine, how was Anita enjoying her summer vacation, how was Joey.

By the time Anita hung up, her panic had collapsed into terror. She punched out the number for the cell phone in the car, praying that Frank would pick up, that he was still in the car; she needed to talk to him now, this instant. He answered on the second ring, his attorney voice smooth, easy. "Frank Benedict."

"Jesus, Frank, it's on CNN, on—"

"I'll call you back in a few minutes," he said, and hung up.

Anita slammed down the receiver, her thoughts moving so fast, they got nowhere quickly. *Sedan, one million.* She paced, paused in front of the TV, then grabbed the receiver again and began punching out her parents' number. Three digits in, she hung up. No way. No way she could call her mom and dad now, what the hell was she thinking? *Hi, Daddy, I made a mistake.*

The phone rang and she snatched up the receiver.

(3)

"It was on CNN at six-thirty this morning."

Benedict stood outside a convenience store on Red Road, less than a mile from his office. Already, the humidity hovered way up there and the sun beat down and he felt like he was being broiled alive inside his jacket. He tugged at his tie, loosening it, and shrugged off his jacket. It helped, but he still couldn't think straight; his wife continued to ramble, to rave, to sob.

"Shut up for a second, Anita," he snapped. "Just shut the hell up."

"Don't talk to me that way," she snapped back.

Benedict squeezed his eyes closed and took a deep breath. *Make it good, Frankie.* "This doesn't *change* anything. Even a million bucks won't bring a witness forward because there was *no witness.*"

The only thing he heard was her breathing. Heavy breathing. Love-making breathing. Panicked breathing. Christ oh Christ. "Anita?"

"Are you sure, Frank? Are you absolutely sure that no one saw the accident?"

"Yes."

No. He suddenly wasn't sure of anything. He couldn't remember what the neighborhood looked like, whether the houses nearby had been lit up or dark. For all he knew, some drunk stumbling home through the storm had seen the entire scenario from beginning to end.

"How can you be so sure?" she prodded, a trace of panic still laced through her voice.

"Because I made it my business to look, Anita." How swift and clean the lie came out. "Because I know."

Her breathing began to even out.

"Look, I've got to get going. I'm due in a meeting in about twenty minutes. We'll talk tonight."

"You say that, but we won't. We won't talk. We don't know how to talk anymore."

He'd been down this road before, the road called Everything That Went Wrong, and he didn't particularly want to travel it right now. "I have to go, Nita. I'll call you after my meeting."

He hung up before she could say anything more, and rubbed his hands over his face, trying not to think about any of it. But, my God, *one million bucks* would tempt even a reluctant witness.

It might even tempt his wife.

One million bucks changed everything.

(4)

Logan's cubicle in the FBI building hardly qualified as a closet, much less a base of operation. And when the red phone rang, the sound echoed loudly between the cubicle's walls, reminding him of all the reasons he'd fled to Minnow Key.

The caller's number, name, and address appeared on the computer screen in front of Logan. He picked up on the second ring. "FBI, Logan speaking."

"I saw it," the breathless woman on the other end said. "I saw everything that happened that night."

"Your name and address, ma'am?"

As she spoke, he highlighted the street address on the computer screen, hit enter, and a map of the accident site and its fifteen-mile radius appeared. The words NO MATCH flashed on the screen. Another crank call, he thought, but listened to her story anyway.

"I was out walking my dog that night and it happened right there in front of me. My God, the biggest crash I ever done heard. The car that did it was a white sedan, seen it with my own eyes, just smacked it and took off."

Yeah. She was out walking her dog in the worst deluge in recent memory, uh-huh, right. "About what time did this happen, ma'am?"

"Time? Well, lemme see. It was late, I know that, probably around ten-thirty. Yeah, ten-thirty, I wanted to be home in time for the news."

You're about two hours off and got the wrong color for the car. "Thanks for your call, ma'am, someone will be in touch with you in the next few days."

He hung up and typed a minus next to her name. Most of the calls so far had been easy to classify as blatant lies. Wells, the assistant director, Logan, and Charlie had decided upon several criteria for identifying calls that might be legit, based on information that had been withheld from the press and which Charlie hadn't revealed on the show the previous night: the exact color of the sedan, the time of the accident, and that Charlie had been found outside the car on the ground.

The color of the sedan—black, a perfect black—had been confirmed from paint chips embedded in the Explorer and jibed with Logan's vision. The official time of the accident now stood at 12:27 A.M., when the clock in the Explorer had stopped. The only people outside the official circle who knew where Charlie had been found were the paramedics, her brother, and her OB/GYN.

If any caller got even one of these criteria correct, an agent would check out the lead in person. Logan had expected to hate this, but found that he preferred it to doing what he'd been hired to do. It brought back all the good feelings he'd had about the bureau before he'd been shot.

"Anything worthwhile yet, Mr. Logan?"

Logan glanced back as Steve Mitchell strolled through the doorway of his crowded cubicle. His tie lay askew against his shirt and the hairs in his Boston Blackie mustache went every which way, as if he'd just blown his nose. "So far, I've got thirty-three cranks and one possible lead. I e-mailed it to the assistant director about twenty minutes ago. It should be in your e-mail by now. I don't know where the other guys stand on their calls."

Mitchell sauntered right up to Logan's chair. "Just for your information, Logan, I know what the fuck's going on. I know you and Wells and Charlie were huddled up there in Assistant Director Feldman's office at four this morning, plotting strategies. I'm a bit puzzled, though, how Wells managed to get Feldman's ear the way he has. But hey, now that there's a million bucks riding on the case, I imagine the director himself is probably listening."

Logan let him rant, but felt his blood pressure rising.

"I also know that Feldman can't bring Charlie back to work in an official capacity until a shrink says she's fit for work and that he can't bring her back in any event to work on *this* investigation. So he's allowing her to work through you."

He leaned into Logan's face, leaned so close he could smell the breath mint Mitchell was sucking on. Logan remained just as he was, barely resisting the urge to grind his fist into Mitchell's mouth. He did the next best thing. "The bigger issue here, Mr. Mitchell, is why you're such an anal retentive."

Mitchell drew back, blood pouring in his face, then he lunged at Logan, grabbed the front of his shirt, and hissed, "You're a dipshit fucker and—"

Logan jackknifed his legs and slammed his feet into Mitchell's gut, knocking him back through the doorway of his cubicle into the hall. Then he shot out of his chair and hurried over to the door. Mitchell, clutching and wheezing on the hallway floor, turned his homicidal eyes on Logan. "You'll . . . regret . . . that."

Logan kicked his door shut and for a brief moment thought of the dock on Minnow Key. The sun. The blue water. The *ease.*

Then the red phone rang again and he sat down at the computer and went back to work.

13

The Squeeze

(1)

Charlie peeked out from behind the living room blinds at the phalanx of reporters and TV vans that had been camped out in front of her home for the last few hours.

She had anticipated this sort of thing for Chico, but not for herself. Her phone had been ringing steadily, her answering machine had half a dozen irate messages from her brother, her e-mail wouldn't stand much more abuse, and she'd had to resort to her fax line for communication with Chico and Wells.

She'd prepared a statement, but every time she read it aloud to herself, it sounded ridiculous, self-serving. She'd said everything she had to say on Chico's show last night.

Her fax line rang again, and she hurried into the den to answer it. "Yes? Hello?"

"Hey, it's Rain. I opened this morning's paper and there you are, on page one. Your phones have been busy for the last five hours. You don't do anything small-time, kid."

"This just sort of happened, Rain."

"Whatever. It's great. This is going to give you the edge you needed. Look, I'm at the end of your street. What do you want me to do?"

"Tell me what to say."

"C'mon, Charlie. That's easy for you."

"Okay, as you drive up, just tell them I'll be out in a few minutes to make an official statement."

"Done. See you in about sixty seconds."

Charlie dropped the receiver into the cradle and ran into the bedroom to put on something more presentable than baggy gym shorts and a Key West T-shirt. She didn't want to look like she'd gone over the hill. She picked out a pair of white cotton shorts with a belt and a cotton blouse with tiny black and white checks on it. White sandals, comb the mop, freshen the lipstick: That would do it. No beauty queen, she thought, but good enough to answer a few questions.

In the living room again, she looked out and saw Rain's pale silver Camaro nosing into the driveway, the crush of media people parting to let her pass. As she got out, they rushed her and she, the very paragon of grace, continued onto the porch before she addressed them.

"If I could have your attention, please," she said. "I'm Dr. Lorraine Sneider, a friend of the family. Ms. Calloway will be available in a few minutes to answer your questions. We appreciate your patience and ask that you be patient just a few minutes longer."

She ducked inside the house and Charlie said, "That was great. Just perfect. Do I looked crazed or anything, Rain?"

"You look fine. What're you going to say to them?"

"I'm going to wing it and make it brief."

"Then I'm taking you to a late lunch."

"Okay. Here goes. Open the door."

Rain opened the door and stepped out ahead of Charlie. Reporters and camera people jostled for a place at the foot of the porch steps. A Latino reporter thrust a mike into Charlie's face. "Ms. Calloway, what's the status of the investigation at this point?"

"Every call that's coming into the special hotline is being checked against criteria that include information about the accident that hasn't been released. All leads will be checked out."

"How many calls has the hotline received, Ms. Calloway?" shouted another reporter.

"Hundreds."

"What's your relationship with Chico Ruiz?" asked another reporter.

"He's a close friend."

"How close?"

"Fifteen years close."

"Isn't it true, Ms. Calloway, that you're on bereavement leave right now?"

"Yes."

"Is that why you're under Dr. Sneider's care?"

Lorraine replied, "I'm an obstetrician, sir, not a psychiatrist. Ms. Calloway and I are former college roommates."

"Despite your leave, Agent Calloway, you're still involved in the investigation, right?"

A trick question. If she answered yes, she would be blatantly violating bureau policy and would alienate the assistant director, who was bending policy already. "Every available resource is being used to see that justice is served. Right now I consider myself a facilitator."

"Ms. Calloway," shouted a guy at the back of the crowd. "You've put up lost-dog posters all over the neighborhood where the accident occurred. Has the dog been found yet?"

"No. And just for the record, Paz is a Rhodesian Ridgeback that weighs about a hundred and forty pounds."

Rain took the mike then and thanked everyone. "When we have any more news, ladies and gentlemen, you'll be the first to know. In the meantime, we ask that you give Ms. Calloway the privacy that she deserves. Thank you very much."

Rain opened the door and they went inside. "How'd I sound?" Charlie asked anxiously.

"Like a facilitator."

"I hope Mitch buys it."

"Screw Mitch. You've got Assistant Director Feldman on your side."

Maybe so, but she knew that Mitch could make her life completely miserable when she returned to work. "You think they'll clear out?" Charlie asked, stabbing a thumb toward the door.

"Sure. It's just a money story. Sex is still bigger. The real challenge is to keep them interested long enough to make a difference."

The phone rang again, but Charlie let the machine get it. "I'm starved. Let's get out of here."

In its heyday, Coconut Grove had been a haven for artists. Now the area was too expensive for artists, most of whom had moved over to Miami Beach, which was rapidly following the same cycle.

Just the same, Charlie enjoyed the Grove. She liked the art galleries, the banyan trees that shaded the road, the nearness of the bay, the odor of the marinas, the neighborhood spirit of the area. Many of her best memories with Jess had connections to the Grove, and it would be appallingly easy to slide back into them, relive them, and get stuck in the past.

"I've been thinking things over," Rain said as they walked toward a seafood restaurant on the water. "Hypnosis might help unlock the memories you've got of the accident, Charlie."

"We've used it at the bureau and it isn't always a reliable tool."

"I'm just suggesting that you try, and see what comes of it."

"I don't want to be hypnotized by a stranger."

"I'd do it."

"You? Since when are you a hypnotist?"

"I've used it for years for patients who don't want epidurals for labor and delivery. It's wonderful for pain management. I've also used it with patients to uncover painful memories and to release them."

"I don't want to relive the accident."

"You don't have to. You'd be a detached observer. What we're interested in finding out is whether you saw the car that hit you and if you did, we want to know *what* you saw. Maybe you saw the driver or the license plate, Charlie. At least give it a try."

She felt deep resistance to the idea. But in the days and weeks since the accident, she'd learned that her resistance to something often indicated a need to explore it further. "All right. I'll try it."

"When?"

"When's good for you?"

"Tomorrow afternoon, my office."

"I don't want to sit in a waiting room filled with pregnant women, Rain."

"The office is closed tomorrow afternoon. It'll just be us."

The resistance now felt like a bull digging its heels into mud. "I'll be there."

(2)

Benedict pulled into his driveway at six-thirty that evening. Anita was gardening out front, wearing a floppy straw hat that she'd bought on a trip to the Bahamas, and very short shorts with a halter top. He saw no sign of Joey.

He drove past her, into the open garage. She didn't glance up, didn't acknowledge his arrival in any way, hardly a positive harbinger for the evening ahead. He was in for a rash of shit and wasn't in the mood for it. But two could play this game, he thought, and got out, briefcase in hand, and went into the house without saying hello to her either.

In the kitchen, no dinner smells greeted him. The stove wasn't on, the table wasn't set, and the inside of the goddamn fridge looked like Mother Hubbard's cupboard. All this because he hadn't called her back after his meeting that morning?

C'mon, Frankie, it's simpler than that. She's pissed because you didn't want to talk about IT.

He left his briefcase on the counter, helped himself to a beer, and turned on the TV in the breakfast room. All day he'd heard people talking about the reward. He'd seen the headline in the *Herald,* had listened to the hype on the radio. And, yeah, it sounded bad. Now he needed to find out how bad it really was.

He tuned the TV to Channel 7, tabloid news at its sensationalistic best. Five minutes into the broadcast, Anita came inside, slamming the door to the utility room. She swept past him without a word and went upstairs. A few minutes later he heard the shower running. The bitch wasn't going to talk to him, and damned if he would break the silence first.

Benedict jerked off his tie, shrugged off his jacket, and drank down half the beer as he listened to Channel 7's star broadcaster, Ricky Sanchez, give the lowdown on the reward. Sanchez, true to form, went through every dirty, gritty detail, from the accident that had killed Jess Calloway and his unborn son, to the woman's appearance on the Chico Ruiz show last night, to the statement she'd released earlier that day.

Charlotte Calloway was a looker, all right, lean and determined and, way back in the depths of her eyes, wounded. He regretted that, he really did. *But shit happens, lady.* And he wasn't going to prison for it.

He caught a whiff of Anita's perfume and glanced back to see her leaning against the doorjamb, hair styled, face made up, her black Levis as snug as a glove on her narrow hips.

"I'm having dinner with one of the teachers, Frank. Joey's spending the night with Bruce. I don't know what time I'll be home."

"What about my dinner?" he blurted out.

She shrugged, obviously relishing the moment. "I guess you'll have to fend for yourself."

"I thought you wanted to talk."

"Talk?" She flipped open her compact and applied lipstick delicately, her mouth puckered into an O. "About what?" She snapped the compact shut, rolled her lips together, and flashed a smug little smile. "This is your problem, not mine. See you later."

With that, she walked out of the room, her hips swaying. Benedict stared after her, fists clenched against his thighs, rage slamming around inside him like some caged beast screaming for freedom. Just who the hell did she think she was, walking out when he'd come home to *talk* because *she* wanted to talk? He'd turned down dinner with Thacker so he and Anita could *talk talk talk,* and then she splits without fixing him anything for dinner, splits with that smug, dirty smile, splits because it suits her.

He shot to his feet and ran after her. He caught up with her in the driveway just as she was getting into her BMW, the Beamer he had bought her, the Beamer she would never be able to afford on a teacher's salary. He grabbed her by the arm and spun her around.

"All day you wanted to talk, you call my office every goddamn hour, you bug the shit outta me to talk. So talk. Let's talk."

She jerked her arm free, color rising in her neck, her cheeks, her eyes livid. "I did *not* call your office every hour. I called four times. I'm tired of being put off, Frank. Everything has to be on your terms. Everything. Your needs are more important than anyone else's needs. Your career is more important. Your fears are more important. Your time is more important. You you you, that's all I've heard since the day we got married, and I'm sick of it. I'm not playing that game anymore. You're not worried about a reward for a million bucks on your head? Fine, I'm not worried about it either." Then she got into the car, slammed the door, and sped down the driveway.

Benedict, literally too shocked to move, watched her white BMW vanish through the lengthening summer shadows. Then rage crashed over him, seized him, and took him away.

When he surfaced some time later—and that described it exactly, *surfacing,* like a whale for air—he sat behind the wheel of the firm's Mercedes, whispering "Come like shadows, so depart." He didn't know what it meant, didn't know why he said it. The dashboard clock read 10:07.

No way. Three hours gone? *Where the fuck was I?*

And more to the point, where was he now?

It took him a few moments to orient himself: He was parked in the trees catercorner to the Miami Lakes U-Haul company. He had absolutely no memory of driving there. *None, nada, zip.* It terrified him, this absence, this hollowness, this vast, flat prairie of the mind that refused to yield its secret.

A bulging backpack rested in his lap. He stared at it for a few minutes, frowning, struggling to find the memory, willing it to come. It finally stirred, and he remembered digging the pack out of the junk in the garage that he hadn't had time to clean up, to sift through. And he'd filled it with things that he'd been accumulating all week and stashing in the trunk of the Mercedes. Tools, a CD-ROM with a computer virus on it . . . yeah, okay, it was coming back to him bit by bit.

He'd been there several times last week and again yesterday, watching the building, casing it out. He'd even gone inside when it was open for business, gone in and stood in line, noting every little detail about the layout. Now here he was, as ready as he would ever be. Ready, even though he couldn't remember the drive here and couldn't dredge up much of the three hours between Anita's departure and now.

As he got out of the Mercedes, pack slung over his shoulder, another memory chipped loose and surfaced. He'd left Anita a little something in the jug of herbal sun tea that she kept in the fridge and drank from nightly before bed. *Sleep tight, bitch.*

But tonight wasn't about Anita. Tonight was about the U-Haul company.

He darted through the shadows and across the street, a blur in the darkness. Hibiscus hedges grew along the front of the building, their pale yellow flowers visible in the spill of the crime lights. Assholes, he thought. They stuck a crime light out front, but let the hedges grow high enough to hide the Jolly Green Giant.

Benedict pushed through the hedge, made his way to the far side of the building, and dropped to the ground. He set his bag down, unzipped it. He picked out his gloves and a glass-cutting device that one of his morally ambiguous clients had given him last Christmas. It was supposedly a joke, but they both knew better.

He put on his gloves, then pressed the cutter's suction cups to the glass. The suction cups allowed him to lift out the piece of glass he'd cut from the rest of the window. He set it on the ground, a section about two feet by two feet. He cut a second piece roughly the same size. Perfect. He put the device back into his bag, then dropped to a crouch again, alert, vigilant, wary. Nothing seemed out of place or unusual in any way. He climbed through the hole, careful not to cut himself on the glass.

Once he reached the main lobby, Benedict turned on his penlight and scrambled over the front desk, where he'd stood in line that day. He booted up the computer. No question about it, he hardly made the grade of a computer nerd like Jess Calloway. But he wasn't exactly a mental slouch either, and desperation had sharpened his skills. He played around with the setup until he bypassed the password, then accessed the program and found his rental file.

Benedict deleted his name, then wiped out every file for the eight days before and after he'd rented the U-Haul. He doubted this would eradicate his name from the home office records, but the virus would take care of that.

He reached into his bag again and brought out a disk that he once had used to test the resilience of the firm's computer system to viruses. The only other person who knew about the virus was the designer, who had died three years before of a drug overdose. Benedict inserted the disk into the A drive and ran it.

Tomorrow morning, as bored employees logged onto the system at the Miami Lakes U-Haul company, a tiny spaceship would appear in the upper right-hand corner of their screens. It would grow in the blink of an eye, grow so fast that most employees wouldn't even know what the hell was happening. By the time they did, the spaceship would wipe their drives clean.

Any system connected to this one—like the home office computers—would be infected as well. Benedict just hoped the ensuing chaos would be sufficient to deflect attention from the real purpose of the virus.

When the disk had loaded, Benedict ejected it, dropped it in his bag, and began going through a stack of hard-copy rental receipts. But these covered only the last week. Where the hell were the receipts from late May? He opened drawers, searched them, shut them.

Time escaped him. The reward and his wife kept intruding on his thoughts, as if the two were inexorably linked. *Would she do that to me? Would she turn me in for a million bucks?* She might be tempted, but the fact remained that she was an accessory. She'd helped him get rid of the Beamer.

And if she gets in front of a jury, Frankie, who's going to believe that?

Joe Smith from some dirt-shit trailer park in South Miami would take one look at Anita and know in his heart that she was not capable of such a thing. He would see that she was a teacher of gifted children, a teacher of the same caliber as the lady who'd gone up in smoke on the *Challenger,* the lady who'd had schools named after her. Then he would look at Benedict, a *lawyer,* and believe he was capable of everything he was accused of—and more.

He didn't want to think about that now, about Anita and the problem she represented.

He found the right stack of receipts in a bottom drawer, each one marked with a neat red check in the upper right-hand corner. His receipt lay in the middle, and when he jerked it out, the clip that held the stack popped off and the pieces of paper went flying.

He scrambled around on the floor, scooping up the receipts, straightening them, then looking for the paper clip. He finally found the clip under the desk, slipped it back onto the stack of receipts, returned the receipts to the bottom drawer.

But as he slid the drawer shut, he heard something, a jingle of keys. He turned off his penlight and the computer. He put the strap of the bag over his head and, hunched over, moved quickly toward the far end of the counter. He needed a space to press into, a closet to hide in, he needed a goddamn miracle.

He backed up to a filing cabinet stacked high with books and manuals and remained very still, barely breathing. Shoes squeaked against the floor. The beam of a flashlight darted around the room. *Security guard.*

Now the squeaking came closer and every muscle in Benedict's body tensed, prepared to spring, to run, to flee, to do whatever he needed to do to escape. The squeaking paused, then the beam of the flashlight struck the floor to his right, twenty feet or so away from him. *I'm fucked.*

But the light slipped away from him again, darting from one computer station to another, buying him a little time. Benedict crept to the side of the filing cabinet. He could see the door way off to his right, a couch and chairs to his left. And in between lay a vast emptiness where he would be exposed.

Is he armed?

He couldn't risk it. He either had to wait or he had to act.

Benedict peered around the edge of the cabinet and saw the guard, an old geezer in a baggy uniform. The man now moved to the employee side of the counter, moved from one computer station to the next, checking to see if any of the machines were on. In fifteen or twenty seconds he would reach the filing cabinet and have a clear view of either side of the counter. He would see Benedict.

Alarms shrieked in the back of his mind, a sour taste flooded his mouth. He saw everything swirling away from him, all that he'd worked for, his entire adult life reduced to a pathetic parody of itself.

He couldn't let that happen.

Then you know what you gotta do, Frankie.

He quickly grabbed one of the books stacked on the filing cabinet, figuring he would use it as a weapon. In his haste he knocked over a heavy metal bookend, and it crashed to the floor, making such a racket that the dead would hear it. Benedict swept it up and sprang to his feet just as the guard rushed toward him.

Benedict swung the bookend and struck the guard in the side of the head. He felt bones give way, blood flew from the wound, and the man stumbled back, arms pinwheeling, and crashed into a chair on wheels. The chair rolled back, the guard's body still on it, his shoes dragging across the floor. The chair slammed into a filing cabinet and the guard slid to the floor, groaning, blood pouring from the wound in his forehead and streaming over his face and the front of his uniform. He tried to turn over, to sit up, to get to his feet.

Benedict, still clutching the bloody bookend, lurched forward and slammed it over the guard's head again, his rage now upon him, riding his back like some sort of demon. "You should've stayed outta here, old man." Another blow. "Outta my way." Again. "Asshole." Again.

He blinked sweat from his eyes and the floor suddenly tilted and he dropped the bookend. It clanked against the floor and the sound echoed in Benedict's skull, a loud, terrible noise that triggered a sudden massive headache. He wiped the back of his hand across his eyes, his knees gave out, and he went down.

He pressed the heels of his hands to his eyes, willing the pain in his head to go away. His heart thudded and knocked in his chest like a car engine badly in need of a tune-up. *Don't panic, take a deep breath, focus focus focus.*

He forced himself to move closer to the body. *Look at him, Frankie, remember what he looks like.* A middle-aged man with a slight paunch, a bashed-in skull, and a bloody St. Christopher's medal around his neck.

Benedict brought his hand slowly toward the man's neck, touched two gloved fingers to his carotid artery. Nothing.

The floor began to tilt, to spin. He felt an abyss opening beneath him and knew that if he passed out now, they would find him here, and the whole nightmare would begin again. With a tremendous force of will, Benedict rocked back on his heels, grabbed onto the edge of the filing cabinet, and pulled himself to his feet. The dizziness ebbed, his mind slammed into high gear, and the entire scene snapped into utter clarity.

He'd been through this once; he knew what to do. He had to cover his tracks. He picked up the bookend, wiped it off with his shirt. Even though he still wore gloves, he couldn't be too careful.

Books. He swept the stack off the filing cabinet, knocking them to the floor.

File cabinet. He yanked open one of the drawers, lifted out a handful of files, and hurled them across the counter.

Motive? Robbery. Yes, perfect. A thief broke in, the security guard surprised him, the thief killed the guard. What could be simpler or more plausible? It happened daily in Miami, people in the wrong place at the wrong time.

Sorry, guy. Shit happens.

He felt calmer then, a false calm, but it worked. He wouldn't be able to carry out much through the window. He needed to leave by the front door. Had the guard locked it after he'd come in? Probably not. But if he had, Benedict knew he would lose more time. He couldn't risk that now. He'd lost enough time as it was. He needed the guard's keys.

He knelt beside the body again, rifled through the pockets of the guard's uniform until he found the keys. He shot to his feet, backed away from the guard. He unplugged a fax and a printer, picked them up, and hurried toward the front door. He smelled blood in the cool air that pumped through the AC vents, the guard's blood. It had settled in his clothes, his hair, in the very pores of his skin. The stink of his sins.

And for moments he saw himself like a figure on a TV screen, a cheap thief scurrying out of a building with his stolen goods and a dead man's blood tainting the very air that he breathed.

Benedict burst through the doors, broke into a run, and tore across the road and into the trees, the fax machine and printer like the weight of a corpse in his arms. He gulped greedily at the night air, hoping his wife would be at home asleep, deeply asleep, hoping he wouldn't be targeted by a cop seeking to make this month's quota of speeding tickets.

I'm going to get away with it because no one saw me or heard me.

He ran on toward the Mercedes.

PART THREE

●

The Sound of Hooves

"The day may come when we can manipulate reality . . . causing what is real and what is invisible to shift kaleidoscopically and calling up images of the past with the same ease that we now call up a program on our computer."
—Michael Talbot, *The Holographic Universe*

14

Piecing It Together

(1)

On the deck of Greg Tillis's oceanside mansion, the air felt sticky and humid to Thacker, the way it usually did in mid-September. He tugged at his tie and shrugged off his jacket. He felt like kicking off his shoes as well and soaking his feet in the pool. But Tillis's housekeeper appeared just then with a mug of coffee and a plate of huevos rancheros.

"Mr. Tillis will be finished with his call in a moment, Mr. Thacker," she said.

"Thanks, Marie."

She put down a basket of warm bread, whipped butter, and an assortment of jellies, then set a place for Tillis. Everything with a touch of class, he thought. That was Tillis. But in recent years the man had never managed to be on time. Even when Thacker came to Tillis's home, Tillis kept him waiting.

In the early days of the firm, when he and Tillis had been the hot young studs in Miami legal circles, the defense attorneys everyone had wanted, Tillis had rarely been late for anything. But as the money had rolled in and the firm had prospered, Tillis had fallen in love with power and now wielded it like some Olympian god. Being late was the way he wielded it with Thacker.

"Hi, Colin, sorry to keep you waiting." Tillis strolled out onto the deck in his golf clothes, a cassette recorder in his hand. "It couldn't be helped."

"Yeah, it never can."

Tillis ignored that remark, set the recorder on the table, and got right down to business. "Mendez removed the bug from the Mercedes about four o'clock this morning."

Shit. He dreaded this moment.

"The chip has a built-in calendar, so the date appears in this window here." He pointed at the slot in the upper right-hand corner. "He didn't have to be using the phone for the chip to pick up sounds. Once a sound within the car triggered the recording capability, then it picked up everything within a hundred and fifty feet of the phone."

"So far, the only thing I hear is static."

Tillis leaned forward and raised the volume—and the static. "It's the radio."

A car door opened, Thacker heard the rustle of clothing, then the door slammed shut. This was repeated as a second person got into the car, then a third.

"Mommy, I'm hungry," said Joey Benedict.

"You had McDonald's at four, honey. That was barely an hour ago."

Thacker had always liked Anita's voice, smooth and soft, the way a woman's voice was supposed to be.

"You didn't eat all your McNuggets," Benedict said. *"That's why you're hungry."*

"Did too, eat it all."

"You left—"

"Oh, stop it," Anita said, her voice weary. *"It doesn't matter, okay?"*

"It does matter," Benedict snapped. *"You pander to him, Anita, you're making him a spoiled brat."*

"I'm not a spoiled brat," Joey shouted. *"Mommy, he called me a brat and I'm not a brat, I'm not, I'm not, I'm —"*

"Jesus, Frank." Then, more softly, *"You're not a brat, honey. But Daddy's right that you didn't eat very much."*

"I don't know if I like chicken anymore. I don't want to eat animals. Aunt Bobbie says it's bad to eat animals, and I believe her. It's like eating Nemo."

Anita, angry: *"I knew it. I knew your sister was brainwashing him."*

"In the civilized world, Joey, people don't eat their pets. But chickens aren't pets." Benedict struggled to keep his voice even now, his temper under control. *"There's a difference."*

"Eating animals makes us mean. It makes wars. That's what Aunt Bobbie says. I don't want to eat animals anymore."

"Then you'd better find some vegetables that you like," Benedict snapped, irritable again.

Indignant, the kid replied, *"I'll eat corn, carrots, bananas, apples, mangoes, yogurt, cheese, crackers, pizza, and—"*

"No meat means no McDonald's," Benedict said.

Anita, under her breath, hissed, *"You tell Bobbie to lay off this no-meat shit, Frank. Or I'll tell her."*

Benedict emitted an exaggerated sigh with which all men with families could identify. Translated, it meant: *Did I ask for this shit?*

After this, Anita called the baby-sitter and said they were on their way. At the sitter's, Joey and his mother got out of the car and Benedict turned the radio on very loud, golden oldies, with Grace Slick singing about that pesky white rabbit. The song brought back a rush of memories for Thacker of the early days of the firm, the hot-young-stud memories.

Neither he nor Tillis was married then, and the money that had rolled in fast and furiously had gone out just as fast and furiously to women and reefer and rock concerts. He had lived two lives in 1969, hotshot attorney by day and stud with a permanent hard-on at night. And now, when he looked in the mirror, he couldn't believe he was fifty-eight years old. Where the hell had the years gone?

He had plenty of money, his health was reasonably good except for his weight and high blood pressure, and his power connections were legendary. But none of this would buy back the years he had lost in his pursuit of the American dream. He drank too much, his marriage had deteriorated into a sham, his relationship with his two sons remained a travesty, and his dick had been deprived so long, it had begun to atrophy.

Screw Grace Slick and her white rabbit, he thought, and then the song ended and Anita Benedict returned to the car.

"I've had it with your sister and her hippie bullshit," Anita said tersely.

"I'll talk to her about it."

They fell silent. There were snippets after that of calls, conversations that related to work, then Benedict's voice again, a phrase here, a word there. *". . . All day . . . wanted to talk . . . call my office every goddamn hour . . . so talk."*

Anita Benedict shouted back, but the recorder caught only bits and pieces. *"Everything . . . your terms . . . your needs . . . your career . . . your fears . . . your time . . . not playing . . . not worried . . . bucks on your head . . ."*

A door slammed shut, a car peeled away.

"I'd say he's having a few marital problems," Tillis remarked dryly.

Thacker didn't say anything. He leaned forward, listening intently to the weird noises that now emanated from the recorder, a loud banging interspersed with heavy breathing. Then he heard mutterings in what sounded like a foreign language "What the hell is *that?"*

"Yeah, that stumped me too," Tillis said. "Until you slow down the speed." He fiddled with the dials, rewound the tape, started it again. Benedict's voice now sounded like he was trying to speak while underwater. But the words were at least identifiable. *"Shittin fucker asshole. Who does she think she is? Where do any of them get off trying to jerk me around? I'll show them, show all of them. Shit happens, he got in my way, what the hell was I supposed to do? What?"*

More banging, more muttering, then Tillis adjusted the recorder to the normal speed again and it sounded like the car was on the highway. *"Gotcha,"* Benedict said suddenly, laughing. *"And I know exactly how to do it. It'll work."* Then the tape exploded with maniacal laughter and Thacker and Tillis exchanged a glance.

Then: *"Come like shadows, so depart."*

Whispered words from Shakespeare, from *Macbeth,* if memory served him. But what the hell did it mean? And why did Benedict whisper it over and over again? He laughed in between too, not that weird maniacal laughter, but an expulsion of air, as if he were forcing oxygen out of his diaphragm.

"That's it," Tillis said, turning off the recorder. "I think it speaks for itself."

"He's got marital problems. So what? So do I. So do you. Everyone I know has marital problems."

"C'mon, Colin," Tillis said irritably. "This isn't just marital problems. The man has gone over the edge."

"People who've gone over the edge don't function. They're in psych units. Frank still functions. He still puts in twelve and thirteen hours a day. He still deals with clients. He still brings in a lot of money to the firm."

Tillis let out an exaggerated sigh. "That phone call that detained me? It was Jerome MacLean. He wanted to let us know that he signed with Becker and Becker."

Thacker hadn't expected this, and Tillis knew it. Tillis, in fact, relished the moment, reveled in it like a pig in shit. The Becker brothers had been their biggest competitors for years and surpassed them in international law, the area where MacLean supposedly had felt Thacker and Tillis were weakest. But all that was beside the point. MacLean had never been about money for either Thacker or Tillis; he'd been about Frank Benedict.

"Has he told Frank?"

"No." Tillis sat down and made a big to-do with preparing himself for breakfast. A flick of the napkin, a bit of sugar and cream in the coffee, a bit of jelly on a piece of bread. "No, he hasn't. He's leaving that up to us."

"Goddamn unprofessional of him."

"He can afford to be unprofessional now and then. He feels— and I quote—that 'Frank is a loose cannon, an accident waiting to happen.' I agree with him. I don't know if his problem is drugs, booze, or something else, but something *isn't right*."

"So we give him some time off and see where things stand when he returns." As soon as he'd said it, Thacker heard Benedict saying, *Don't poke me in the goddamn chest, Colin,* and wondered why he continued to defend the man.

Because you don't want to admit that Tillis is right. Because he couldn't stand the thought of Tillis's smug I-told-you-so smile. Because Benedict was supposed to be his golden boy.

"Frankly, Colin, I don't think that's going to make much difference." Tillis dabbed at his mouth and leaned forward, his expression skewed with earnestness. "If he'd signed up MacLean, I'd be inclined to keep him on, with steady adjustments in salary and bonuses, and give him another couple of years to prove he's really partnership material. But without MacLean and in light of the material on the tape, I feel we should give him his walking papers."

"That's too drastic, Greg. We've never fired anyone just because they didn't bring in a big client."

"Christ," Tillis spat out, leaning forward. "Haven't you heard a word I've said? We're not firing him because he didn't bring in MacLean. We'd be firing him because he's a fucking loose cannon."

"That's only your opinion. I haven't seen any evidence of it." *Don't poke me in the goddamn chest . . .*

"What the hell kind of evidence do you need, Colin? You waiting for him to walk into the firm with a gun some morning and open fire?"

"Cut the dramatic shit."

"My point is that I will *not* have the reputation of the firm tarnished in any way."

Thacker rolled his eyes in exasperation. "We've always agreed on that point, Greg. And so far, Frank hasn't done anything to tarnish our reputation."

"I'm telling you, something in him has snapped, Colin."

Shit happens, he got in my way, what the hell was I supposed to do? What? Who got in his way? Thacker wondered. He sensed that everything on the tape related to a specific event or emotion or relationship. It was too simple to dismiss it all as just the ramblings of a man who had gone over the edge.

"I want to think this over before I decide."

"Fine. However you want to handle it. And if it comes down to letting him go, we can give him a very generous severance package. He's got nearly two hundred thousand in his pension plan, so we can give him half of that, a year's salary, and health benefits."

Thacker nodded and pushed to his feet.

"How long do you think you'll need to make your decision?"

"I don't know."

"Don't think about it so long that it's suddenly too late, Colin."

(2)

The phone woke Anita. She groped for it, murmured "Hello," and heard the chipper voice of a woman whose name she couldn't summon. Bruce's mother. Bruce, the kid with whom Joey had spent the night.

"You sound under the weather, Anita."

"I, uh, must be coming down with a cold." She sat up, rubbing her eyes, a ball of panic gnawing at the inside of her chest. Her body felt weird, sort of rubbery, and her eyes felt dry and puffy. "How'd they do last night?"

"Fine, just fine. I was thinking about taking them to the beach and wanted to check with you first."

"That'd be great. We don't have any plans."

"We'll swing by the house in a while and pick up Joey's suit and whatever else he wants to take."

"Great. Thanks. May I talk to him for a second?"

"He's outside."

"Then I'll see him when you get here."

She hung up and glanced at the clock on the nightstand. *Noon?* Anita hurried over to the bureau and looked at her wristwatch. Noon. She ran into Joey's room, where the Power Ranger clock on the wall said 12:01.

Impossible. She couldn't have slept twelve hours. She'd gotten home early last night, around eleven, and hadn't been surprised to find that Frank wasn't home. She'd figured he'd gone back to the office or over to Colin Thacker's place for a nightcap. She'd poured herself a glass of ice cold sun tea and had gone upstairs, relishing the time alone. She'd probably fallen asleep around midnight and had slept so soundly, she'd never heard Frank come home or leave this morning. *But twelve hours?*

Anita couldn't remember the last time she'd slept twelve hours straight. It had to be stress. And last night's argument with Frank hadn't helped the ol' stress levels one iota, so, yes, it made sense. But why should twelve hours of sleep make her feel so physically strange?

She showered, dressed, blew her hair dry. Her body still didn't feel like her own, but a couple of Tylenol would fix that. Anita opened the medicine cabinet and *stuff* tumbled out: an old razor, a tube of Crest, and a plastic vial of Valium. The cap had come loose and the little pills now stuck to the sides of the sink.

Anita picked them up one by one and dropped them back into the container. Her dad had prescribed them for her last fall, when she'd developed insomnia. She'd taken them about a week, long enough to regulate her sleeping pattern, then stuck the container away.

According to the label, the prescription had been for twenty-one pills. She knew she'd taken seven, which would have left fourteen, not ten. She must have miscounted.

Anita counted the pills again, setting each one down on the counter. But there were only ten.

Maybe Frank had been taking them.

No. He drank, he didn't take pills. The only pills she'd ever seen him take, in fact, were Tylenol with codeine, for the headaches that had plagued him ever since that nasty concussion had laid him up several years ago.

So why are four missing?

Perhaps she'd taken the Valium longer than a week last fall. Or maybe she'd gotten up in the middle of the night and had taken four of them and couldn't remember it. That would explain why she'd slept so late and felt so physically weird. The other possibility suddenly loomed before her, a forbidden country, a darkness so horrifying that she wrenched away from the counter and stared at the ten little pills lined up neatly in a row.

Ten little Indians . . .

He wouldn't. Not Frank. Not her husband.

He isn't the same guy you married. The man she'd married wouldn't have hit a car and fled.

A wave of dizziness crashed over her, and she grabbed on to the edge of the counter to steady herself. In the mirror, her image trembled and blurred. She looked down, down at the pills, and plucked them up one by one, counting them as she dropped them back into the container.

. . . Two . . . six . . . ten . . .

Twenty-one minus seven equals fourteen. No two ways around it. The math hadn't changed.

Apprehension fluttered in some deep place inside her. She suddenly wished she had a close friend, a close female friend whom she'd known since they were kids, the sort of friend she could call now and say, *Tell me if you think I'm crazy.*

But her friends were also Frank's friends, or they were teachers or the mothers of Joey's buddies, women with whom she had superficial relationships. At some point early on in her marriage she'd let old friendships lapse and had discouraged new friendships from developing. On the rare occasion that she'd thought about it, she'd told herself that she didn't have time for new friendships. But the truth wasn't that simple. The truth, she thought uneasily, was that Frank poked fun at her friends. The few times that she'd brought someone to the house who also wasn't a friend of his, he'd embarrassed her with his bragging, his arrogance, his show of temper, even his drinking. Always, he'd had a tumbler of something nearby, a glass from which he sipped. It looked like ginger ale; she knew it was scotch. She knew and she ignored it.

She could call her father or her mother, but what the hell would she say? *Frank drugged me.*

It was the only explanation. He knew that she had a glass of sun tea every night before she went to bed. He knew and he'd put four Valium in the jug in the fridge to make sure she didn't wake up when he came in.

Anita pressed her fists into her eyes and for one long, surreal moment, felt Frank's hands against her breasts, his fingers sliding between her legs, his mouth on her. She wrenched back from the sink, arms swinging to her sides, her breath coming in short, panicked spurts.

What the hell did that mean? That she'd stuck around for all these years because of good sex?

Good sex and a beautiful home, exotic trips, and no financial worries, a wonderful son who loves his father: the whole tidy package, Anita. That's why you've stuck around.

All those things were true, of course they were, even though they hadn't had good sex since the accident. Hell, they hadn't had sex at all. But what about love? Where did love fit into any of this?

I love him, I've always loved him . . .

But did he love her as much as he loved himself?

She had backed into her bedroom, shaking her head, the container of Valium clutched in her hand, and now she sat down heavily at the foot of the bed. She spilled the pills into her hand again for a final count.

Ten. Always ten. Ten goddamn little pills.

But why had he drugged her?

Because he drove back to the quarry to see if the car was visible and he didn't want her to know about it. He needed to know if the water level in the quarry had dropped, so he'd made the long trip alone and . . . what? What had he done when he'd gotten there?

He sat there on the hill in the dark, staring down at the quarry, the water struck through with moonlight. Or maybe he'd forgotten to remove something from the trunk and had gone back to get it. But she knew that nothing had remained in the car when they'd ditched it. She had seen with her own eyes, crawled inside it, checked under the seats. She had even removed the license plate and had stashed it up in the attic with Frank's disgusting collection of spiders.

But still, his paranoia seemed feasible to her because these fears had been her own. How many nights had she lain awake, going over every little detail, worried that they'd missed something?

On the other hand, maybe she was just mistaken about how long she'd taken the Valium last fall. And it seemed reasonable that the stress of the last few weeks had put her into a twelve-hour deep freeze last night. She almost had convinced herself of this until she went downstairs to get Joey's bathing suit out of the dryer and found it and the washer empty. A week's worth of laundry lay neatly folded in the basket on the shelf.

Frank had done a wash. He'd folded clothes. My God, this was a first. Not once in all the years they'd been married had he ever done a wash or folded an article of clothing. Never. Why now?

She wanted to believe their argument had prompted it, that Frank had realized their marriage was headed into oblivion if things didn't change. But even if that were true, the deeper issues remained. The hit-and-run, her participation in getting rid of the car, the tantalizing reward.

Just then, Joey burst into the house in all his youthful exuberance, shouting for her, his bare feet slapping the tile floors. "Hey, hon, in the laundry room," she called, and he came running in.

"I need my suit, a towel, my bucket and shovel, and—"

"Hey, don't I get a hug?"

He threw his arms around her, hugging her close, then jabbered on about the fun he'd had at Bruce's last night. Hand in hand, they went into the garage and collected the beach stuff, a bag for his suit and towel, and flip-flops. A while later she stood in the driveway, waving good-bye to him. The tightness returned to the center of her chest. She began to ache all over inside. She knuckled her eyes, certain she could no longer live like this.

She ran back into the house, reached for the jug of sun tea. *I have to know. For Joey, for myself.* Her fingers touched the cool glass. Something started breaking up inside her, that tightness in her chest, and she emptied the tea into a glass jar before she could change her mind.

Anita put the jug in the sink and washed it well. Then she filled it to the same level with fresh water, tossed in a handful of tea bags, carried the jug out onto the deck, and set it in the sun. Fresh tea would be done in a few hours. Frank wouldn't know the difference.

She hurried through the door with the jar in her hands. She had a friend who worked in the lab at the hospital, the mother of one of Joey's classmates. She would be able to test the tea, to tell her yes or no.

If the answer was yes, the woman would wonder who had put the Valium in the tea and why and Anita couldn't tell her the truth. *Oh, my husband did it.* Maybe she could say it was for a science experiment for her gifted class next fall.

If you really believe your husband drugged you, what the hell are you still doing here? Hello, what's wrong with this picture?

Anita shifted the jar to her other hand and dug inside her bag for her keys. As she inserted the key in the lock, the jar slipped from her hand, crashed to the driveway, and shattered.

"Shit." The tea ran down the driveway, a dark stream.

I would've remembered getting up in the middle of the night and knocking back four Valium. Of course she would. She was a physician's daughter, she'd grown up hearing about the perils of drug overdoses, she'd always been careful. Frank had done it—not to kill her, it hadn't been enough to kill her, just to put her to sleep for twelve hours. The only question was what she should do now.

* * *

Lily doesn't feel so good today. She's sitting in the day room watching TV and Doris keeps pacing back and forth, talking on that funny little phone she carries in her pocket. Lily is sure that Doris is talking about Pan, who keeps running around here with his pants unzipped, his shirt unbuttoned, muttering that the zebras are coming.

"Un loco," whispers the lady across from Lily, gesturing toward Pan.

Lily doesn't know what "loco" means. "He's on new meds."

"Meds peds. He's craaazzeee." She draws the word out and laughs.

"Hi, sweetie." Lily looks up at the woman who stops in front of her, a pretty woman, very tall. She doesn't recognize her. "How're you doing today?" the woman asks.

"I'm doing fine. But I'm worried about Henry."

"Oh, Mom, don't worry about Dad, okay?"

Mom: this woman's face suddenly pops into Lily's mind with a name attached to it. Chrissy. Her daughter. "Where've you been? I haven't seen you for months, Chrissy."

"It's been only a couple of days, Mom. I was swamped with patients when I got back from my vacation."

"He's missing, isn't he." Lily starts to cry and Chrissy sits beside her on the couch and puts her arm around Lily, holding her close.

Lily blows her nose and watches Doris go over to Pan. She takes him gently by the arm, gently even though he's screaming about the zebras now, the sound of hooves, and leads him out of the day room. "He's crazy. Pan's crazy. That's what she said to me."

"That's what Doris said to you?"

"No. Someone else. I can't remember who it was. What's your name again?"

"Christine. I'm your daughter."

"Chrissy. You got so big!"

She hugs her again and Lily likes the way she smells, of that world out there beyond the fence, of sweetness and light and everything good. "You're not missing anymore."

"I wasn't missing, Mom. I've just been busy." She touches the

book in Lily's lap. "I'm glad to see you've been writing in the journal I gave you. Have you done any sketching lately?"

"I don't know." Lily opens the journal, sees her own printing and a few puzzling sketches. "I guess I have," she says with a laugh. "Sometimes I write, sometimes I live it. Sometimes I draw, sometimes I'm in the drawings."

"May I look through the journal?"

"Not yet." Lily slips it hastily in her pocket. "Maybe later."

"I thought you might like to go down to the office with me for a few hours. I've got four pups in the kennels that need some TLC."

Office. Kennels. Pups. The words are keys that open certain memories. Smells do it too, Lily thinks, scents like Chrissy's perfume, for instance. "But I can't leave Henry."

"Mom, listen to me." She takes Lily gently by the arms. "Dad is dead. He died . . ."

"Oh, I know *that*," Lily says irritably. "I'm talking about a different Henry. He needs food. I have to feed him."

Chrissy suddenly gets up and goes over to the TV and turns up the volume. She sits beside Lily again, but her attention is on the TV. "Did you hear about this, Mom? The hit-and-run? The million-dollar reward? That accident happened the same night you took off out of here. One man died, the woman lost her baby, and her dog took off."

Photos appear on the TV screen of a man, a woman, and a dog. Lily's heart nearly stops. It's Henry, her Henry. The dog was in the accident, the dog is missing, the woman is an FBI agent, it's all coming at her so fast, she can't put it into any order.

But suddenly she sees herself hiding under some bushes as a car races through the rainy darkness and slams into another car. Then the car races backward through the rain and rams the car again and pretty soon someone stumbles out of the car and falls to the ground and doesn't get up again. A dog scrambles out after whoever fell to the ground, a big dog, a monster dog, and he tries to get the woman up, but he can't and he limps off into the rain, howling, and Lily whistles and he crawls under the bush with her.

She vaguely recalls something else, how the ramming car stopped and someone got out. A man. A man got out of the car and gazed through the rain at the ruined car. "Mom?"

"I have a secret, Chrissy."

"What's that?"

"If I tell you, it wouldn't be a secret anymore."

"I won't tell anyone."

"You promise?"

"Cross my heart."

They're in the garden now and Lily goes over to the fence and starts taking food out of her pockets. "Henry," she says softly, and whistles.

"There's nothing out in those bushes, Mom. Except lizards and ants."

"Is too." Lily tugs on Chrissy's hand, pulling her into a crouch too. "He doesn't know you, so he's probably a little shy. I feed him. He's starved. His ribs are starting to show."

"Mom, you shouldn't stuff food in your pockets like that. It's . . ."

"There. Look, Chrissy. The bushes are moving."

"It's the wind. C'mon, I'll take you outside the fence and we'll have a look."

"Can't. Can't go outside the fence. Doris will put the bracelet on me if I go."

"You're with me, Mom. It's okay."

And just like that, they're beyond the fence, where life is happening, where the air smells free and rich and filled with magic. Chrissy is magic. The grass is green and soft and Lily suddenly wants to fall into it, roll around in it, lick it, bury her face in it.

"Okay, here's the mound with all the bushes on it, Mom. Nothing here."

"Henry's just being shy." Lily whistles again and suddenly he pokes his nose out, then his whole head.

"My God," Chrissy whispers, and holds out a piece of cardboard with clumps of food on it.

"Henry won't come to you. He doesn't know you." Lily takes the cardboard from her and moves closer to the dog.

"Mom, don't." She grabs Lily's arm. "He might be rabid."

"Oh, silly. He won't hurt me. He's my secret."

She lets go and Lily moves closer to Henry. He's wary at first, eyes flicking about nervously, his body still hidden in the bushes. Then he crawls out of his hiding place, his huge body visible now, ribs sticking out, his nub of a tail wagging when he realizes the fence doesn't separate them.

Lily throws her arms around his neck and he barks and licks her face and they roll around in the grass, just the two of them. Then he hurries over to the food and wolfs it down.

"My God," Chrissy breathes. "A Rhodesian Ridgeback. That's the dog who— His leg's hurt, Mom."

"I know. He limps. Can you fix it?"

"Not here. I'll have to take him to my office. Will he follow you to my car?"

"I don't know."

She digs into her purse and pulls out a phone. "Doris, it's Chris. I'm outside the fence with Mom. I'm going to be taking her with me for the afternoon, down to the office . . . Right, I've got some new pups who need a lot of loving . . . okay, thanks."

Lily loves her for not telling Doris about Henry. Now Henry is their secret.

Chrissy drops the phone back into her bag, stands slowly. "Okay, Mom, I'm going to back away and I want you to call Henry. We don't have too far to go. My car's in the closest parking lot."

"Henry, want to go home?"

He looks up, cocks his head to the side, moves hesitantly forward; Lily takes a step back.

"It's okay, boy. Chrissy is going to fix your leg." Lily whistles and Henry limps alongside her, licking her hand as they follow Chrissy.

She keeps stroking his head, loving the silky feel of his coat, loving him. In the light, his leg looks bad, all swollen and puffy and matted with blood and dirt. It hurts her to look at it.

"Not much farther, boy."

But he suddenly stops and just sort of drops to the ground, like his legs are refusing to support all his weight. Lily falls to her knees beside him and Chrissy comes over real slow and careful.

"I want to help you," she says quietly, and holds out her hand so Henry can sniff it.

It reminds Lily of when Chrissy was small and they used to rescue wounded birds on their lake. She rolls this memory around inside of her for a while, loving its texture. She doesn't have any trouble with the long-ago memories. She has all the animal memories tucked inside her, in a special room. She knows other memories hide in there too, like

(the rain, the storm, the man getting out of the ramming car . . .)

. . . But some of those memories scare her.

Henry licks Chrissy's hand and she finally touches his head and talks to him in that soft, beautiful voice that she uses with Lily and with her animals. "That leg looks like it's cut to the bone. Mom, I want you to stay here with Henry. I'm going to run to my car for a tarp. If we can slide it under him, we can pull him over to the car."

"Okay."

"What'd I just say, Mom?"

Chrissy, testing her. "To stay with Henry."

"And where am I going?"

"To your car." Lily looks at her, at her beautiful daughter. "I'm not deaf or stupid, you know."

Chrissy hugs her quickly. "Of course you're not. I'm sorry. Be right back."

She runs off toward the parking lot. Lily stretches out on the grass beside Henry, her lungs filling with the smell of grass and sky and sunlight. She rests her head on Henry's chest. He whimpers and licks her hand and lays his head on the ground again.

15

In the Between

The room felt comfortable and snug to Charlie. No baby posters or pregnancy reminders adorned these walls. Rain's various degrees hung in a neat row behind her desk, and a huge clay pot in the corner billowed with red and yellow impatiens.

"Just make yourself as comfortable as possible," Rain said, pulling a chair over to the recliner. "Take a couple of long, deep breaths, kick off your sandals, loosen your clothes."

Charlie's resistance to hypnosis had peaked around midnight last night. Now she actually anticipated it. She trusted Rain implicitly and knew she would take her through the events of that night without causing her any more trauma. And yet, despite her anticipation, a small pocket of fear remained, fear that the hypnosis might blow open this seventh sense that Rain had told her about, that it might do to her what it had done to Logan.

Rain fiddled with the knobs on her recording equipment, tested it to make sure it worked properly, then clipped a mike to the collar of Charlie's blouse. "I'm going to give you a suggestion that you can come out of the hypnosis at any time just by opening your eyes, Charlie."

"Okay."

"Is your cell phone off?"

"No. Leo's supposed to check in with an update on the hotline calls."

152 · T.J. MacGregor

"If we're going to do this, let's do it right." Rain reached into Charlie's purse on the floor and dug out the cell phone and handed it to her. "Forward your calls to my number. It'll ring out front; the machine will take the message."

Charlie reprogrammed the phone, dropped it into her purse, and sat back. "Now what?"

"I want you to take several very deep breaths, Charlie. With each breath, the tension runs out of your body through the soles of your feet," Rain began. "Close your eyes too."

She had a soothing voice, the human equivalent of water running over stones in a stream. Within minutes, Charlie felt so relaxed, her body seemed to have grown into the chair. She sank deeper and deeper into relaxation until she hovered at the edge of sleep.

"I'm going to touch your forehead, Charlie, and the level of your relaxation will double. Then I'm going to count backward from ten, and with each number, your relaxation will triple."

Images flashed across Charlie's closed eyes. Vague, disconnected images, some in black and white, others in color. Then the images began to fill in, to come together into something she recognized. A door. She faced a tall metal door.

"I'm going to count back from ten again and your right arm will become so relaxed, it will feel like part of the chair. At six I'll ask you to lift your arm, but you won't be able to do it . . . ten . . . nine . . . eight . . . seven . . . six . . . Lift your arm, Charlie."

She tried, but couldn't. "Can't," she said hoarsely.

"Good. When I reach number one, you'll be back on the night of the accident. It will be like you're watching a movie. You'll be a detached observer, able to report what you see and experience, but you won't feel any emotional or physical pain."

The metal door remained foremost in Charlie's mind, but as Rain continued the countdown, the door began to slide open.

"What do you see, Charlie?"

Rain's voice reached her as if from a great distance. When she finally spoke, her voice was so soft, it was nearly inaudible even to her. "Metal door. It's sliding open."

"That's good. It's going to continue to open until you can walk through it. I want you to touch your hand to the door and ask it to keep opening."

Charlie did what Rain suggested, and the door kept moving.

"When it opens, you're going to walk through it and find yourself in the car on the night of the accident. At no time will you experience fear or pain. You can always come out of the hypnosis by simply opening your eyes."

The metal door swung silently open and there she was, within the vibrating image of her own past, inside the Explorer with Jess and Paz.

"Where are you now, Charlie?"

"Driving to Alex's. Jess wants to get to higher ground. He's driving too fast. I keep telling him to slow down."

"Is Paz with you?"

"Yes. The thunder frightens him. He whimpers, tries to get into my lap. So much rain. Hard to see the road."

"I want you to move forward in time to the moments right before your car was hit and tell me what you see and hear. Tell me what's going on."

And suddenly she was so fully immersed in this movie of the mind that she could see what she saw then, smell what she smelled then, hear and taste what she heard and tasted then.

They're arguing about where they are. Jess isn't watching the road and she's leaning forward, rubbing at the glass with her hand because the windshield has fogged up. Light explodes through the car, and in the circle she has cleared on the glass she sees a car racing toward them, aimed straight at them. The headlights glare like the eyes of some primitive, predatory beast.

She screams that it's going to hit them, and in the instant before impact Charlie sees the car clearly, a dark Mercedes or BMW, the driver hunched over the wheel like some madman. Then the world ruptures, glass flying everywhere, metal crunching against metal. The Explorer spins out of control, and before it has stopped, the madman slams into them again. Then: blackness.

When she comes to, pain burns through her body and warm liquid rushes out between her legs. Her water has broken, the horn is blaring, and Jess is calling to her. The air bag has impaled him against the seat and he can't move. Behind them, in the backseat, Paz barks and howls.

"Get help, Charlie. Jesus, I can't breathe . . . my eye . . . my legs, I can't feel my legs . . ."

Sobbing, she presses her hands against the air bag that holds her back against the seat. But the pain, my God, the pain sweeps over her in hot, powerful waves that suck the air from her lungs, the will from her bones. Worse than the pain is the sound of Jess's staccato breathing interspersed with a terrible keening.

She presses her hands as hard as she can against the air bag and realizes it didn't fully inflate. She's able to get her left arm free and gropes for her purse on the floor. There. She touches it. Thrusts her hand inside. Finds her pocketknife.

"Hurry, Charlie," Jess wheezes.

She struggles with one hand to open the knife, then stabs the air bag with the blade and suddenly she is free, she can move, she can breathe. Still sobbing, she stabs the air bag that impales Jess and he shrieks as it deflates, shrieks in pain and crumples over the steering wheel.

She grabs his arm and screams his name, screams at him to say something, begs him to speak. He coughs and slowly lifts his head, one hand cupped over his eye. The horns keeps blaring, blaring, blaring, the noise slamming around inside her skull, getting mixed up with his voice, the rain . . .

"I . . . hurry, Charlie. Hurry."

Still sobbing, Charlie kicks open the door and stumbles out into the storm to get help. The baby, her son, rolls around inside her, she feels another rush of warmth between her legs, and the pain seizes her again. She clasps her stomach and, gasping for air, tries to ride out the pain. But it drives her to her knees and she sinks into the wet grass, the rain drumming her back.

Then Paz is there, nudging her, barking, trying to get her to put her arm around his neck. But she doesn't have the strength. And suddenly her body collapses to the ground and she can't move, can't get up, can't do anything but lie there.

Her fingers twitch against the wet grass; she tries to push herself up. Paz appears at her side, whimpering, limping, blood running down his leg, and presses his own body against hers for support. But she's too weak to get up, and he limps off into the storm, howling. The stink of blood settles in the air, thickening in her nostrils.

Rain streams into her eyes. Paz's howls grow more distant; she can no longer see him.

Headlights again. The glare spills across her body, stalls there, blinding her. If she can raise her arm, if she can signal the driver . . . Tires shriek and the headlights race toward her, and she realizes it's the car that hit them, that the driver is coming for her. She rolls onto her side, brings her knees up against her protruding belly, and somehow manages to roll onto them. She crawls across the grass to escape the black beast, her fingers digging deeply into the saturated soil, pulling her body forward. But there's no place to hide, no trees, no fence, nothing at all.

The tires shriek again and the headlights turn abruptly away from her as the car veers off in the opposite direction. She drops to the grass, on her side, her hands pressed against her belly to hold Matt inside until help comes. She screams for Jess, screams. . . .

Charlie bolted out of the chair, wheezing and sobbing, and stumbled across the room to the nearest door. She threw it open and lurched into a hot, deserted alley. Sunlight poured over her and beat against the black asphalt, sending up waves of heat that quivered in the air.

She sucked the heat into her lungs, sucked and coughed, sucked and coughed, and doubled over at the waist. The ice floes of unexpressed grief were now breaking apart in her chest, in her womb, in the deepest part of her being. She couldn't stop it from happening, couldn't push it back, couldn't delay it anymore with her missionary zeal. Her denial had shattered and the truth rushed into her.

Life without Jess.

Like without Matthew.

Life with her future torn away from her.

Her knees buckled and she went down in the alley, her knees slamming hard against the hot asphalt, her palms landing a heartbeat later. And there she remained, on all fours, panting from the heat, beads of sweat rolling down the sides of her face and hitting the ground.

"Jesus, Charlie." Rain's hands touched her back, her shoulder, and Charlie wrenched away.

"No." The words whispered out through her clenched teeth. "Don't touch me."

Rain took her hands away.

Charlie's head spun as she rocked back onto her heels, pressed her hands to her thighs. She pulled air in through her teeth and saw Jess with his hand cupping an eye, saw him, heard him, and squeezed her own eyes shut. She rolled her lower lip against her teeth to cut off her sobs.

"Charlie, it's okay," Rain said softly, touching her again.

Charlie's right arm snapped upward and slammed into Rain's wrist. *"It's not okay!"* she shouted. *"Nothing's okay, it'll never be okay, you hear me, Rain? Nothing is okay."*

Then Rain's face swam into perfect clarity and Charlie saw the compassion in her eyes, and her anger fled. Rain's arms went around her and everything inside her seemed to come undone. She sobbed and sobbed, vaguely aware of Rain's voice whispering, "Get it out, Charlie. Let it come."

At some point she realized she felt empty, dry, hollow. She had nothing left inside her. She lifted her head and wiped her face with her gritty hands and gazed down the long, deserted alley lined with bougainvilleas that exploded with red. Waves of heat trembled inches above the asphalt; it was like watching heat rising from a kettle in the seconds before the kettle begins to whistle and emit steam.

Then, suddenly, the waves began to congeal, to clot like blood, and seemed to form a shape. She stared, spellbound, as the shape became recognizable. Jess. It was Jess, all six foot two of him, standing there in the alley, as real as the blackness of the asphalt or the red of the bougainvillea vines.

He smiled, that was all, just one of those weird Jess smiles that spoke tomes about who and what they were together and apart. Just as quickly, the shape disappeared. He was gone. Only the waves of heat remained.

"Charlie?"

Rain was no longer touching her.

Charlie looked over at her, at Rain holding out her arms, showing her the hundreds of tiny bumps that covered them. "Goose flesh," she breathed.

Charlie quickly rubbed Rain's arms and said, "Let's go back inside, where it's cool."

She pushed to her feet and headed for the open door to Rain's office. Rain fell into step beside her, rubbing her own arms now. Neither of them spoke until they were back in Rain's office, sipping from tall glasses of iced water.

"He was there, wasn't he, Charlie."

Rain spoke so softly, Charlie could hear the hums and clicks of the building behind her voice. "Take me under again," Charlie replied. "I want to know what happened when I died."

"No way. Not now. Maybe tomorrow or next week, but not now."

"I need to know, Rain. I need to know what else I haven't remembered." She sat back in the recliner, set the glass of water on the side table. "Please. I won't freak. I just need to know."

Rain looked at her for a moment, then nodded reluctantly.

Charlie drifted away in a navy blue sea, here but not here. A fog surrounded her.

"Where are you now, Charlie?"

"Rising above the fog."

"What fog?"

"The fog where my body is. The fog that hides Chiloé."

"Tell me about Chiloé."

"It's the beginning and the end."

An embryonic peace washed through Charlie as she spoke, a state of mind or being that she'd imagined belonged to holy men, yogis, and saints. She realized she could dip into a vast ocean of knowledge and information with nothing more than her *intent*, her *desire*. So she dipped and she drank and she immersed herself in this collective memory. And through it, she reached a master record that contained everything her soul and every other soul had ever been or would be. Every life, wish, travesty, relationship, intention, every minute detail recorded and encoded for eternity.

"I don't understand what you mean, Charlie."

"Chiloé is like the River Styx. It's in the between. It stands between the land of the living and the land of the dead, and when you go there, you forget."

"What did you forget?"

"That life continues."

"Tell me about Jess and Matt. Where they are now, how you perceive them."

"In many lives," Charlie whispered, and saw those lives flash past her like scenes from dozens of movies. "Scotland. Mexico. Ancient Egypt. Atlantis."

"I know you're speaking to me now, Charlie, from a higher perspective. I'm going to touch your forehead and you'll sink twice as deep and be able to tell me the larger reasons behind this tragedy."

Something cool touched her between her eyes, and she seemed to sink down into the navy blue depths of her own being. "When she had the chance, she denied the ability and died for it anyway. When she didn't have the chance, she sought desperately to develop the ability and died in the trying. Now she has the chance *and* the ability."

"What ability is that?"

"To perceive what isn't readily apparent to others."

Rain touched her forehead again. "You'll remember everything you've experienced very clearly but without pain. You'll feel comfortable with your ability, with this seventh sense. You'll be able to use it in new ways. On the count of three, you'll open your eyes and feel completely rested, confident, and certain about your next step. One . . . two . . . three . . . Open your eyes, Charlie."

And she did, and they felt as dry as tissue paper. "Paper. A pencil."

Rain dropped a notepad with a pen clipped to it in her lap and Charlie briefly described the car that had hit them. Color, number of doors, that it was a Mercedes, a BMW, or maybe an Infiniti. The driver was male.

Then the stuff that she'd felt and seen and learned faded away from her, like a dream upon awakening, slipping beneath the surface of that vast, magnificent ocean.

Charlie handed Rain the notepad and rubbed her eyes. "Rage," she said softly. "The whole thing was about rage. The driver's rage."

Rain stopped the tape, rewound it. "Let's not worry about that now. We know for sure that the driver is male. From the car he was driving, we can assume he's probably a well-heeled professional. Did you get a look at the license at any point?"

"No. But I had the feeling that he has a wife and a kid. It feels like a hunch."

Actually, it felt like heartburn.

"Good, this is good. What other intuitive nudges do you have?"

She thought about it, shook her head. What she wanted most just then was to go home and sleep.

"The bottom line is that you've got this incredible intuitive ability that you've used all along in your work, but not in this way. Dying changed all that. Now you have to use it consciously. If you catch this guy, it's going to be because your intuition has led you in the right direction."

"Not *if*, Rain. *When*."

Charlie called Wells in the lab and when he didn't answer, she tried his cell phone and he answered on the first ring.

"Wells here."

"Leo. It's me."

"Hey, I was just about to call you. I've got news."

"Me too. You go first."

"No, you."

"The driver was a man and the car was a BMW, Mercedes, or an Infiniti."

"What the hell. How'd you know that?"

"I'll explain when I see you."

"No, I mean, you're right, girl. I finally got an answer back on those paint chips. And they're from a BMW or Mercedes, built between 1994 and 1997. I got the word from Germany this morning."

"We're closer, Leo. Much closer."

"Bet your ass. How about you, me, and Logan have dinner tonight? We need to plan our strategy."

"My place, eight. We each bring something. Rain's coming too."

"I am?" Rain asked.

Charlie nodded. "Eight, Leo. *Ciao*."

(2)

In the long afternoon shadows, her home looked serene, Benedict thought, tranquil, untouched by tragedy of any kind. The property itself reminded him of a little Eden, lush with mango trees and citrus, a veritable treasure chest of vitamin C.

Poking out here and there, he saw bougainvillea vines, brilliant orange firecracker plants, cactuses, palms. A large landscaped mound provided ample privacy from the road, hiding the front windows, but not the porch or driveway. He recognized both from the local news piece he'd seen.

Benedict already knew she wasn't home; he'd called her number on his cell phone. He also realized his presence here was sheer insanity, that he should turn the hell around and get as far from Charlie Calloway's home as possible. But he couldn't. He needed to know something about the woman whose life he'd altered so dramatically.

He parked one block over and hurried toward her place on foot. Neighbors were out, kids playing ball and Frisbee, people walking dogs. But no one looked at him. Even if someone later remembered him, what would they remember? A man in jeans and a baseball cap, a guy with dark hair and dark shades, he could've been anyone.

Benedict cut through the side yard and loped toward the screened porch at the back. He pulled a hanky from his back pocket and used it to cover the porch door handle before he touched it. Unlocked, of course. No South Floridian ever locked a screen door.

He figured the sliding glass door would be locked and he would have to climb in through a window somewhere. But the door wasn't locked and he slid it open and slipped inside. The dog, he thought. She and her husband probably hadn't locked their doors very often because they had a monster guard dog and Charlie Calloway, widow, hadn't broken the habit yet. Besides, she was a fed and undoubtedly kept a gun in the house. A fearless woman. He liked that.

He stepped into the silent kitchen. The air felt abnormally cool; big electric bills, he guessed. He pulled on a pair of Latex gloves and trailed his fingers over the clean, uncluttered countertops. Once upon a time, before Anita had gone on strike, his own home had looked this tidy. Fearless and neat, he liked the combination.

The first door in the hall was shut. He pressed his ear to the wood, listening, then turned the knob. The hinges didn't squeak; he liked that too. But he didn't like what he found in this room. A ruin, a heap of debris. The crib in the corner looked as if someone had taken a hammer or a bat to it. Strips of wallpaper lay everywhere. The pine dresser had nicks in it, gunshot nicks, that was what they looked like. The drawers had been hurled against one wall, which bore the dents, the peeling plaster. Pieces of a shattered mirror littered the floor.

Charlie Calloway, he thought, had gone into a rage in here.

He could identify with that.

He left this room and continued down the hall to the rest of the rooms, where tidiness prevailed again. Good, one room just for rage. Maybe he ought to try it. Go into that room, shut the door, and lose it big-time. Then, when the rage was spent, you walked out again and shut the door behind you. It had possibilities.

In the den, he stood for a while in front of the computer, noting that the box that held the hard drive was at least twice the size of his own. The monitor was also well beyond standard. Hell, the monitor was probably larger than his TV screen. Jess Calloway, computer genius. He was tempted to boot it up, but began to feel a certain urgency about time. He moved on to the array of photos on a bookshelf.

Here stood pictures of Charlie Calloway with her husband, of the two of them with their dog, of Charlie with people who were probably her immediate family. A brother or sister, nieces and nephews, parents. In the last photo, Charlie stood sideways, her T-shirt raised, her pregnant belly exposed. She was laughing in this photo, her head thrown back, her hair wild.

Something about the photo made him hard. Before he consciously realized it, his gloved fingers had seized the photo and slipped it in his back pocket.

No, no, Frankie. Better not.

"Shut up," he whispered, and walked down the hall again and into the master bedroom.

The bed dominated the room, a king-size with a brass headboard that had strange markings on it. Benedict leaned close to the markings, frowning, and ran his gloved fingers over them. Chinese? Weird. He sat down on the bed, testing it. Good mattress, not too hard, not too soft. He slid open the drawer of the nightstand, fingers touching the neatly arranged items: a pair of Chinese coins with square holes in the middle; an *I Ching* book, the original translation by Richard Wilhelm that had been so popular in the late sixties and early seventies.

The husband's side of the bed.

Curious about the symbols on the headboard, Benedict glanced through the hexagrams and matched one of them, hexagram 11, Peace. He looked at the second symbol on the headboard and realized it was the same as the first, that all four symbols, in fact, were the same. Peace, Peace, Peace, Peace. How quaint.

He put the book back into the drawer, shut it, opened the drawer on her side of the bed. A gun, two boxes of cartridges, a notebook. Benedict removed the notebook and, heart speeding up, opened it.

5/27: Jess & I are in a cafe in Chiloé. We have a glass of that local golden liqueur, that stuff called Oro, and suddenly everything goes sort of hazy and we're on the bar, making love. This is absolutely real. I feel his hands on me, I feel his fingers when they slide into me, I feel his mouth on my nipples, sucking them. I feel his hardness inside of me. Then Alex taps my shoulder and says, "Charlie, what the hell are you doing? You're fucking in full view of everyone."

Interpretation: Well, hey, Freud would have a field day with this one. I woke in the middle of an orgasm.

Benedict began to stroke himself, first through his clothes, then he unzipped his jeans and slipped his hand inside.

6/1: This time Jess & I are on hill somewhere. I think it's that hill on Chiloé where we waited that night for the ghost ship. It's cold, we make love to keep warm. And it's just like the other dreams, so real that I wake with my body twitching and tears on my cheeks, and my own hands bunched between my thighs.

Interpretation: Pound sand, Freud. Give me Jung any day. Jung would say it was real, a perceptual shift. Or he would say I'd tapped

an archetype. I say that it's real, just as real as my day-to-day life,
which right now is very pathetic.

Benedict read on. Some dreams were common, almost boring.
But others were erotically charged, like touching a live wire with
your cock. And it was these dreams that kept him stroking himself,
harder and faster as he lay where she had lain. And when the feeling
swept over him, it was like the purge of his rage, a total release, a
spiritual cleansing.

He lay there for a few moments, curled up on his side, inhaling
the smell of her body in these sheets, drifting in it. Then reason
clamped over him and he shot to his feet and zipped up his jeans
and looked wildly around, shocked that he had been so stupid, so
goddamn stupid.

Benedict jerked the top sheet off the bed, the sheet he'd been
lying on, and bunched it up under his arm. He drew the quilt back
over the bed, fixing it at the corners. He shook out the pillows, put
them back where they'd been, fluffed them up. He left everything
as he'd found it and backed out of the room, his breathing fast,
uneven.

Get out. Now.

He ran back down the hall and paused only long enough to find
a garbage bag. He stuffed the sheet inside, ducked out the doors,
raced into the yard. Shadows had lengthened, he felt the approach
of evening in the air.

On the next block, he lifted the lid of a garbage can and shoved
the bag down deep. Then he hastened on to his car, smiling to
himself, his cock still hard.

16

Shadow Man

(1)

When Charlie pulled into her driveway at six that evening, she felt drained, used up. All she wanted to do was go through Jess's clothes and belongings, pack them up, and get the boxes into the attic. She wanted to clean out the nursery. She wanted closure. She didn't feel like having dinner with Wells, Lorraine, and wacko Logan. She didn't feel like being with anyone. The feeling went so deep, in fact, that as soon as she set the groceries on the counter, she made a beeline for the phone.

She still had time to cancel.

But as she punched out Wells's number, she felt distinctly uneasy, eerie. Charlie turned, sniffing the air like an animal, and reached into her purse for her gun. She slipped off her shoes and moved slowly, puzzling over what felt *so wrong*.

Once, years ago, before she and Jess had gotten Paz, their house in Country Walk had been robbed. They'd had a fancy security system in those days, locks on every window, and it hadn't helped. The intruder had gotten in anyway. After that they got Paz and never locked the goddamn doors again because she realized that no security would deter a determined thief.

She'd felt then as she did now, an amorphous sense of wrongness that wrapped itself around her like thin tendrils of cold fog. She moved faster when she hit the hall and stopped outside the nursery door. She stood to one side, listening, then turned the knob and kicked the door open and swung into the room, the weapon sliding slowly from one side of the room to the other.

Nothing.

Just a ruin, the way she'd left it the night she'd gone ballistic. But in here, in this stale air, in this permanent twilight, she felt something bad. Something evil. Something so malign that goose bumps erupted on her arms. Her body suddenly seemed to bristle with awareness, that hunch sensation moving around inside her, nowhere and everywhere at once.

She backed out of the nursery, shut the door, and ran up the hall to the den, expecting to find the computer equipment gone. But it was all just where she'd left it. Nothing appeared to have been disturbed. Nothing, so far, was missing. She glanced at the bookshelves, at the line of photos that she'd arranged in front of the books, and knew immediately which photo was gone. The one of her with her big belly, clowning for Jess's camera, a little thing in a frame.

Gone.

Whoever had come in here had taken the photo and left.

Jess's gun.

Charlie raced into the bedroom, jerked open her nightstand drawer. His gun hadn't been stolen. Nothing looked out of place. Frowning again, she sat at the edge of the bed and looked slowly around. On impulse, she shut her eyes and told herself that she needed to know who had been in her house. As she tried to relax in the same way the hypnosis had relaxed her, she laid back against the quilt. Cold air from the ceiling vent blew directly on her legs, so she crawled under the quilt, on the top sheet.

She began to breathe evenly, slowly, directing her mind in the way that Rain had done, counting down, counting slowly. Before she reached a mental count of ten, she realized that something felt wrong about the bed and she sat up, threw the quilt off, and ran her hand over the sheet.

She was lying on the fitted bottom sheet.

Where the hell was the top sheet?

Charlie threw off the quilt, picked it up, and shook it, thinking the top sheet had gotten tangled inside.

No top sheet.

But her journal fell out, the journal where she'd been writing down her dreams, trying to make sense of what had been happening to her. The journal that had been in her nightstand drawer.

She opened it up, read the first dream, slapped the journal shut, and leaped off the bed, shouting, "You come in here and steal a photo of a pregnant woman and then read her dream journal? What kind of fuck are you?" She hurled the journal across the room, started to strip off the fitted sheet, when she noticed something damp in the center, something that caught the light.

Charlie got onto the mattress on her hands and knees and leaned close to the stuff. "Jesus," she whispered, and leaped off the bed and ran into the kitchen for a clean spoon and a bowl. She scooped the semen off the sheet, put the spoon in the bowl, and ran to the phone and dialed Wells's various numbers. He didn't pick up on any of them. He was in transit, on his way to her place.

She went back over to the bowl, pressed her fist to her mouth, and backed away from the nightstand, backed out of the kitchen, backed up the hall to the bathroom doorway. Then she turned and ran inside and slammed the door shut.

Sobbing now, she stripped off her clothes and turned on the water as hot as she could get it and stood under it, sobbing and scrubbing herself with soap until the doorbell rang.

Charlie's stomach growled as she paced the length of the forensics lab, where the air stank of cleansers and chemicals. Now and then she paused to watch Wells as he ran a series of tests on the semen sample. She knew the basics, that the semen would yield blood type, race, an approximate age, a blueprint of information. But it wouldn't give her a goddamn name. It wouldn't give her an address, a profession, anything *tangible*.

Maybe Logan could read semen. But Logan wasn't here, he had told Wells he "couldn't make it" to dinner. And Rain was helping Wells, the two of them trading medical jargon that Charlie didn't understand. So she paced and fumed, struggling with a pall of gloom that had clamped down over her and wouldn't let go.

She finally stopped at the window that overlooked Miami. Lights had blinked on all over the city, creating a false beauty that hid the imperfections, the ugly pockets of poverty where crime and desperation flourished. At night the city seemed magical, the way it had when she was a kid. But even the magic couldn't touch her gloom. All she could think of was that somewhere out there the man she sought went on about his life.

A life that includes jerking off in my bed.

"Hey, Charlie. Snap out of it."

Wells stood next to her with a computer printout in hand. "He's A positive, Caucasian, probably in his forties. No venereal diseases. He has an elevated white count that indicates he's fighting off an infection of some sort, nothing major. He's—"

"Give me his name, Leo. Or an address."

Wells shrugged. "Hell, at least we've got an approximate age now. And we know that he knows where you live."

"We don't know for sure this is the same guy who hit the Explorer," Rain said, walking over to them. "You're making a lot of assumptions, Leo."

"Who the hell else would it be?" Charlie snapped. "All he took was a photo of me with my belly exposed. It's him. I know it's him."

"Would Logan read her house?" Rain asked Wells.

"I doubt it. Logan wants out of this whole thing."

"So here we are," Charlie said. "A little wiser but no closer to this fucker."

Wells folded the printout and slipped it into a drawer. "I say we go out to dinner and talk about where we go from here."

"There isn't anyplace to go from here," Charlie replied. "We've hit a dead end. And he knows it. The reward hasn't flushed out any witnesses, and we haven't been able to get any lead on his car or his identity or anything else."

"I'm running a search on the MVD's computer for every Mercedes and BMW, 1994 model or later, that is registered in the tri-county area," Wells said. "And until we've gone through that data, it's not a dead end."

"Shit," Charlie muttered. "Just in the city of Palm Beach, every other car on the road is either a Mercedes or a BMW. We'll be lucky if the final tally is under ten thousand cars."

Neither Wells nor Rain said anything, and who could blame them? There was nothing more to say.

Charlie slung her purse over her shoulder. "Let me know when you've got the list of ten thousand, Leo." She headed for the door.

"What about dinner?" Rain called after her.

"I've lost my appetite," she said. "You guys go on."

Neither of them stopped her, and moments later she strode to her car, the pall of gloom pursuing her like some faithful pet.

(2)

Daybreak. On Minnow Key, sunrise had been a good time for Logan, the day fresh, the possibilities unlimited. Just then it was not a good time. He felt like heading back in the direction he'd come. The last thing he wanted that morning was contact with the local-yokel cops.

He was here only because Wells had asked him to help out, had practically *begged*, citing the numerous favors that he owed Metro Dade's chief of police. Wells had assured him his personal contact with the locals would be minimal. But judging from the sheer volume of police cruisers in the parking lot of the U-Haul company, "minimal contact" was a pipe dream.

He slowed as he approached the barricade and pulled out the bureau ID he'd been carrying around. The local yokel strutted over to the window, dark shades in place, thumbs hooked in the belt of his pants. "Sorry, sir, no one is being permitted to enter or leave."

"FBI." Logan held out the badge.

The cop tilted the shades back onto his head and scrutinized the badge as though he'd never seen one before. "No one said anything about feds being involved."

"Then ask Special Agent Leo Wells. He's supposed to be here."

"No Wells has come through here."

Great. "Then how about if I pull over there and wait while you find out, Sergeant."

"How about if you can the attitude and get out of the car, *sir.*"
He opened Logan's door and stepped to the side. "Now."

Like I need this shit. Bad enough that he and Wells had arrived
at Charlie's the other night for dinner, only to be shown a glob of
come in a bowl. Bad enough that Wells had come by his camper
around nine last night and hauled him over to the Calloway woman's
house to read the place. The woman hadn't been too thrilled to see
him and he hadn't been too thrilled about being there. Bad enough
that the only thing he'd gleaned was an energy pattern, the equivalent
of a whisper in the cosmic wind. Now this.

Logan got out and leaned against the car.

"I'd like to see your license and registration," the cop said.

"Why? You've got my badge."

The cop snapped his fingers in Logan's face. *"Now."*

Logan just folded his arms across his chest. "I'd like to see your
superior officer."

The cop grabbed the front of Logan's shirt, jerked him forward,
then slammed him back against the car. In that brief moment of
contact, Logan saw him knocking a woman around, beating her up
with his fists. "Turn the fuck around," the cop snapped, and pulled
his gun.

"If you beat her up again, she'll press charges and call your wife,"
Logan said quietly.

"What?" He stepped back, obviously nervous, uneasy. "How
. . . I mean, what . . ."

"Your wife already suspects there's someone else. She found
something . . ." He groped for the image that had come to him and
nearly laughed. "Lipstick on your collar. That's what she found.
And that's what you'll be confronting when you get off your shift
tonight. An irate wife."

The blood drained from his face and he took another step back.
Over his shoulder, Logan saw an officer loping toward them, a man
he recognized as the chief of Metro Dade. Everything, he thought,
had now come full circle.

"Hey, Sergeant," Chief Perkins shouted. "Put that goddamn gun
away!"

The sergeant glanced back, looked at Logan, then at the chief again, and holstered his weapon.

"What the fuck do you think you're doing?" Perkins snapped.

"He . . . I . . ." the sergeant stammered.

"Get your ass outta here before I suspend you."

The sergeant took off and Perkins shook his head. "Christ, I'm really sorry about this, Logan. Good to see you again."

"You too."

"Leo's inside the building. C'mon, I'll take you to him. I really appreciate your doing this."

"The sergeant is trouble, Chief."

"He's new."

"He beats up regularly on his girlfriend."

Perkins rubbed his large, square jaw. "That's spooky, Logan. Downright spooky."

"Hey, you think it's spooky for you? You ought to be where I am."

"No, thanks. I'll check out the situation with the sergeant. You have my word on that one. How much do you want to know about this scene?" He gestured toward the U-Haul building. "Wells wasn't sure about it and said to ask you."

"Whatever you know."

"The janitor found the security guard at six-thirty A.M. the day before yesterday. The intruder broke in through a side window and stole some office equipment. Looks like the security guard got in the way. That's all we know. Prints are of absolutely no use. On a busy day, they get anywhere from two to three hundred customers in here. They employ fifty people. We sealed off this building and they've set up in another building out back."

He might as well try to read a crime scene at an airport, he thought. "How was he killed?"

"He . . ."

"No, on second thought, keep it to yourself. If I get it right, then it means I'm hooked in to him. You have anything that belongs to him?"

"Personal effects. I got his watch out of property because Leo said metal is, uh, easier for you to, uh, well, do whatever it is you do."

"I'll start with the watch."

He brought it out of his back pocket, a simple, inexpensive watch sealed in a transparent bag. "It was still on him when he was found."

"It'll do. Just hold on to it for now."

"I heard you were helping Leo out with the Calloway investigation. I jumped on the possibility that maybe you'd give us a hand here because, frankly, in the last two days we haven't turned up anything and I don't think we're going to find lead one without some kind of, uh, special help."

"How many people are in the building now?"

"Just our people."

They went inside, into a cool stillness that smelled faintly of blood and violence. Wells spotted him and hurried over. "I thought you'd gotten lost."

"Held up. Where do you want me to start, Chief?"

"Wherever you want." He handed Logan the bag that contained the watch.

"Hold on a second," Wells said. "Charlie Calloway's around here somewhere. She wanted to watch how you work, Doug, if that's okay with you."

"She didn't get enough of that last night?" Logan drolled.

Wells shrugged. "If it's a problem, I'll ask her to leave."

"No, no, it's fine." Logan didn't give a damn who watched; he just wanted to get this over with. "I'm just going to move around in here for a bit, get my bearings. Where was the body found, Chief?"

"Over here."

Perkins headed toward the long counter lined with computer monitors, and Logan fell into step beside him. Part of him recoiled at the thought of holding the guard's watch, of being possessed so completely by the images that he had no control over his own actions. He didn't want a repeat of what had happened when he'd read Calloway's Explorer.

But when he'd been in the Explorer, the emotional residue of the accident had been everywhere, buried in the seat, clinging to the steering wheel, stuck to the dash. He'd breathed it. As soon as he'd gotten out of the Explorer, the impressions had dried up. That was how it usually was with people too, like with the sergeant outside. Once the connection had been broken, he was generally okay, despite any aftereffects that might linger briefly.

If the emotions were strong enough, however, then he risked being swept away, swallowed up, subsumed. So the trick would be to somehow create distance between himself and *the other* before he touched anything. He needed grounding, the very thing that had eluded him for the last three years.

Logan followed Perkins behind the counter and stopped at the chalk silhouette of the guard's body. A moment later, Wells and Charlie joined them. "Is it okay with you if I observe, Logan?" she asked.

"Sure, Calloway." No first names between them, he thought, and wondered what, if anything, that meant.

The four of them stood there for a moment or two, staring at the silhouette, saying nothing. *They're waiting for me to do something,* Logan thought. *Get on with it.*

He crouched, his knees popping, pain flaring briefly in his hip. He set the bag with the watch in it on the floor beside him. He didn't want to touch the floor with his bare hand, so he moved it through the air, about an inch above the inside of the chalk silhouette.

He began to breathe more deeply and with each breath, told himself he would maintain his equilibrium. He realized that if he couldn't achieve this now, he might as well reconcile himself to spending the rest of his life isolated on a tiny key, talking to the trees and his fishing pole and his cat. He might as well hang up any hope of a different, better future.

Here and there within the silhouette, he sensed hot spots. He held his left hand over the hottest of these areas, at the silhouette's head, and reached into the bag with his right. His fingers touched the watch, but he didn't pick it up.

A psychic current ran through him from his left hand to his right, the energy pattern unique to the guard. Logan familiarized himself with it and suddenly knew that he needed to release it before he proceeded. He directed it down through his body and out through the soles of his feet and back into the floor. A definite difference. Was this what he'd never done before? Was it going to be this easy?

Logan pressed his left hand down over the watch and placed his right flat against the floor, within the shape of the silhouette's head. Impressions and images sprang at him, hungry for recognition, but he pushed them back, shoved them into a mental closet, and slammed the door shut. He took his hands away from the floor and the watch.

Not so fast, he thought. *Let's do it again.*

"You want us to get out of your way?" Perkins asked.

"It's not you, it's me. I'm having trouble grounding myself." He raised his eyes to Wells's face. "I don't want a repeat of the Explorer."

"Hey, *kemo sabe.* I understand. What do you want us to do?"

"Maybe this will help." Charlie stepped closer to Logan and put her open palms against his back. "Send it through me."

"Send what through you?" Perkins asked.

"The excess," she replied.

Logan wondered how she knew, then stopped wondering because it felt so *right.* He touched the floor and the watch again. This time he didn't feel threatened or nearly overwhelmed. The images came more slowly, but with shocking vividness, as if to compensate for the lack of speed.

"He was hit in the head with something metallic. Hit hard. Hit . . ."

". . . in a rage," Charlie finished, her voice soft and strange.

"Yeah, a rage. The intruder was hiding . . ." Logan turned his body slightly and Charlie turned with him, hands still on his back, as if she'd felt the movement seconds before he had. "Over there . . ."

". . . behind the filing cabinet," she said.

Logan stood, but not before Charlie had also moved, once again anticipating what he would do. He went over to the cabinet, put his hands against it, and Charlie, standing behind him, put one hand against his back, between the shoulder blades, and the other at the top of the metal cabinet.

"He swept something off this cabinet and hit the guard with it." Logan realized he'd left the guard's watch on the floor next to the silhouette and, without it, could sense the intruder's energy more strongly. It exerted a magnetic pull on him, as though he were a grain of metallic dust, and he suddenly knew that he'd felt this same energy before.

At Charlie's. In her house. Sweet Christ.

He didn't think she felt it; she was too busy being hooked in to him, anticipating his movements. She moved seconds before he stepped into the energy's slipstream.

It was awkward for them to walk with her hands on him, so she fell into step alongside him. He grasped her fingers, drawn to them by the same inexorable energy that had pulled him into the intruder's slipstream.

He didn't understand what was going on. He didn't know what, exactly, had changed about her since the night he'd read the Explorer. He only knew that when she touched him, he felt grounded. The energy of whatever he was reading yielded information, but then it moved on, through her and out of them both. She allowed him to do what he had to do without being swallowed alive.

"If I'm not doing this right, just tell me," she whispered.

Logan almost laughed. She seemed to think he knew what he was doing; what a goddamn joke. "I don't know what's right in this situation. But whatever you're doing works, so keep doing it."

Wells and Perkins hurried along behind them.

"You feel him?" she asked. "The intruder?"

Logan nodded. "Strongly. What about you?"

"Yeah, and it scares me. Everything I feel here scares me."

"Just remember that what happened here is over."

"No, it's not over at all. It's over for the guard, but it's not over for this guy. He's . . . he's a shadow man, Logan. Know what I mean?"

There. A name. She'd named the evil, tagged it, categorized it, given it a shape, brought it out into the open. What she hadn't done—and what he had no intention of telling her right now—was that Shadow Man had been in her house. In her bedroom. He'd jerked off on her sheets. But he didn't understand the connection between that incident and what had occurred here. He stopped. "Right here."

They had reached the room where Shadow Man had entered. The window he'd come through lay directly in front of them, a neat, professionally cut opening in the glass. Logan brought her hand up to the windowsill. To the glass to the right of the opening. She seemed to understand what he was doing because she brought her other hand to the glass and shut her eyes.

"What do you feel?" he whispered.

She gasped and he suddenly knew that *she* knew this man had been in her house. "It's him," she whispered.

Logan put his hands on *her* shoulders, to ground *her,* to absorb the excess. Her breathing evened out. She shut her eyes. "A leak. I see a leaky boat. What the hell does that mean?"

"Describe the boat."

"I feel it's a metaphor. That he's plugging a leak."

"A leak in what?"

She hesitated, shook her head. "I don't know."

Logan stepped out from behind her and put his own hands to the glass, the sill, the glass again. She wasn't touching him then. Maybe it was that, maybe it was just the overpowering *blackness* of what he sensed, but the emotions of the other, of the intruder, seized Logan and swept him away.

When he surfaced, the ceiling tilted at a nauseating angle above him. "He got rid of the car," Logan said.

"What car?" Wells asked.

"The car. He got rid of the car by renting a U-Haul. I had an impression of water but seen from somewhere above the water. Like a cliff."

"A cliff?" Perkins shook his head. "Son, the day I find a cliff in Florida, I hang up my badge for good. And what car are you talking about?"

Logan still saw it in his mind's eye: the U-Haul, the cliff, and the intruder's shadow spilling over the guard, a shadow with its arms raised, hands clutching something. Although the images seemed clear, the connections were mixed up, frames of one movie spliced together with frames of another movie. The characters were the same, but the plots had no connection whatsoever.

"I'm confused," said Wells.

Then it came to him, came with such lucidity, it literally rendered Logan speechless.

"What?" Charlie said, grabbing his shoulders, shaking him, not hard, but hard enough to snap him back from the edge of a seductive abyss. "What is it?"

Logan found his voice. "All along we've assumed that the driver who hit you took his car to a garage to be fixed. Or found someone to fix it. But suppose he got rid of it? Suppose he rented a U-Haul to transport the car somewhere and then sank it?"

"You mean"—Wells crouched next to Charlie so they were both eye level with Logan—*"this break-in?"*

"And the break-in at Charlie's . . ." There, he'd said it. "And the accident. Same man."

"Jesus," Wells whispered, and locked eyes with Charlie. "It's no dead end, girl."

"Where's the body of water?" Charlie asked, her face so pale, it was as if she hadn't seen sunlight in the last twenty years. "Do you have any idea?"

"No."

Charlie stood, paced, stopped at the window. "If he got rid of the car, what'd he tell his family? His coworkers? His friends?" She turned, facing them, her frizzy hair struck through with light coming through the window. "He'd have to have some explanation. And he'd want to recoup part of the cost of the car. To file an insurance claim, he'd have to report the car stolen!"

Wells pressed his fist to his forehead. "Of course. It was right in front of us the whole time, and we didn't see it."

"Goddamn," Perkins said. "I'll get right on it. Give me some dates."

"May twenty-fourth to June fourth," Charlie said. "That would give him ten days."

"As far as the press is concerned," Perkins said, "this was a simple B and E in which a security guard was killed. We don't want this guy to know we've made any connection. We all agree on that?"

"Absolutely," Wells replied, then hurried after the chief. At the door, he glanced back at Logan and Charlie. "Don't go anywhere."

Once they were alone in the room, Charlie moved away from the window, plopped down in one of the desk chairs, pulled a notebook out of her purse, and began to scribble. Logan paced around the room, working the kink out of his hip. He wanted to talk about what had happened, but didn't know where to start. She finally broke the silence first.

"Is this how it always works for you, Logan?"

"How what always works?"

"Your ability."

Logan laughed and shook his head. "Look, for the last three years I've kept to myself because it's damn unpleasant being overwhelmed by other people's secrets every time someone touches me. I've never done this kind of stuff before, so I don't know what works and doesn't work. I wouldn't even be here if it weren't for Leo."

"Teach me to do what you do," she said.

"Hell, I should be asking you to teach me what you did. Somehow, you absorbed the excess. How'd you know about that anyway?"

She shrugged. "I don't know. It just came out. Then, when I was touching you, I could feel things. Here." She touched her fist to her solar plexus. "As soon as I acknowledged the feeling, I got impressions. Say this, turn here, do that." She leaned forward. "I need direction, you need grounding. Maybe we can help each other, Logan. I need to know how to defend myself against this . . . monster. I need an *edge*."

Yeah, and maybe he needed to hightail it back to Minnow Key. Back to the easy life on his dock. Back to talking to his cat and the trees. "I don't know. I don't know if I can work with anyone else in that capacity."

"You just did."

"Yeah, but that wasn't planned."

"We could try."

"I have to think about it."

"What's there to think about? It either works to our mutual benefit or it doesn't."

"Nothing is ever that simple."

"This is."

"Look, Charlie, it worked once and I'm grateful that you enabled me to be able to come up with a few answers without drowning in what I saw. But just because it worked once doesn't necessarily mean it'll work again."

"Jesus, Logan. You know what your problem is? Your misery is your closest friend." With that, she got up and walked out of the room.

Logan stared after her, anger slamming around inside him. What goddamn nerve. She didn't have any idea what was involved here. The one time he'd taken her hand, that night in the bureau warehouse, her sorrow had crashed over him like a tsunami. She'd been an open emotional book. If they worked together in the capacity she had suggested, he would become a walking wound filled with her psychic debris. It would be endless incidents like what had happened with the sergeant outside. He would be constantly on the defensive, trying to protect himself.

Your misery is your closest friend.

Screw it, he thought. Give him the hotline phones any day. He got up to go find Wells and Perkins.

17

Crossroads

(1)

Benedict braked for a light at the intersection. For moments he couldn't remember whether it was morning or evening or whether he was on his way to work or on his way home. The clock on the dashboard didn't help: 7:45 wasn't followed by A.M. or P.M.

He felt sharp stabs of panic at his lack of focus. Then it occurred to him that it had to be morning and he was on his way to work because he wasn't hungry. He always had breakfast. Relieved of this worrisome lapse, he recognized the intersection and his heart literally leaped into his throat.

Here. This is where it happened. Here, Christ, here.

He was at the very intersection where he'd rammed the Explorer, catercorner to where it had happened. It was like seeing an old scene from a different perspective for the first time, from above it, for instance, or behind it. He noticed a building that had escaped him before, that he hadn't realized existed until that very second. The sign at the front of the lushly landscaped grounds read:

WE CARE HEALTH CENTER
ALZHEIMER'S UNIT

He felt a sudden constriction in his throat, a tightening in his gut. Benedict turned left, trying to get a better view of the place, but a wall of pines and banyans surrounded the building. He nosed into a parking space two blocks over and walked quickly back toward the intersection.

An Alzheimer's unit probably would have shifts, like a hospital. Suppose someone on the graveyard shift had stepped outside that night for a smoke?

No, not in that deluge. But it was possible that someone had arrived or left and had seen him. Seen everything. Then why hadn't the individual come forward to claim the reward?

Because there weren't any witnesses.

Just the same, here he was at the scene of the crime.

He nearly turned around and ran back toward the car. But the same compulsion came over him that he'd felt when he'd driven by the Calloway home, that he had to see the place, get some sense of it. Otherwise he would lie awake at night, the possibilities gnawing at him. One look, that was all he needed.

As he crossed the end of the clinic's driveway, a navy blue Volvo turned in. He glanced at it, and to his utter horror it stopped and the passenger window went down. An elderly woman with short, stylish gray hair stared at him, her puckered mouth moving silently, as if in prayer. The driver, a younger, very attractive woman, leaned across and called, "The front of the building is on the other side, sir. This is the dependent care section."

"Thanks. I wasn't sure."

"Just follow that sidewalk on the far side of the banyans."

The old woman stuck her head out of the car. "Have you seen Henry?"

"Henry?"

"He doesn't know Henry, Mom."

"But I know *him*," the old woman said, grinning and pointing a gnarled, arthritic finger at Benedict. "I know him, Chrissy."

Benedict's blood turned to thick sap in his veins. Never mind that the woman obviously lived in this place, her brain barely functional, her mind no longer focused in the here and now. Never mind that. Something about the way she said, *I know him,* spooked him too deeply for words.

"Thanks again," Benedict managed to say with his most charming smile. He turned away from the car and moved quickly, but not too quickly, toward the sidewalk on the far side of the banyans. He heard the Volvo drive on, and glanced back only once as the rear fender flashed briefly in the light, then vanished down the driveway.

He knew he should run. He knew he should turn right around and run the fuck out of here. But if he did and the driver of the Volvo later asked the front desk if a man in a suit had come in for information and the receptionist said no, she might remember his face. He could see this entire scene in his head, see it unrolling with frightening precision. And if he could see it, then it was possible.

Best to go forward, to walk through the front doors, march his ass up to the information desk and ask for a brochure. *For my mother,* he would say. Then he would go on his way and no one would remember him.

His shoes squeaked against the sidewalk. The thick, sagging branches trapped the morning heat, and he began to sweat profusely. He pulled off his jacket, draped it over his shoulder, and went inside.

A tidy, colorful lobby, but not opulent, Benedict thought. That was good. It meant all the money wasn't going into appearances. He liked the pleasant music, the vases of fresh flowers that adorned the coffee and end tables. It would be fine for his mother, just fine. *Okay, good, you're in character now. Do it and get out.*

He approached the desk and the receptionist glanced up and smiled. "May I help you?"

·"I'd like a brochure, please."

"In that stack to your left, sir."

Oh, hey, that was terrific, Frankie. They'll remember the sweating guy who came in and asked for what was right the fuck in front of him. "Thanks."

He picked up a brochure and glanced through it as he left. The words melted together. A bad move, a really bad move.

Benedict neared the driveway. Almost off the grounds, he thought, not much farther. Little balls of panic bubbled against the underside of his tongue. But here came the navy blue Volvo again, sunlight and shadows dancing across its shiny hood. Benedict quickly bowed his head and pretended to be reading the brochure. He didn't look up until it had pulled out into the road.

(2)

Wells made two stacks of files. The first included files on every Mercedes stolen in the tri-county area within the two weeks following the accident. Next to it lay the files on stolen BMWs. In all, there were thirty black cars reported stolen within the tri-county area between the specified dates. That figure, Charlie thought, was high enough to qualify as a pattern called "foreign car theft ring."

She, Wells, and Rain divided the files equally, ten each, with a mix from the two different piles. They found their spots on the living room floor, none of them too far from the snacks that Charlie had put out on the coffee table.

"First thing we've got to do is whittle this pile way down," Wells said.

"So someone enlighten me," Rain said. "I'm looking for a Caucasian male in his forties, but what other criteria do we have?"

"The owner should live or work within a fifteen-mile radius of the accident site." Charlie gestured at the laptop she'd set up on the coffee table. "If you aren't sure of the street's location, punch it into the computer and it'll be highlighted on the county map. If he lives seventeen or twenty miles from the accident site, check it out anyway."

"The max should be about thirty," Wells said.

"The owner should be a white collar professional," Charlie added.

"I don't know too many blue collar folks who drive cars as expensive as these," Rain said. "What else?"

"Anything irregular," Charlie replied. "It's a subjective call. But you'll know it when you see it."

"*You'll* know it," Rain said. "I can recognize something odd or irregular about an ovary, guys, but I don't know about police reports."

"Shit," Wells said with a laugh. "What about me? Give me a pathology slide or a thread of fabric, no problem. But a police report? Ha."

"One more thing," Charlie said. "We're assuming that the driver himself reported the car stolen. But maybe it was his wife. Or his grandmother. So what matters is that the owner of the car fits the specs."

For the next two hours they read in silence. Now and then papers rustled or one of them nibbled at a snack or got up to use the bathroom. It reminded Charlie of her last week in the Quantico training program, when cramming had become the center of her existence and the rest of her life had gone on hold.

The first three reports she read held a ring of truth. One car had been stolen in broad daylight, from the parking lot of a local grocery store in South Miami. Another had vanished at Lauderdale beach. The third had been taken while the owner dined at an expensive restaurant in Palm Beach. Of these, only one qualified in the home address department and he lived nineteen miles west of the accident site.

Charlie put this file to her right; it would have to be checked out.

Now and then beepers went off, cell phones pealed. Charlie's own phone rang and the machine took the messages. Her brother called twice, Mitch called once, media people called. The office of the shrink she was supposed to see the next day called and verified her appointment. She'd already decided she wouldn't make that appointment. Screw Mitch and his rules. She would do this her way.

By eleven they had whittled the stack of thirty to eighteen that needed to be checked out. Charlie felt discouraged as she thumbed through the stack. "This is impossible. How the hell can all these people own a Beamer or a Mercedes and live within thirty miles max of the site?"

"Easy," Rain said. "This is Miami." She hit a key on the computer that enlarged the map. "Look at the area this covers, Charlie. The thirty miles maximum includes affluent neighborhoods like Coral Gables, Miami Beach, and Coconut Grove. It even dips over into some of Broward County's affluent neighborhoods. And it includes banks, attorneys' offices, medical facilities . . . Personally, I think it's a miracle we've ended up with just eighteen."

"Optimist," Charlie grumbled. "The bottom line is that it could take us days to check out every one of these leads."

Wells clicked his tongue against his teeth. "C'mon, Charlie. It's not that grim. Six leads apiece."

Rain shook her head. "Count me out on that end of it, guys. I've got patients back to back for the next few days."

"Okay, nine apiece," Wells said. "We can get it down to six apiece if I can get Logan to pitch in."

"Just curious, Leo. But he seems to think he owes you a lot. What'd you do for him when you worked together in the Jax bureau?" Charlie asked.

"Got him out of a building before it blew. I managed to keep him alive long enough to get to the ER, but then he died for something like eleven minutes during surgery on his hip."

"You mean eleven seconds, don't you?" Rain asked.

"Nope. Minutes."

"Christ," she said softly. "He should be brain damaged."

Wells shrugged. "He thinks he is."

"No." Rain shook her head. "I mean *seriously* damaged, Leo."

"Hey, I got the same med school curriculum that you did, Rain. Ten seconds of interrupted oxygen flow to the brain produces unconsciousness. A few minutes of oxygen starvation can turn a Mozart into a kid playing tiddledywinks. If the body temperature is unusually cold, this rearranges the rules somewhat. But Logan's body wasn't cold. They had pulled the body bag over his head, when he suddenly started breathing again."

"And he's *normal?*" Rain asked.

Charlie let out a sharp, clipped laugh. "That depends on your definition of normal. By social standards, he's a misfit."

"By bureau standards, so are you," Wells shot back.

"Gee, thanks, Leo."

"Hell, the three of us are misfits for sure," Rain said. "By normal, I meant mental functions."

"Normal except that he reads shit with his hands."

"Rain's got a theory about near death experiences," Charlie said. "It's called the seventh sense theory."

"I wouldn't go so far as to call it a theory," Rain said.

"Let's hear it," Wells said.

"The way I see it, humanity is about to make a quantum leap in consciousness . . ."

"Bullshit," Wells retorted. "Every time I get optimistic about humanity's pending quantum leap, I get cut off in traffic by some dude with a loud horn. We like to think we're at the brink, Rain, but frankly, the momentum just doesn't seem to be there."

The look on Rain's face told Charlie that she obviously felt passionate about this subject. "It's everywhere, Leo. It's global. And I feel that people who undergo unusual transformations in consciousness are the pioneers. NDEs, alien abductions, even dementia patients, all the recent research in quantum physics: This stuff is the equivalent of LSD in the sixties. It busts open our habitual perceptions and forces us to acknowledge that something new and unusual is happening, even if we don't know what the hell it is. We're talking about new paradigms, Leo. And it sounds to me that Logan may be one of those pioneers."

"A very reluctant pioneer," Charlie added.

Wells grinned. "For sure."

"So at least call the reluctant pioneer. Enlist his help."

Charlie's phone rang again and a softly spoken woman said, "Hi, my name's Christine Lincoln. I'm a vet over in Gables. I think your dog is one of my patients."

She shot to her feet and raced to the phone. "Yes, hello, this is Charlie Calloway."

"Ms. Calloway. I'm so glad you're home. I've had a Rhodesian Ridgeback as a patient since last week. My mother, who lives in the vicinity of the hit-and-run, befriended him."

"What's your address, Dr. Lincoln?"

"Four two seven Red Road."

"What was wrong with him?"

"His front paw was cut nearly to the bone and it had gotten horribly infected. I didn't want to call until I was sure he'd come through surgery okay."

"I'm leaving my house now."

Doris sits beside her on the couch and touches her hand. "What's wrong, Lily honey?"

"Nothing. I just don't feel like talking."

"You miss that pooch, don't you."

"Henry. His name's Henry."

"You can remember his name, Lily. That's wonderful."

"I remember your name too."

She laughs. "That's because I'm always in your face. Listen, I don't want you to worry none about that dog, okay? Your daughter says Henry's going to be fine."

"But he's not here anymore."

"He's got to stay at your daughter's office until his leg's better. You stayed with Chrissy last night and she dropped you off this morning, hon. She'll be back to pick you up tomorrow."

Tomorrow means nothing to her. She wants it to be now. This moment. All sorts of feelings wash through her, and she suddenly feels like crying.

"How about if you and me go walk in the garden?"

Lily doesn't feel like going out into the garden, but she doesn't want to stay in the day room either. So she nods and picks up her journal and off they go.

Outside, they sit in the sunlight, where the birds twitter and sing. Her hand moves across the open page of the journal, sketching something. When she looks down to see what it is, her hands stops. It doesn't want her to see.

"What're you drawing there, hon?" Doris asks.

"I don't know. My hand doesn't want me to know."

"Oh. But if you don't look at it, how do you know what you're sketching?"

"My hand knows."

Doris just shakes her head, like it's all a mystery to her. But Lily catches her watching as she sketches and her hand doesn't seem to mind that she watches. When Lily's hand finally stops, Doris says, "Can I take a good look at it, hon?"

"Sure."

She studies it, turns the journal this way and that. Her eyes get bigger by the second. "This is really a good drawing, Lily. I think you should show it to your daughter when she gets here. You have any other drawings in here?"

"I don't know."

Lily takes the journal from her and pages through it, looking for drawings. At the back, she finds dozens of drawings—of flowers and trees, of Doris and other people Lily doesn't recognize, of Henry *the dog. Then she takes a good look at the most recent and feels something in the pit of her stomach that she doesn't like. Fear, she thinks. It's fear. She slaps the journal shut.*

"What is it, Lily?" Doris asks.

"Bad." She clutches the journal to her chest and rocks back and forth on the bench, eyes squeezed shut. "Bad."

"Bad? No way, Lily. It's fantastic. Incredible detail. I mean, look at it." Doris reaches for the journal, opens it, points her plump finger at the rain, the trees whipped by the wind, the two cars, the face in a windshield. "But where'd you see this?"

Lily snatches the journal back, slaps it shut. "Bad, bad, bad," she whispers, and starts to cry, she can't help it, the tears just come. Then she suddenly shoots to her feet and races for the fence, the wind biting her eyes, her body remembering its former strength and glory, her legs remembering how it used to be in the marathons.

Everything blurs together, the sky and the sun and the fence, the flowers and the trees and the grass. She wants out, wants to fall into the blue, into the light. She wants Henry, she wants— And then something rises up out of the blur and she slams into it. She sinks like a stone through silence and darkness.

18

Awakening

(1)

The sprawling Spanish-style building stood on a wide, shaded road in a Coral Gables neighborhood that smelled of old money, Charlie thought. The branches of a pair of banyan trees out front braided together overhead, forming an intricate canopy in which wildlife thrived.

Charlie hurried up the sidewalk that wended through the trees. It seemed unlikely that two Rhodesian Ridgebacks would be loose in the area near the accident site, but she didn't want to get her hopes up.

She entered a spacious lobby in which a dozen pet owners waited with an assortment of dogs, cats, and birds. "Hi," she said to the receptionist. "Dr. Lincoln called me about a Rhodesian Ridgeback that she's treating?"

"You're Ms. Calloway?"

"Yes."

The young woman flipped her long ponytail over her shoulder, grinned, and got up. "Let me take you back to the kennels. Dr. Lincoln is on the phone, but asked if you would wait a few minutes. She wants to talk to you."

She followed the woman through a door off the lobby and down a brightly lit hallway. "He's such a sweet-tempered dog," the woman said. "We've all just fallen in love with him."

"Dr. Lincoln said her mother found him."

"Right. Lily's a patient at the We Care Health Center, that Alzheimer's unit right near where the accident happened."

Charlie nodded.

"Near as we can figure, your dog must've wandered onto the clinic grounds and Lily had been feeding him. She used to raise hounds and has always loved animals. Anyway, I'll let the doc talk to you about all that."

The woman pushed through double doors into a tremendous indoor kennel with skylights and gardens. A raucous barking erupted and the sounds echoed as they headed down a row of clean cages with long runs behind them. The woman unlocked the last cage, where a Rhodesian Ridgeback lay curled like a plump, misshapen comma, snout tucked into the space between his hind legs. Charlie couldn't tell for sure if this dog was her dog; she needed to see him up close.

"Hey, big guy," the young woman called. "You've got a visitor."

The dog didn't even lift his head.

Charlie stepped into the cage, crouched, and whistled, using Jess's special whistle, and the entire kennel fell silent. The dog raised his head, cocked it to one side, and gazed down the long run at Charlie.

"Paz? It's me."

She whistled again and suddenly the dog struggled to his feet and limped toward her, barking, the rear part of his body wagging as though his entire spine were a tail. Charlie's eyes filled with tears and she ran toward Paz, the last vestige of her old life, of her husband, her pregnancy, of that road that would never be taken now.

Even with his injured paw, he reared up and literally bowled her over. She sat there on the floor of the concrete run, her arms clutched around his neck, her face buried in the familiar scent of his fur. He barked and licked and she laughed and wept and kept running her hands over him.

He seemed pitifully thin, ribs protruding, one ear torn at the tip, a new scar against the side of his muzzle. She couldn't begin to imagine what he'd been through and felt enormous gratitude toward whatever providence had brought him back to her.

Barking erupted in the kennel again, and moments later a tall, slender brunette stopped at the door of the cage. She wore a white

190 · T.J. MacGregor

lab coat over jeans and a cotton shirt and stood there with her
hands on her narrow hips, smiling and shaking her head.

"I love happy endings, Ms. Calloway."

Charlie got up, rubbing her hands against her shorts, Paz limping
along behind her. "I can't thank you enough."

As Charlie grasped the vet's outstretched hand, something passed
between. It felt like a mild electrical current to Charlie, and she
suddenly knew she could dip into this current if she wanted to and
come out with information about this woman. She sensed the current
connected somehow to that vast ocean of knowledge that she'd
experienced when Rain had hypnotized her.

"He's doing remarkably well and should have full use of that
leg within a month. My mother had been feeding him and bringing
him water, but I can't vouch for his diet. I don't think he would
have lasted much longer hiding out on the clinic grounds. He was
running a three-degree temp and that leg was so infected that for
a while I was afraid I would have to amputate it."

"Your receptionist told me your mother's a patient at the Alzheimer's unit at the intersection where the accident happened."

Lincoln nodded. "For the past two years."

Paz dropped to the floor in front of Christine Lincoln's feet, rolled
over onto his back, and offered his belly for a scratch, something he
did only with people he trusted. She accommodated him as she told
Charlie about her mother. "She used to be a marathon runner and
got out quite a few times the first year she was there. Then I started
bringing her into the office with me a couple times a week and she
stopped taking off. Her memory actually seemed to improve.

"When I went on vacation in late May, her visits here stopped
for a few weeks, and she seemed to backslide. She even took off
again. That happened on May twenty-third or twenty-fourth, sometime after the ten P.M. bed count."

"The night of my accident."

"Right."

"You think that's when she found my dog?"

"Or he found her." She gestured toward a bench just outside
the cage. "Let's talk over there." She patted her leg as she stood.
"You too, Paz."

He limped along between them, alternately nuzzling each of their hands. When they sat on the bench, he settled to the floor between them. Charlie kicked off her sandals and rubbed her bare feet over his sides.

"When was she found?" Charlie asked.

"Around four A.M. on the twenty-fourth. She was huddled under a cluster of thick bushes and shrubs just outside the clinic fence. The same spot where we found Paz. She was drenched and totally out of her head, calling and sobbing for Henry. That's my dad's name. He's been dead about three years, but Mom doesn't remember it and we try not to remind her.

"Anyway, they got her inside her room and put her to bed and the next morning she wakes up and starts rattling on about Henry. That he needs food. Water. That he needs her. That kind of thing. Naturally, the employees figured she was talking about my father. Then when I got back from vacation and went by to see her, she told me she had a secret. Turns out she'd named your dog after Dad and that when she was talking about Henry, she meant the dog, but everyone else thought she was talking about Dad." She paused and leaned over to stroke Paz. "Christ," she said softly. "It's so complicated."

Charlie heard grief and despair in her voice, the inevitable horror at watching her mother descend into a kind of madness. She reached out and touched the vet's arm, a touch intended only to impart comfort. Instead, that current reared up, a strange thing with serrated edges, sharp and hurtful. Part of her turned instinctively away from it. But another part of her embraced it, opened to it, and dipped, sank, tasted, sought to understand.

It didn't seize her and sweep her away. It didn't swallow her. She didn't feel subsumed or overpowered. Instead, the current seemed to plug the empty spaces in her soul, to fill in the pockets of nothingness that Jess's death and the loss of her baby had left inside of her.

Charlie didn't know how long it lasted, probably only seconds, maybe less than that. But when it ended, when the current abruptly stopped, she knew that she had crossed some invisible boundary and would never again be quite the same.

She spoke slowly, working her way through what she'd felt in the current. "You feel that your mother's interest in life was rekindled through taking care of Paz. You're afraid she'll backslide now that Paz is gone. But that—"

"My receptionist talks too much. I apologize, Ms. Calloway. She shouldn't have told you any of that."

"She didn't."

Dr. Lincoln frowned. "Then you're very insightful."

There was other stuff she could have said then, things about the doc's failed marriage, disappointments, and worry about her son, questions about the man she was currently seeing. But none of it seemed relevant to this. "I just want you to know your mother's attachment doesn't have to end. I'd be glad to have your mother visit Paz anytime. Or he can go to the center. Whatever you want to work out."

"I appreciate it. I really think it would make a difference in my mother's life."

"Can I take him home?"

"You'll have to flush that drain in his leg three times a day and continue with the antibiotics, but sure, you can take him home. Oh. I almost forgot." She reached into one of the deep pockets of her lab coat and brought out several sheets of paper. "When you got here, I was on the phone with the clinic." She kept creasing, then straightening the sheets of paper. "Mom's been very depressed since Paz left the clinic grounds, and today she and one of the nurses were in the garden and she—I don't know—she freaked, I guess. She started running and slammed into the fence and now she's laid up with facial lacerations.

"Right before it happened, she was sketching in her journal. That's one of the things they encourage people to do. Keep a journal. My mother used to draw as a hobby, and she does quite a bit of it now. This is what she was drawing right before she freaked. The nurse copied them from the journal, then faxed them to me."

She handed Charlie the papers she'd been holding. Charlie unfolded them, three sheets with pencil drawings on them. The sketches seemed bizarre at first, nothing in proportion to anything else, the perspective skewed. But the longer Charlie looked at the drawings, the more sense they made: an intersection in a rainy darkness, streetlights that swung in the wind, casting eerie shadows against the wet streets; trees bent to one side; water gushing down curbside drains.

In the second sketch, the detail in the intersection had been expanded. One car headed toward another, its headlights glaring, cutting a swath through the darkness. Seconds away from impact, she could just make out a figure in the windshield, a face. The face of a man.

Charlie quickly went to the third sketch. Her breath stalled in her lungs; her heart slammed into the walls of her chest; her body seemed to come undone all at once. She knew the shape on the ground was herself. She knew that the dog with its snout to the shape was Paz, that the car in the distance was the Beamer or the Mercedes that had intentionally hit them. She knew that she had a witness.

A witness with Alzheimer's who lived eternally in the present tense.

Charlie finally breathed again. "She saw what happened."

"It sure looks that way. But the memory isn't the kind that she can tell you about. That's how it is with this insidious disease. When Dad was still alive, she used to wake up asking him who he was and if they were married and why he wanted a divorce. All that in one sentence, Ms. Calloway."

"I understand. Just the same, I'd like to talk with her. And bring Paz with me when I do."

"She's not in any shape to talk to anyone right now. But maybe we can get together tomorrow afternoon. I'll be going by to see her and will call you then."

Charlie gave her a card with her phone numbers jotted on the back. "Anytime, I don't care how late it is."

(2)

Shadows lengthened, falling across the suburban street where Logan and Wells walked. A wind had kicked up out of the east and to Logan it smelled of the easy life. Caribbean ports, beaches as white as popcorn: His life on Minnow Key expanded to foreign shores.

He imagined himself living in some hooch, the expatriated American, a character in a Jimmy Buffet song.

Great fantasy. But in his heart he knew that the same phantom would haunt his life. A handshake or a caress in a foreign country would be no different from its counterpart here. It would besiege him, swallow him. He would still be a psychic voyeur.

"One more down," Wells remarked, and crossed out another name on his master list of suspects. "If I have to listen to another alibi, I may lose it completely."

"It's only the fifth," Logan reminded him.

"Exactly my point. That leaves thirteen more."

"So let her follow up some of these names, Leo."

"Hey, man, she just got her dog back. She won't be doing shit until tomorrow. In the meantime, I got Mitch riding my ass, nosing around, making trouble in the lab because I'm never there."

"So quit and come live on Minnow Key. We've got room."

Wells laughed, but even his laughter sounded tired and discouraged. "I'd bug out living like you do, Logan."

"You've never tried it."

"Got no desire to either." He tucked the master list into the back pocket of his jeans. "You should've known Jess. You'd have liked him. No bullshit with him. You ask him a question, he gives you the straightest answer he's got. Charlie's like that too."

Yeah, he'd noticed. "Correct me if I'm wrong, Leo, but it sounds like there's something there between you two."

Wells just smiled. "Mighta been, some other life, some other place and time. But I liked Jess too much to ever try to mess around with his woman." He unlocked the driver's door and looked at Logan across the roof of the bureau's Ford. "Look, I don't pretend to know how you do what you do. Me, I'm just a guy who studies what the dead leave behind. But you? Christ almighty, Logan. You've got a gift. Instead of embracing it, you take off in another direction. It scares you shitless."

Logan opened the door and got into the car. He didn't want to discuss it. He couldn't learn squat by going over every little goddamn thing that had gone wrong in his life since the day he'd come sliding out of his mother, shrieking at the indignity of it all.

Yes, he was a self-centered, selfish prick who was scared shitless by what dying had given him. But so what? Working with the Calloway woman wouldn't change any of that. And wasn't that what Wells was really talking about? Yeah, he could just see it, he and Charlie as a psychic duet, a metaphysical Nick and Nora, a cabaret act for law enforcement personnel.

"Forget it, Leo. I don't want to read some old lady with Alzheimer's."

"Hey, did I even mention it?"

"Not in the last thirty minutes."

"That old lady may be our best shot, Doug."

"Your best shot, not mine."

"Okay, you don't want to do her? Then do the dog."

Right. The dog. *Do the dog,* like it was a new dance.

"Forget the old lady, forget the dog. Tomorrow you pick me up at seven and we'll hit the other names on your list."

Wells veered into the parking lot where Logan had left his car, pulled up next to it, slammed on the brakes. He turned to Logan with his jaw thrust out and his nostrils flaring. "You got shot, it fucked up your life. Well, hey, too bad. You're not the only person with problems. So get over it and get on with it, Logan. Use what you have."

Logan stared straight ahead, hands flat against his thighs. His head ached, his stomach growled, he wanted to throw open the goddamn door and walk back to Minnow Key. But his hip hurt and he smelled rain in the air. He felt like weeping for himself, for Calloway, for Leo, even for that stupid-ass cop at the crime scene the other day. The whole sorry lot of them didn't know what they were doing or why they were there or where they were going.

Logan didn't have any answers either. Even though he could see what they could not, it hadn't made him any wiser. It hadn't made him more tolerant. He still couldn't control the impressions he got when he touched someone. He still didn't know how to control the ability or manage it or meld it into his everyday life.

He got out of Wells's car and shut the door. Wells leaned out the window. "Hey, Logan, you change your mind between tonight and tomorrow, give me a call. Charlie, the doc, and I will be over there sometime tomorrow, probably in the evening."

Then he stepped on the accelerator and sped away from the curb, headed into the sinking sun.

(3)

Charlie lost track of the time. She no longer lived in a world of clocks. Her life now seemed to be measured by how much information she could download before someone or something realized she'd accessed the computer at the Motor Vehicle Department in Tallahassee. The state's computer. The master brain.

Her needs were simple. She wanted a photo of every driver in the stolen-car files that Wells had culled. She wanted the photos enlarged so that an old woman with Alzheimer's stood a chance of identifying the driver. She knew the odds were stacked against her, that it was the longest shot she'd ever taken on a case. None of that mattered. She had to give the old lady something to work with.

By nine that evening she'd downloaded fifteen of the eighteen photos. Her body hurt, she knew she should stop to eat, but she couldn't, not yet, not until she had them all. Now and then Paz got up and limped over to her, nudged her leg or her arm. Then he continued his endless roaming through the rooms, sniffing at everything, as if seeking Jess's scent.

Paz started barking seconds before the doorbell rang, a furious barking that made the hair on her arms stand on end. *It's him. He doesn't have to break in this time; he just rings the doorbell.*

Charlie quickly got out of the MVD computer, pulled her gun from the bottom desk drawer, and went into the living room. Paz bared his teeth and backed away from the door to make room for her. "Who is it?" she asked.

"Mitch."

"If you're with Harnson, you can just pedal on home, Mitch."

"I'm alone."

She removed the chain and unlocked the door. Mitch wore jeans that were obviously new, much too blue and much too stiff. He moved stiffly as he stepped into the house, glanced at Paz, and ran his fingers under his nose, messing up the hair in his thin mustache. "I'm glad you found the dog, Charlie. But could you call him off?"

"Sit, Paz," she said, and he did. "So what brings you over here?"

"You don't return your calls and you're never home." He gestured at Paz, who continued to sit but kept growling. "Leo told me you found the pooch."

"No offense, Mitch. But you're not here for dog talk."

"You have a few minutes?"

"That depends on what you've got to say. I'm not in the mood for threats or conditions or any of that bullshit."

He held up his hands and shook his head. "No threats, no conditions."

"Fine." She shut the door and leaned against it, not inviting Mitch to sit down. "So what's on your mind?"

"A truce."

"In other words, you want to know what leads I have and in return you'll . . . what? What can you do for me, Mitch?"

"Reinstate you."

"At my desk job? No, thanks. I could call Assistant Director Feldman tomorrow morning and convince him to do that much for me."

"You'd be reinstated as assistant field supervisor, with full field privileges, just like you had before your pregnancy."

"When can you do that?"

"By tomorrow morning."

"How about right now?"

"Okay."

"And what do you want in return?"

"Everything you, Leo, and Doug Logan have pulled together on this case."

"And what're you going to do with it? Turn it over to Jay Harnson so he can fuck things up?"

"Harnson has been fired."

The picture began to come together now. "Really. And when did this happen?"

"At three o'clock this afternoon."

"So let me get this straight, Mitch. The deal is that I get reinstated with full field privileges, except that I can't touch this investigation. Right?"

"Policy."

"Bereavement leave and my seeing a shrink were also policy until sixty seconds ago."

"Policy is more flexible on those points."

"So I turn everything over to you, get reinstated in my job, and you crack the case and get credit for it."

He looked mighty uncomfortable now. "You're twisting the whole thing around, Charlie."

"Am I? Let me put it another way, then. I can do what I need to do without your help or intervention, Mitch. Feldman has already given me that freedom. And I have Leo and Logan to back me up."

"Logan is a special consultant without any clout whatsoever. And Wells is forensics. He can't get you a chopper or a boat or even a backup team."

"He can get them through Feldman."

"But he'll have to wade through five miles of red tape to do it."

He had a good point. "Is Feldman riding your ass now, Mitch? Is that what this is about?"

"Yeah, more or less."

Charlie would bet the farm that Mitchell's job was on the line. Good. That put her in the stronger position. "I've got a couple of conditions."

"Such as?"

"If I share what we have, you stay out of my way unless I need you. You get credit for cracking the case, but I get to bring the fucker down."

"Fair enough. Anything else?"

"Yeah, I get my badge and gun back tonight."

"They're in the car."

"So you agree?"

He stuck out his hand and Charlie grasped it and felt the current. She sensed the dark tide rising. Then the vast invisible ocean opened in front of her. She needed to know specifically whether she could take Mitch at his word or whether he had another agenda. She held on to his palm several moments too long and he broke the connection first. He frowned and rubbed his hand, as if he'd felt something that he didn't like.

"Your annual evaluation put you on a probationary status, didn't it, Mitch?"

His thin brows shot up and his mouth puckered as if he'd bitten into something bitter. "How . . . I mean . . ."

"You need a big win, and because of the million-dollar reward, cracking this one would get you off probation. You fired Harnson because he wasn't doing shit on this case and it reflected badly on you."

Mitch stepped back, astonishment etched permanently into his features.

"So I'll play your game, Mitch. But if you fuck with me, if you interfere, I'll take credit for everything, even if it means losing my job."

"That's cocky as hell. You make it sound like you already know who the perp is."

"I'm close."

He didn't bother trying to disguise his eagerness. "How close?"

"Very."

"I won't interfere. I'll supply you with whatever you need, whenever you need it, and I'll supply it fast."

"Then come on back into the den and I'll show you what we've got."

Lily wakes with a headache and a heaviness in her chest. Not a cold; nothing like that. This heaviness is about lack and absence, loss and guilt and death. It's about unrelieved sadness.

She glances toward the window. Dark, curtains pulled shut. It's night. Very late. No sounds anywhere. Henry, she thinks. She really wants to see Henry. But she remembers Henry on an operating table, a scalpel slicing open the festering infection, pus draining out. She remembers Henry in a cage afterward, being monitored by her daughter.

He will be okay, she's sure of this. She sees him trotting toward her, his injured leg free of bandages. She feels this Henry exists in the future because the trees are different. The ones with the bright red blooms, the ones whose name she can never quite recall but which she can see from the garden, are completely bare, like they are in the fall and winter. The sky is a perfect blue, a winter blue, and the grass is much dryer than it is in the summer.

She turns on her bedside lamp and gets out of bed to find her journal, then sits down again and begins to sketch this Henry in the future. But suddenly her hand jerks in another direction, away from the sketch of Henry to something else, something that takes shape with the urgency of a living thing.

Lily is somewhat alarmed, and when she tries to look at what she's drawing, her hand stops. Her hand doesn't want her to look. So she glances at the walls, at the pictures that adorn her dresser, at her brightly colored room and the beckoning light in the window. She wonders why her face hurts, why her head hurts, why she feels like she ran into a wall or something.

And while she isn't watching her hand, it moves in grand, graceful loops across this page and the next and the next. When it finally stops, Lily sets the pencil down and goes through the pages. She doesn't understand what her hand has drawn.

Cobwebs. Spiders. A car. People on a sailboat. Fire.

"Stupid," she whispers, and throws the journal across the room and gets out of bed to find Doris.

Lily nearly runs into her in the hall, Doris in her baggy robe, her floppy slippers.

"Doris, I . . ."

"Lily." Her eyes grow wide, startled, and she rushes over to Lily. Her large, strong hands touch Lily gently and hustle her back into her room. "You sit down and I'll get you some tea. How're you feeling, hon?"

"Okay." But she doesn't want tea. She doesn't want to sit on the couch. She wants . . . she can't remember.

She sits there until Doris returns with a cup of hot tea, but she feels anxious, nervous, inexplicably restless. Doris's beautiful dark face looms in front of her.

"Lily hon, you feeling okay?"

"I ache. My face hurts."

"No wonder. You ran into a fence."

"Chrissy wanted me to call her as soon as you got up. It's real late, but I'll call her if you want."

It takes her a moment to place that name. "I want to know how Henry is."

"You remember what happened with Henry? With the dog?"

"Yes."

"Good, hon. This is good."

She pulls the funny phone out of her robe pocket, starts to punch out a number, but Lily suddenly remembers what she wants to tell Doris. "Wait. I need to show you something."

She hurries across the room and picks up her journal before she forgets.

When she rises up, the sight of moonlight through the curtains captures her attention and she pulls the curtains open. She drifts away then, floats out through the glass, out into the air, and touches the leaves, melts into the leaves. She becomes the essence of moonlight and green. She becomes a single leaf, rustling in a summer breeze.

"Lily?"

She turns, frowning.

"You were telling me about the journal. And I got the phone right here. . . ." She holds it up. "With Chrissy's number all ready to be dialed."

Lily looks down at what she clutches to her chest. The journal. She pages through it, frowning, puzzled, and then she sees them. The sketches. The ones she wants to show Doris. "These, Doris, look at these."

Doris looks. Doris shakes her head. Doris studies and clicks her tongue against the roof of her mouth. Then Doris sits heavily at the foot of Lily's bed. "Lily, you know how much I love your drawings. I've got dozens of your sketches on my walls at home. But these are—"

"You don't like them?" Lily blurts out, her heart already sinking.

"Like them?" Doris laughs. "They're the best you've ever done. But they scare me." Her voices drops. "I can't explain it exactly. They're . . ."

"Dark."

"Yeah."

"Eerie."

"Uh-huh."

"They haven't happened yet."

Doris looks up at Lily, her eyes shiny, bright, like pieces of polished fruit. "You're spookin' me, hon. Really you are."

"I'm spooking myself."

Doris moves over to the window. She still holds the funny phone in her hand, but she seems to have forgotten it.

"When I was a young thing, Lily, back in Jamaica, I heard hooves in my yard one night. Hooves, can you imagine?" *She glances at Lily, smiling at the memory.* "It woke me outta a sound sleep, those hooves did. I thought the zebras were loose and I started crying. My mother came running in and I told her about the zebras. She reminded me that zebras are found only in two places, in the zoo and in Africa. I felt better about it. But a couple of days later a bad storm destroyed a lot of homes in our town. In my heart I knew those hooves were a warning." *She pauses and looks at Lily.* "Your sketches are like that. A warning."

"You think a storm is going to hit here?"

"Not a physical storm. There's not a tropical depression or a hurricane anywhere out in the ocean now. This is some other kind of storm, that's what I think. Maybe it's a storm to the people connected with the dog, to Henry's owner, maybe, or someone around her."

"We don't have to call Chrissy now. Would you sit with me till I go to sleep, Doris?"

" 'Course, hon."

"And tell me that story about the zebras again."

Doris tucks Lily into bed, and she pulls the covers to her chin. The lamp goes out. When she shuts her eyes, she sees spiders, a boat, fire, death, ruin, devastation. And it's close, so close she can smell the smoke, the ruin.

Lily rolls onto her side and curls up into a ball and prays that sunrise comes fast.

PART FOUR

●

Dark Tide Rising
June 17—18

"If only you knew the things I have seen in the darkness of the night."

—M. C. Escher

19

Loose Ends

(1)

At seven A.M. June 17, Benedict stood in front of the bathroom mirror, combing his hair and practicing what he would say to Colin Thacker over lunch that day. "I'd be delighted to accept the partnership, Colin. You won't regret your decision."

No, scratch the last part. He didn't need to grovel or kiss ass. Even though MacLean hadn't signed yet, Benedict had every confidence that he would, and he knew that Thacker felt that way too. Last Friday, Thacker had stopped by his office and invited him to lunch today "to talk things over." That could mean only one thing. An offer. *The* offer.

As he stepped back from the mirror to straighten his tie, another face appeared in the glass next to his own. A floating phantom face, that of the security guard from the U-Haul company. Benedict rubbed hard at the image, fingertips squeaking against the glass. The image didn't vanish. Instead, it assumed greater clarity, crushed skull now visible, blood running down the side of his face, bits of gray mush and flecks of bone taking shape.

Benedict grabbed the bar of soap and frantically rubbed it against the glass, streaking the mirror with soap. He yanked the towel off the rack and scrubbed at the glass, his breath exploding from his mouth. "Go away, go the fuck away," he spat out.

He could see the man's eyes now, dead eyes drifting in sockets. He wet one end of the towel and kept rubbing, rubbing, rubbing, panic building inside him.

"Daddy?"

Benedict whipped around and saw himself reflected in Joey's expression.

"You . . . you look weird, Daddy."

"Mirror's a mess," he managed to say, and dropped the towel to the floor. The bar of soap slipped out of his hand and landed with a thud in the sink. He turned on the faucet and thrust his hands under the water, not daring to glance in the mirror.

Can Joey see it ? Can he see that hideous face?

"Grandpa's coming to pick me up today. To stay overnight. We're going to that summer carnival we always go to."

"You'll enjoy that. You see anything in the mirror, Joey?"

"No. Just your back."

Benedict turned around again. The image had vanished. Only the soap-smeared glass remained. He laughed, a high, nervous laugh, and glanced at his son in the mirror. A small frown creased the space between Joey's eyes. "You okay, Daddy?"

"Sure. Sure, I'm fine. Just tired." He left the towel and the soap where they'd fallen, left the mirror smeared with soap, and hustled his son out of the bathroom. He felt better once they were in the bedroom, where sunlight streamed through the windows. Better until he saw the room as it really was, clothes piled everywhere, the furniture coated with a thin layer of dust, cobwebs strung in the shadowed corners.

Not only had Anita stopped fixing meals, she no longer cleaned the house either. Next week it would be worse. Her creative writing class would start so she would be late getting home in the afternoon, and at night she would be grading papers.

Even more to the point, though, was how long he could stand living like this. She'd been sleeping in her den since their argument last week, and when he saw her, they spoke to each other only when necessary. She'd shut him out completely. If she suspected that he'd put Valium in the sun tea, she hadn't voiced it. If she'd made a connection between him and the security guard at the U-Haul company, she hadn't voiced that either. For all he knew, she planned to turn state's evidence against him and collect the million bucks.

Everything seemed to be hurtling away from him at the speed of light, and he could almost feel that familiar beast, chaos, hovering nearby, ready to leap in to fill the vacuum.

"Daddy?"

Benedict blinked and looked down at his son. At that innocent, perplexed face. He suddenly put his arms around Joey and swept him up into his arms and hugged him close. "You're squeezing me too hard," Joey said. "I can hardly breathe."

"Oops, sorry." Benedict put him down and took his hand, and they walked toward Joey's room. "When you get back from Flagler Beach, we'll do something special, Joey. Go sailing again. Or go to a movie."

"Everything's always tomorrow or next week, Daddy. How come we can't do something fun right now?"

"I've got to go to work, sport." Benedict crouched so that he was eye level with his son. "As soon as I make this partnership, I'll have more time. I promise." He hugged Joey, his thoughts scurrying furtively back to Anita.

If she suspected about the Valium or the security guard, she would be incapable of keeping it to herself. She would want to talk, analyze, dissect. She always had been like that and always would be. Therefore, it was likely that she didn't suspect.

"Are you and Mommy having a fight?" Joey asked when they reached his room.

Bitch has been talking to him, poisoning him against me. "Whatever gave you that idea, sport?"

"Mom's been sleeping downstairs. You don't talk much."

"She's sleeping downstairs because now that school's out, she's been going to bed later than I do. She doesn't want to keep me awake."

"So you're not fighting."

"Nope." Benedict hugged him again. "I've got to scoot. See you tonight, sport."

He whistled as he trotted down the stairs, his mood vastly improved now. He strolled into the kitchen and his whistle died on his lips. Anita stood at the stove, making pancakes. Behind her, the TV was on, morning news unrolling with the usual horror stories.

"Morning," she said cheerfully, as if the last six days have never happened.

He could play the game too. "You're up early."

"I've got to get Joey packed to head to my parents' place. Want some pancakes?"

"Thanks, but I'm in a hurry this morning. I've got lunch with Colin and a million things to do."

Anita poured two mugs of coffee, handed him one. "So why're you meeting with Thacker?"

"I think they're going to offer me the partnership."

"Really? Even without MacLean?"

"I haven't written MacLean off, Anita."

She started to say something, but glanced back at the TV, where a photo of the guard from the U-Haul company flashed on the screen. Anita turned up the sound. "So far, the police don't have any suspects. They believe the break-in at the Miami Lake U-Haul company was . . ."

Benedict forced himself to say, "My God, that's the same place where we rented the U-Haul." He hoped that by voicing what she was undoubtedly thinking already, he would deflect whatever suspicion she might harbor. It would also serve to remind her that she was an accomplice in the incident. "When did it happen?"

"The same night we had our argument." She looked at him then, eyes narrowed, her expression inscrutable. "You weren't home when I got here."

There. Her suspicion. It already had rooted inside her.

"I drove over to a bar on the beach and tried to sort through everything. When I got home, you were asleep. I tried to wake you, to apologize, Anita, but you were gone."

"Yeah, I slept twelve hours that night."

Her gaze lingered on his face for a beat or two, but he couldn't tell what the look meant. So he abruptly changed the subject. "Since Joey's going to be with your folks for the next few days, how about if I take time off and we sail the sloop up to Sebastian like we used to do? We could anchor in one of those coves on the Indian River. We haven't done that for years."

She looked surprised. "You feel you can take the time off right now? Or that you should?"

"It's sort of a tradition at the firm. When you're told you're going to be a partner, you get paid leave for three or four days."

This time he couldn't mistake her expression. Her eyes teared and she came over to him and put her arms around him. "I've missed you," she whispered.

"Same here." He stroked her hair and shut his eyes and knew that the beast of chaos had backed off for now. Anita had always grounded him. "We'll get through this, Nita."

"I know we will."

Benedict kissed her quickly. "I've got to scoot. Maybe I can get away early this afternoon and we can head out this evening."

She walked him to the door, her hand soft and gentle against his back. "We need to get away more often by ourselves, Frank."

"We will. From now on, we will."

He hugged her again, then hurried down to his car. Maybe things between them would be all right, he thought. Maybe all they needed was to get away by themselves.

As he headed down the driveway, he pulled out his wallet and removed the photo of Charlie Calloway. He'd taken it out of the frame and had been carrying it with him since he'd stolen it. He had no good reason to keep it with him and knew he should get rid of it, burn it, bury it, something. But he liked the feeling of power it gave him and he liked that it aroused him. Even then he felt himself getting hard just at the sight of her.

As he sped down the driveway, Benedict rubbed himself with the photo, thinking of Anita, of Charlie, of Anita, and gradually their faces melted together. He quickly slipped the picture back into his wallet.

(2)

As soon as the door shut, Anita sat down hard in a kitchen chair and buried her face in her hands. She didn't know what she felt just then, relief or suspicion, euphoria or grief. All of the above. None of the above.

She still didn't know for sure about whether he'd drugged the sun tea. But she felt reasonably certain that he'd had nothing to do with the death of the security guard. Otherwise, he wouldn't have said what he had when the newscast about the guard had come on. All along, it had been as simple as her breaking the ice, that was all she needed to do. Instead, she'd made them both miserable since last week, driving a wedge further between them.

The hit-and-run had been an accident and bad judgment, but not outright murder. Frank wouldn't willfully extinguish a life. Until she knew otherwise, her marriage deserved the benefit of the doubt.

(3)

Thacker sipped at his martini and gazed through the window that overlooked South Beach. The tropical light glinted against the white beaches. Bikini babes rollerbladed through the hot light. Models on a photo shoot posed in the public playground. A white stretch limo cruised past, windows too darkly tinted to glimpse the celebrity inside. Life on South Beach, Thacker concluded, had nothing to do with the real world.

And yet, life here fueled the real world. On a given day, the dramas that were played out on South Beach were reflected in suburban homes all across the country. Kids who rebelled, kids who bought into the glamour, kids who snorted so much white dust, their sinus cavities collapsed before they hit twenty. He knew a thing or two about all that; one of his sons had a major coke habit and was now drying out at the Betty Ford Center. He claimed he'd found God, but Thacker had serious doubts that God gave a shit.

You waiting for him to walk into the firm with a gun some morning and open fire?

Tillis's words rang in his ears. He realized that he believed his own son might be capable of such a thing, but Benedict? How could a man like Benedict be the loose cannon that Tillis seemed to think he was? He was too educated, too bright.

Don't poke me in the goddamn chest. . . .

Thacker froze that moment in his mind, scrutinizing the expression on Benedict's face, in his eyes. Violence. Rage. And suddenly, in his heart, he knew that Tillis was right. Knew it with a certainty that had eluded him all these weeks. Knew it in his goddamn bones.

He glanced back out the window and spotted Benedict hurrying up the sidewalk in chinos, a shirt, and tie. He wore three-hundred-dollar shades and shoes that probably had cost twice that amount. You could tell he was an attorney, a look that had eluded Thacker for most of his life.

Benedict stepped into the restaurant and strolled over to the table with a million-dollar smile. A smile, Thacker thought, that could mean only one thing. Benedict believed this lunch was about a partnership offer.

"Hi, Colin. Either you're early or I'm late."

"I'm early. What would you like to drink?"

"Whatever you're having."

A safe answer, Thacker mused, and signaled the waiter. He ordered a martini for Benedict, and they placed their lunch order.

"I'd like to take a couple of days off before Anita goes back to work, Colin. If that's all right with you."

A permanent vacation, Thacker thought, and decided to get right down to it. "Have you spoken to MacLean recently, Frank?"

"I called him this morning and left a message. Why?"

"That time frame he gave you is just about up."

"He'll sign. I'm not worried about it."

"Actually, he signed with Becker and Becker last week." Thacker blurted the words. "He called Greg Tillis and told him."

Benedict looked as if he'd been punched in the stomach and hadn't gasped yet. Blood rushed out of his face. His eyes seemed to bulge in their sockets. Thacker thought Benedict might even puke. Then Benedict burst out laughing.

"C'mon, this is a joke, right, Colin?"

"I wish it were."

A dark tide rose in Benedict's eyes, hints of that same darkness Thacker had seen that day in the hall. But hell, who wouldn't feel that way?

"The bastard didn't even have the professional courtesy to call *me?* Jesus, what the hell's wrong with him? Nine months of barbecues and bullshit and this is how he makes his decision?"

He went on like this for several minutes, blowing steam, venting his frustration. All very human. "Look, Frank, there are always going to be clients who don't sign. That's the nature of the business we're in. You just put it behind you, chalk it up to experience, and move on."

"He should have called *me,*" Benedict spat out.

"I can't argue with you on that point."

"What reasons did he give?"

"He thinks Becker and Becker are stronger in international law."

"Maybe."

"And he thinks you're a loose cannon."

"*What?* Where the hell did he ever get that idea?"

"Like I said, Frank, you've got to just put it behind you and move on."

Benedict lowered his eyes and didn't say anything. He kept rubbing his thumb over the crease in his napkin, a hard, repetitive action. His thumbnail turned white. The waiter brought their food and left. Soup, salad, shrimp smothered in a white wine sauce, a basket of warm, homemade bread. Benedict didn't even look at it. He just kept folding his goddamn napkin, making Thacker uneasy.

"I suppose now it's going to take an act of God to get Tillis on our side about the partnership," Benedict said finally.

Thacker knew this was the opening he'd been waiting for. But Christ, he felt low, mean, and cruel doing it here, now, on top of the news about MacLean. "I'm afraid it's going to take more than that, Frank."

Benedict's eyes darted to Thacker's face. "Meaning what?"

He knows. "He's offering a generous severance package, Frank. All the money you've put into the pension plan, a year's salary and health benefits, and the usual bonus . . ."

"I'm being *fired* because I didn't nab MacLean?" He leaned forward, his face skewed with incredulity. "Is that what you're saying, Colin?"

Actually, Frank, you're being fired because we bugged your goddamn car and heard the ravings of a lunatic. "Look, don't make this any harder than it already is for me, Frank. I've been in your court since the beginning. But Greg and I have been equal partners for—"

Something terrible happened then to Benedict's eyes. The dark tide surged and collapsed into a blackness so utterly terrifying that Thacker forgot what he was going to say. Forgot where he was. Forgot everything. Those eyes impaled him, pinned him to his chair, pierced him like metal stakes. He felt an irrational and overpowering urge to shoot to his feet and flee, but he couldn't move. His body refused to move. His muscles and bones had turned to dust.

Then Benedict abruptly catapulted to his feet and leaned across the table, into Thacker's face, and hissed, "You double-crossed me, you fat fuck."

He grabbed the edge of the table and jerked upward and everything slid into Thacker's lap. Bowls of steaming soup, shrimp smothered in white sauce, salads covered with ranch dressing, hot coffee, martinis, glasses of ice water. Silverware clattered to the floor. Glasses and plates shattered. Thacker wrenched away with such violence that his chair toppled and back he went.

His arms flailed impotently, bits of lettuce and clusters of broccoli clung to his slacks and the front of his shirt, his crotch burned from the hot soup and coffee. The chair crashed to the floor, and for seconds he just lay there, dizzy with astonishment, his ears ringing, his skull filled with the roar of his own blood rushing through his veins.

Then people surrounded him, waiters and waitresses, busboys and customers, a blur of faces, a cacophony of voices. Hands reached out and pulled him to his feet and someone pushed a chair over and he fell into it.

He looked around for Benedict, but he was gone like the wind.

(4)

The call came just as Charlie finished downloading the last of the drivers' license photos. "Charlie Calloway."

"Hi, it's Christine Lincoln. How's the patient?"

"Doing just fine. He's eating well and seems happy to be home."

"Great, I'm glad to hear it. How about meeting me at the center this evening at six? Mom should be in shape for some questions by then. But I wouldn't count too heavily on this, Ms. Calloway."

"Would you mind if I bring a couple of people with me?"

"Other agents?"

"Two agents and a friend who's been helping with the case."

"That'd be fine. See you at six."

Charlie glanced at the clock. That gave her a little more than three hours to prepare. With the weeks that now lay behind her, three hours was nothing more than spit in the wind.

(5)

At 3:03 P.M., Benedict cruised through the parking garage that most of the employees of the firm used. No one was around. This level was reserved for the firm, and few of the employees ever left early during the week.

Most of the attorneys, in fact, would slave away until six or seven, then go out with a client for drinks or dinner or both and wouldn't roll home before ten or eleven tonight. Stupid fuckers, he thought.

He located Thacker's silver Porsche easily enough. It always occupied the spot closest to the elevators because the fat man couldn't walk too far without gasping for air. Aside from the fact that he was overweight, he also had high blood pressure and a rotting liver. An immune system so compromised, Benedict thought, that it wouldn't stand much more abuse.

Benedict pulled up behind the Porsche, jerked on his emergency brake, and reached for the heavy gloves between the seat. He put them on, then picked up the small glass cage on the seat beside him.

The brown recluse scurried diagonally across the inner wall of the cage, her sac of eggs as clearly visible through the glass as the fiddle on her back. Benedict tapped on the glass to get her full attention. She went still, anticipating some morsel of fresh food other than the dead fly he'd put in the cage before he'd left the house. "Okay, sweet thing. You know what to do."

He got out of his car and went over to the Porsche. Thacker never locked the car; it was his way of playing Russian roulette with Miami car thieves. Besides, the Porsche had been insured to the hilt and Thacker could afford to be cocky.

Benedict opened the driver's door, balanced a corner of the cage on the headrest, and lifted the trapdoor. The recluse scampered out, over the headrest, paused briefly at the top of it, then vanished.

He shut the door and hurried back to the Mercedes, smiling to himself, the scene already unrolling in his head. That evening Thacker would get into his car and head out for drinks and dinner with some client. On the way, he would feel a sharp sting, hopefully in the neck or someplace close to his head.

Within an hour the bite would be swollen, red, and painful. Thacker would scratch at it, probably slap some Calamine lotion on it, but by then he would be into dinner and drinks. By the time he got home, he'd be six sheets to the wind and probably wouldn't realize the itching and swelling had increased.

By tomorrow morning he would be dead.

And who would ever suspect? This was South Florida, after all, home to all sorts of disgusting and poisonous critters.

Shit happens, Colin.

20

Reversals

(1)

Charlie had an hour to kill.

Everything had gotten pushed back because Christine Lincoln had forgotten that her mother ate with the other patients at six every evening. So now Charlie sat alone in a park several blocks away, making notes about the files and nibbling at a vegetarian taco.

Half a dozen kids played in the park, and their laughter kept distracting her. One little boy in particular caught her attention, a towhead in a swing with a pure, sweet face. Watching him, she felt grief welling in her chest and quickly looked away, back down at the files.

But the tears fell anyway, fat drops that splattered against the file, smearing the type, and she didn't try to stop them. She thought of herself outside Rain's office, her sorrow busting loose from the room where she'd sealed it, and knew this would happen to her for months to come. And that was okay, she couldn't keep it all bottled up inside of her indefinitely. But she also knew that as long as she remained alert to the hidden, the unseen, there would be signposts for her.

One of the most obvious was that she had gone to the U-Haul company only to observe Logan; Logan had gone there only as a favor to Wells. And Wells had asked Logan to do it out of some obligation that he felt toward Chief Perkins. None of them had suspected the break-in and the murder of the security guard were connected to the hit-and-run.

Synchronicity, she thought.

And was it also synchronous that moments after her sorrow had exploded from her she had seen something in the alley? Seen— *what? C'mon, Charlie, go ahead and say it. You saw a ghost. You saw Jess. You saw him in broad daylight and—*

She stopped the thought.

None of this had diminished her anger or her need to find the man responsible.

Her cell phone rang and she fished it out of her purse. "Calloway."

"Leo here. I just wanted to let you know Logan won't be joining us at the center. He's on his way back to Minnow Key."

Odd, how that made her feel. It didn't really surprise her, but she'd hoped . . . hell, forget what she'd hoped. It didn't matter. "We don't need him, Leo. Maybe Rain can hypnotize the woman."

"Yeah, maybe. Anyway, sorry about Logan."

"It's not your fault, so stop taking the blame for his decisions, okay? See you in a while."

She hung up before he could say anything else.

(2)

Logan had little use for ritual. He'd gotten too much of it during his years with the bureau. But right then he felt the need for something like ritual, some small gesture that would symbolize his intent, his desire, his decision.

He sat on a deserted strip of beach with pines and seagrape trees and the camper to his back. The sun hadn't set yet and the surface of the ocean reflected the thunderheads in the distance, stacking up against the horizon. Buffet weaved in and out of his legs, purring. Now and then the cat darted out to play tag with the waves or to follow some stray scent across the dune of sea oats. He always came racing toward Logan again to dive for cover.

Buffet, he thought, knew they were headed home, back to Minnow Key.

He'd called Wells, told him he was headed home, and Wells had just hung up on him. Logan didn't blame him. If he'd been in Wells's shoes, he would have done the same thing. Anything Wells might have tossed his way, any accusations and recriminations, wouldn't be anything new. Logan had heard it all before, from his ex-wife, from Charlie at the U-Haul company, from his brother and everyone else who had known him for any length of time. And all of it, he knew, was absolutely true. He couldn't hack intimacy of any sort, but he especially couldn't handle the variety that came with his curse.

He picked up his sandals and stood, then walked down to the edge of the water. He pressed his palms into the froth of a breaking wave, then down deep into the sand, and something moved under his hands. He pulled them back and a hermit crab emerged in the sunlight, its little conch house inching along the sand.

He rarely saw hermit crabs along the shores of the ocean. They tended to proliferate in less salty water, in the briny rivers that merged with the intracoastal. He turned this one on its side, and in a few moments the crab itself crept out and darted up the beach, seeking another home.

Transition, he thought. Hermit crabs lived in a constant state of transition. He sensed that it wasn't merely odd that he'd found one just as he was blowing town; it was significant. It hinted at some deeper order in the world that he'd perceived often but had never really understood until now.

And suddenly, the message to him seemed abundantly clear. If he split now, he would simply become more of what he already was, darting like the hermit crab from one refuge to another but never really going anywhere. The door to other possibilities would slam shut forever. He would grow old and die on Minnow Key.

Logan leaped up and whistled for Buffet as he trotted back toward the camper. Buffet, figuring they were still headed home, raced past him and bounded into the camper. Only later did Logan realize that he still held the conch the hermit crab had abandoned.

(3)

Thacker left his office at 7:10 that evening and walked across the street to the parking garage. He anticipated dinner with a potential client whose burgeoning computer company would help compensate for the loss of Jerome MacLean. Not that it would make any difference for Benedict.

He'd already had Benedict's office cleaned out, and his belongings had been packed into several cardboard boxes. Tomorrow someone would swing by his place to pick up the Mercedes, and the first of his checks would be deposited in his account. Thacker would never have to see the lunatic again.

He tossed his briefcase into the passenger seat and heaved his corpulent body behind the Porsche's steering wheel. It annoyed him that his belly pressed against the wheel. Too much food, too many martinis, too much excess. Tomorrow he would start doing laps in the pool again, and maybe he'd go back on that diet he'd tried last fall, when he'd lost thirty pounds.

As he braked for a light at the intersection, he felt something brush against the back of his neck. "Goddamn gnats," he muttered, and slapped at it. Summer on the peninsula brought out not only gnats, but those little bastard no-see-ums.

The next bite didn't feel like a gnat or a no-see-um; it felt like an overfed mosquito hungry for more. He slapped again, and this time he squashed it. He looked at his palm: no blood, just a few legs and insect matter. He pulled some tissues out of the box on the dash to wipe off his hand.

Hundreds of tiny spiders scampered up his arm, darted between his fingers, and vanished under the sleeve of his jacket. Thacker shrieked, slammed his arm against the seat, and threw open his door. He stumbled out and staggered across the road, screaming, *"Get them off me, get them off!"*

The spiders now scurried up the side of his face and into his hair, and he kept screaming and slapping at himself, trying to get the little fuckers off. But they just kept coming, a relentless marauding army. He vaguely heard horns honking, shouts. Cars sped past him; no one stopped to help him.

Thacker stumbled over the curb and sprawled in the grass, slapping at himself and screaming. He rolled, trying to crush the spiders, but they seemed to be everywhere now, inside his shirt and his trousers, hidden in his sleeves, dancing across his eyelids. He rolled to crush them and his head crashed into a circle of decorative concrete blocks around a tree. He struggled to push up on his hands and knees, but he felt too dizzy, his head spinning, blood seeping into his eyes now, darkness spilling into his peripheral vision.

He managed to crawl forward several feet before his arms and legs simply gave out and he collapsed against the ground. His mind shrieked at him to get up, to get help, but he could feel the baby spiders dancing into his nostrils and ears. Then darkness spilled over him like a viscous, suffocating liquid and swallowed him whole.

(4)

Logan pulled into the health center and parked in a visitor's spot, between Wells's vintage Mustang and Charlie's van. His hands started to sweat as he got out. He grasped the shell and thought, *You can do this.*

Even in the moonlight, the lush, tropical foliage was visible. Logan distracted himself by naming them first by smells—jasmine, roses, gardenias. Then he named them by sight: black olive trees; acacia trees in full crimson bloom; a thick, climbing poinsettia vine; a tree with bright yellow flowers that he'd always called poohee trees. The door loomed in front of him and he felt suddenly short of breath.

You will do this.

He pushed through the doors and went over to the information desk. A short, perky woman came right over, all smiles and courtesy. "May I help you, sir?"

"I'm Doug Logan. I'm supposed to meet Charlotte Calloway and—"

"Through the double door, take a left, and follow the yellow line to the end."

Directions to the city of Oz, he thought, and thanked her.

The yellow line, as bright as a new lemon, led him through a maze of hallways, past rooms that smelled of roses and gardenias, with a faint undertone of illness and decay. As he turned a corner, an elderly man stopped him. "Did you see the zebra?"

"The zebra?"

"She went flying by here. . . ." He slapped his hands. "I can still hear the sound of hooves." He cupped his ear, listening. "Hear them?"

Yeah, Logan heard them all right. The hooves of the impossible galloping toward him.

"I'll tell whoever's in charge," Logan said.

"Thanks, thanks very much," the man said, and hurried on down the hall.

The yellow line led Logan into a brightly lit wing with a skylight filled with waning light and tremendous windows that overlooked a garden. He watched a thin woman with white, frizzy hair coming down the path, her arm hooked through that of a much younger and very attractive woman. A huge dog limped alongside the older woman, its front paw bandaged.

When the two women sat on one of the benches, the dog sat in front of them. Now and then the old woman reached down and stroked the dog's head with obvious tenderness. Lily Lincoln and her daughter and Calloway's dog, he thought, characters in his redemption play.

He was so engrossed in watching them, he didn't hear Calloway approach him, didn't even know she'd come up behind him until she spoke. "I thought you'd blown town, Logan."

"I changed my mind."

"I appreciate it."

"Let's see if you still feel that way when we're done." He looked at her then, those soft blue eyes filled with an infinite hope that rested on him. "This is a real long shot, Charlie. I'm not the Oracle at Delphi. I'm not even sure it's possible to pick up anything from an Alzheimer's patient."

"So now you'll find out one way or another." She patted the large bag slung over her shoulder. "I've got photos to help her out."

"Listen to me, Charlie." He touched her arm then, the first time he'd done so since that night in the warehouse. Nothing came to him, no impressions, no images, no emotions. He realized he'd touched her at precisely the moment when she had found her deepest calm, the calm from which her own ability emanated. He promptly forgot what he intended to say.

"What?" she asked.

"Nothing."

"Leo's getting the room ready. There's something I want to show you first." She opened the bag and brought out half a dozen photocopied pencil sketches. "What do you make of these?"

It took him a few moments to figure out what he was even looking at. The perspective seemed skewed, like peering through beveled glass at a scene where nothing was where it should be. He kept turning the sketches this way and that and finally recognized a sailboat, a man and woman, a knife or a knifelike object. "I don't know. They're—"

"Pertinent?" The word rolled off her tongue with all the softness of a kiss or a caress.

He felt the truth of what she'd said, but didn't have a clue what it meant. "You first."

"When I first saw these, I felt . . ." She hesitated, glancing down at the sketches. ". . . weird. I got goose bumps, okay? My reaction was here." She touched her fist to her solar plexus. "It was visceral."

"Yeah, but how does it pertain to the reason we're here?"

"I'm not sure yet. I just know that it does."

"Let's get started." Logan thrust his hand into his pocket, fingers seeking the abandoned conch shell.

(5)

The center's conference room had pale pink walls that had been decorated with artwork by the center's patients. Most of the paintings and drawings seemed bizarre to Charlie, perceptually distorted somehow, and yet all showed originality and perhaps even genius. These artists, she thought, had struggled to express the ineffable, and in doing so had broken all the rules and forced others to expand or discard their own way of perceiving reality.

Charlie felt like an intruder, an impostor, a goddamn phony.

Her stomach churned, telling her to get out of there, to leave this old woman alone. But Lily Lincoln now sat comfortably in a leather recliner and her daughter leaned over her and asked, "You okay in this chair, Mom?"

"Just keep Henry here," Lily said, and rested her hand on Paz's head.

He licked her hand and turned his eyes on Charlie, who smiled and mouthed, *Good dog.*

"I'll be just fine as long as Henry's here." She looked at Wells, who stood near the window, fiddling with a recorder, and at Rain, who had come just in case anything went medically wrong, and at her daughter, and at Logan, who now pulled a chair alongside her. "What's your name, young man? I'm Lily. Have you ever heard of Wink, Texas?" She'd asked this a dozen times since they'd entered the room, but this time she stuck out her hand.

"Doug Logan. Nice to meet you. And no, I've never heard of Wink. What's it close to?"

Lily frowned. "You know, I'm not sure. But what a pretty place it is."

"You were born in Wink, Mom," said Christine Lincoln.

The old woman's face lit up. "That's right."

Logan still held the old woman's hand, and now Charlie saw him wince with pain.

"Charlie, Doug, and Leo are FBI agents," Christine said, leaning over her mother, handing her a glass of water. "They want to ask you some questions about what happened the night of the storm. The night you found Henry."

Lily reclaimed her hand, frowning. "What're you talking about, Chrissy? Henry's always been here."

Wells set the recorder on the table and Charlie moved closer with her own recorder, her own mike. A rumble of thunder outside turned Lily Lincoln's head toward the window. Her hazy eyes narrowed, and she suddenly threw her arms over her head. "So scared."

"Of what, Mrs. Lincoln?" Charlie leaned forward and touched Lily Lincoln's leg. "Can you tell me?"

"Don't like thunder. Thunder scares me. I hide under a bush so the thunder can't find me. I'm wet."

Logan got up and moved behind her. He pressed his hands to her shoulders, began to knead them. "Just relax, Mrs. Lincoln. You'll be okay. There's nothing to be afraid of."

"Such a crash," she whispered, and began to cry.

Logan's hands lingered for another moment, then Christine Lincoln stepped forward and calmed her mother again, and Logan backed away from her chair. He looked helplessly at Wells, then at Charlie, and she mouthed, *Anything?*

He rocked his hand back and forth and went over to the window on the other side of the room. Charlie quickly followed him. "What?" she whispered. "What the hell's wrong?"

"This is impossible," he whispered back. "She's too far gone. I pick up only white noise."

"I can't accept that."

He turned on her then, turned with more than three years of frustration leaping like flames in his eyes. "Some things you have to accept, Charlie. Your husband's dead. Your son's dead. You can't change it. This won't bring them back."

The words struck her like arrows, piercing all the places inside where she hurt. Instead of turning away from him to lick her wounds, as she might have done last week or even a few days ago, she grabbed his arm and leaned toward him. "Then bail out now if it's too much for you, Logan. I don't need you. I don't need anyone."

Charlie walked away from him. Rain was talking to Lily now, talking in her soothing, hypnotic voice, giving her suggestions to relax, priming her for whatever would come next. Charlie stood off to the side for several moments, letting Rain perform her magic, then she opened her bag and brought out all the photocopied drawings.

"Can you tell me about these, Mrs. Lincoln?" she asked, setting the sketches in Lily's lap and handing her one. "Tell me what these are about."

For the longest time, the old woman did nothing. She simply gazed off at something in the window that had seized her attention. Then she straightened the sketches and picked them up one by one.

(6)

They hit the water about fifteen minutes before sunset, with the wind blowing at twenty-six knots and the sail billowing above them. Anita loved the sting of salt in her eyes and the tug and pull of the muscles in her arms and across her back. Years of swimming had conditioned her to this kind of physical activity. She relished it, reveled in it. She was good at it.

The Indian River merged with the intracoastal canal and served as a juncture where fresh water met the ocean, a boundary of the mind. She and Frank sailed for miles before they ever saw another boat. The sun set and twilight hung in the air, as thick and pervasive as the heat.

The lush, isolated islands in the river looked inviting in the twilight. But most of them were mangroves, their curved exotic roots flourishing in the briny water, their appearance of solid ground a deception, an illusion, a trick of the mind. Finally, four miles from the mainland, they anchored in a sheltered cove off a *real* island, one with solid ground.

Australian pines fringed the shore, and here and there a spit of beach glinted in the fading light. She was hot and sweaty from sailing and needed to cool down. She stripped off her tank top first and her breasts sprang free. Then came her shorts and panties and she dived into the dark purple waters and sank.

Moments later, she heard a splash and Frank came up behind her, his hands running over her body. She turned in his arms and they surfaced together, bubbles surging around them, and exploded, laughing, into the twilight. He kissed her then, a long, deep kiss that tasted of old times, of better, simpler times.

Maybe, she thought, there was still hope for their marriage.

They made love there in the shoals, her legs scissored around his waist, his hands and mouth indistinguishable from the caress of the warm water. He slipped into her easily and for a long while they clung to each other, barely moving, listening to the rhythms of each other's blood.

This dance, this wordless choreography, dated back to the first time he'd taken her sailing. It had become a landmark in their marriage, a port they visited during rough times, as if to reaffirm their commitment to each other. She hoped that was what it meant now.

He moved slowly inside her, the way he always did in the beginning, his rhythm perfectly matched to hers, his voracious hunger expressed mostly through his mouth and his hands. "It's still good between us," he said softly, nibbling at her ear.

"That never changes." She dropped back to look at him, her fingers sliding through the hair at the sides of his head.

Maybe it was the twilight, maybe it was the shadows, but his eyes suddenly seemed to deepen in color, to change shape and even texture. Anita pulled back a little more, frowning slightly, head cocked to one side. Frank's hands suddenly tightened against her buttocks, and he thrust hard and she gasped and ground her hips against his and buried her face in the damp hollow of his shoulder.

She wanted him to slow down, it was too quick, too intense, but when she whispered "Not so fast," he didn't seem to hear her. He just kept thrusting and plunging, faster and faster, and she sank her nails into his shoulders and dropped her head back, the twilight against her throat, the river splashing between them.

She cried out when she came, her voice echoing across the deserted waters, a strange and hollow sound. He clutched her body against his, his mouth open against her shoulder, her neck, his hands cradling her head. He whispered that he loved her, he was sorry and he loved her and he would always love her, and Anita started to cry.

Lily knows that something is required of her now. She understands this is a kind of test. She senses the man sitting next to her is at war with himself and that she is the battlefield on which the war will be played out.

"The rules aren't fair," she blurts out.

"There aren't any rules, Mrs. Lincoln," says the woman who brought Henry to the center tonight. "There are only the sketches. We need you to tell us what the sketches mean."

Thunder rolls across the sky again. It frightens her. Reminds her of something, but she doesn't know what. She wants to run, to hide, to make herself as small as possible. The rain will start soon, a torrent of rain, and she and the dog must hide where no one will find them. No one.

The woman touches Lily's arm. "Please help us," she says softly.

"Can't." Lily shakes her head and turns the sketches facedown in her lap. "Can't."

Lightning sears across the glass, and in the cracks that it creates, Lily sees writhing shapes, water, another world, someone else's world. A shudder ripples through her and she squeezes her eyes shut, not wanting to see, but forced to see even though her eyes are closed.

"I run into the storm. I run and run because it feels good to run, but I don't like the storm. I don't want to be in the storm."

The man beside her suddenly rises, moves behind her, brings his hands close to her body but doesn't touch her yet. She feels his presence behind her, feels it like a solid wall and, for some reason, it makes her feel safer.

"Go on, Mom," Chrissy says.

"I hate the fence, Chrissy, I know you don't like to hear that, but I hate the fence. I have to find Henry, so I climb the fence and Pan sees me do it, Pan shouting into the rain about the stupid zebras, that the zebras are going to get me."

The man's hands now touch her shoulder and the crown of her head. She wiggles, not entirely sure she likes the feeling, but after a moment or two, it's not bad. His hands make her feel safer too, and more secure, and she suddenly understands this is part of his private battle.

"I climb that stupid ol' fence and hit the sidewalk like I'm running a marathon." She laughs, her head thrown back, but she can't sustain it. In some ways, the laughter is like her memories, quick, elusive, here one second, gone the next.

"And then I hear the crash and I dive into the bushes. I'm scared. The zebras are coming . . ." She brings her hands close to her face, looks at them, and suddenly remembers a Gypsy reading her palm when she was about fourteen. At a carnival.

Before she can retrieve the memory of what the Gypsy said to her, another woman steps forward, the woman with the soothing voice. "Mrs. Lincoln, I want you to listen to the sound of my voice, okay?"

Lily likes this woman's voice. Her voice is a thread that her senses follow in the same way that she follows music and certain parts of

228 · T.J. MacGregor

her past. Lily looks through her sketches, then rests her head against the chair and closes her eyes.

At the count of ten . . . yes, okay . . .

Seven . . . eight . . . nine . . . ten . . .

And Lily is there. "The dark car hits the larger car. Bad. Bad. Why would someone do that on purpose? He backs up and hits the car again, I see it, see it with my own eyes, and, dear God, I want to run. I want to leap out of that hedge and run. But I don't. I can't do it, see, because a dog comes limping across the street, a dog that's dizzy with grief. My heart breaks and I whistle for it, whistle for the dog, and he comes right under the bush with me, just crawls under it and crouches beside me, shaking and whimpering."

21

Mind Swells

(1)

"Tell me about the man, Mrs. Lincoln. Did you see him at any point?" Charlie asked.

The question seemed to pull Lily out of whatever space she'd been in. Charlie looked over at Rain for help, for guidance, for something. But Rain merely opened her arms, as if to say it was all Charlie's call from there on in.

"Man?" Lily blinked as she looked up. "What man are you talking about? What's your name again?"

Charlie ignored the last part and directed the old woman's attention to the sketches again. "Tell me about the bad man. Describe him."

She slapped another sketch in front of Charlie and stabbed a gnarled finger at it. "Here, he's here. See him? See that light glowing in his face? That's him. Dark hair, tall, taller than Chrissy, taller than you. That's him. Fancy suit. Fancy car. I could see. My eyes are better than yours." She sat forward, pointing at Charlie. "You think I'm crazy, all of you." She made a sweeping gesture with her thin, wrinkled hand that not only encompassed the lot of them, but the entire facility. The world. The universe. "And I don't care. I can still see better than you. Sometimes I can see so well, I see tomorrow," she finished with a whisper.

Charlie pulled out some of the license photos from her bag. "Is he anywhere in here, Mrs. Lincoln? Do you see him in any of these pictures?"

She sped through the first batch, shaking her head. "No, no, no."

Charlie handed her the next batch. And the next. Small batches, five or six photos. Even so, it didn't take her long to empty her bag of thirty photos. Lily finally stopped on photo twenty-eight . "Him." Frowning, she rifled back through the photos and slapped number fifteen beside it. "Or maybe him."

"Which one?" Charlie prodded.

"Both."

"*Both?* There were two men in the car?"

"What car?"

"Mom, listen, you have to—"

Charlie grabbed the two photos and hissed, "Which man, Mrs. Lincoln? *Which man is it?*"

Then Lily Lincoln shook her head wildly, back and forth, back and forth, and she started to cry, to sob, and she flopped forward in her chair, hands covering her face, and Wells pulled Charlie away from her.

"Knock it the fuck off, Calloway," he snapped, and walked her hastily to the couch near the window and pressed down against her shoulders, forcing her to sit.

After that, Charlie wasn't sure what happened. One moment she shrank into a couch, and the next she knelt in front of Mrs. Lincoln again, begging her to narrow it to one picture, pleading with her to remember what the most recent sketches meant. This time Rain pulled her away from the old woman and walked her outside, into the starlit garden.

"Chill out, kiddo. You're not going to get anywhere by doing it that way. The more upset Lily gets, the less she's going to recall."

"I know, I know. But—"

"But nothing," Rain said harshly. "Let the reluctant pioneer in there do his thing. Logan doesn't have a personal connection to this, and he'll probably get more than you can."

Rain didn't understand jackshit, Charlie thought. She didn't get it. Then Charlie felt her face crumbling and Rain put her arms around her and patted her on the back as though she were a very young child. "I know how you feel, really I do. But give Logan and the old lady time, Charlie."

Minutes ticked by. Charlie paced in front of the fence, thinking of Paz living for weeks under the bushes just outside. *Weeks.* And every day Lily Lincoln had stuffed her pockets with food and fed Paz through the fence.

A long while later, the doors exploded open and Logan hurried out and hustled them over to the lights that illumined the fountain. "Take a look at this. It's him. I got it." He thrust a photo into Charlie's hand. "Frank Benedict."

Charlie stared at the picture. She'd expected him to look like a monster or a movie star, one or the other, nothing in between. Instead, he looked ordinary, a man in his early to mid-forties with dark hair and a pleasant face, someone she might pass on a busy street. He could have been her neighbor or a coworker.

You. You killed my husband and son.

Logan handed Charlie the file, sat on the bench with her laptop on his thighs, and booted it up. Charlie opened the file, her mouth dry, a pulse beating at her temple. Frank Benedict, forty-four, an attorney with Thacker and Tillis. Wife, Anita, a teacher of gifted kids. Six-year-old son, Joey.

Wife reported the vehicle stolen three days after the accident. Did that make her an innocent victim or an accomplice?

"Does the address fit the accident radius?" Charlie asked anxiously.

"Hold on," Logan said. "It's coming up."

She peered over his shoulder as a red, pulsating X appeared within the original fifteen-mile radius of the accident site. A home on a canal. "We need warrants," she said. "And backup." She hurried back inside, where Lily and Christine Lincoln were. Wells was on the phone, pacing the length of the window, his voice hushed, urgent.

Charlie went over to the old woman and hugged her. "I can't thank you enough, Mrs. Lincoln. We're going to get this guy." And Lily Lincoln was about to become a millionaire. Or she and Logan would split the reward. She didn't know. "Would you watch Paz for me until I get back?"

The old woman drew back, head cocked to one side. "Is it allowed?"

"Of course it is," her daughter replied. "You're coming to my place tonight, Mom. You and Henry."

Charlie nuzzled her face against Paz's fur. "I'll be back tomorrow morning to get you, big guy."

Paz whimpered and licked her face, then dropped his head on Lily's knee.

As Charlie stood, the old lady's eyes followed her up. "What's your name again?"

"Charlie."

Lily crooked her gnarled finger at Charlie. "I have a secret I want to share with you."

Charlie hesitated, reluctant to be drawn into Lily's fantasy world again. She needed to call Mitch for a backup, needed to get moving, to get out of there. But without Lily she would have nothing. She went over to Lily's chair. "What secret?"

Lily put her mouth close to Charlie's ear and whispered, "They think I'm crazy. But I'm not."

Charlie drew back and looked at Lily, looked hard and deep, her hands still on the woman's thin arms. Her eyes had turned toward the window, but Charlie knew she wasn't really seeing the window or the lightning beyond it. Her gaze had gone inward. "Fire," she said hoarsely. "So much fire. The rug gets him."

Fire. Rug. Uh-huh. "I don't understand."

Lily giggled and sat back. "Me either."

Charlie flew up the sidewalk toward her van. Thunder sounded in the distance and another flash of lightning brought back the night of the accident. *No rain,* she thought. *Please don't rain. Just hold off until I find him.*

"Hey, Charlie, hold on."

She turned to see Wells racing up the walk behind her. "You can't go off half cocked. We know who he is now, and unless you want him to beat the rap, we've got to do this by the book."

"Fuck the book, Leo."

"I've already talked to Feldman. We'll have warrants in ten minutes. He's faxing them here. I also talked to Chief Maxwell. He says Colin Thacker of Thacker and Tillis, the firm where—"

"I read the file, Leo," she said impatiently.

"Yeah, well, Thacker's dead."

"What? How?"

"Anaphylactic shock, from what appear to be spider bites."

Coincidence? How could it be? "I'll meet you at Benedict's place. I won't jeopardize this. We may need backup, so call Mitch."

"Mitch?"

"I promised him I would." She held up her badge. "In return for this. Tell him this can't be any sort of commando thing. It's got to be very quiet, very quick."

Logan joined them, his body literally vibrating with energy, her laptop slung over his shoulder. "Let's get going. Leo, my cat's in the camper."

"I'll get the doc to take him."

Charlie snapped, "I don't want company, Logan."

"Tough. I'm not doing this for you, Calloway. I'm doing it for me."

Then he touched her arm and hurried her on toward her van.

(2)

They ate on deck, beneath the stars, just like the old days, he thought. He'd grilled chicken and baked corn in the hot coals and Anita had made a salad and opened a bottle of wine.

Benedict felt better than he had in months, his thoughts clearer. The lunch with Thacker, the events of the past several weeks, all of it had assumed a pall of unreality, like episodes from some other man's life, tales heard around a campfire. For the first time since the night of the accident, Benedict saw his way clear into the future. And what he saw felt good to him.

"How much do you think we could get for the house?" he asked suddenly.

Anita draped a dry towel around her shoulders; the wind had kicked up out of the east and rustled her hair. "I don't know, probably two hundred or two and a quarter. Why?"

"Remember how we used to talk about sailing around the Caribbean for a year? Or two years? Or living permanently on the sloop?"

"Yeah, so?"

"I want to resign from the firm, Anita."

Her mouth literally fell open.

"Working seventy and eighty hours a week, never seeing you and Joey . . . it's not worth it. If we sold everything and I took out the money I've put into the pension plan, I figure we'd have between three fifty and four hundred thousand. We could sail the Caribbean for six months or a year. Then we could find someplace to settle down. It'd be great for Joey. He'd be exposed to new cultures, new things. . . ." The look on her face made him stop.

"All this because Thacker didn't offer you the partnership?"

He almost told her the truth then, that Thacker, that fat fuck, had fired him. But if he told her that, she would think he was running away. And he wasn't. For the first time in a year, he wasn't running.

"I don't care about that, I don't care about MacLean. I just want to have a life."

She sat back against the railing, her hair frizzy in the lantern's lambent light, her lovely face pensive. "It would solve a lot of things," she said finally, quietly.

He knew she referred to the incident and waited for her to go on, to bring it all up again, to hash and rehash the particulars. Instead, she asked, "How long do you think it would take us to sell the house?"

"We wouldn't have to wait for the house to sell. We could set up an account in the islands and the money would be wired there. I could give my notice on Monday, call the broker and tell him to sell out, and have my pension check in the bank by Friday. Our passports are current. We could be sailing by next weekend."

"I'd have to get together some sort of home schooling program for Joey and find someone to teach the creative writing course."

"You could have that done in two days, Anita."

"What about Nemo?"

"He'd come with us."

"Could my folks meet us once in a while in some port? Would you mind that?"

"Look, I don't care who meets us where, Anita. I just want to do it."

She stood in a single, graceful motion, and went over to the railing, straddling it like a saddle. For a long time she didn't speak. Then: "What we did was wrong, Frank. But we did what we had to do. I understand that."

Don't start. "There wasn't any other way."

"We're not running, are we?"

"Of course not. This whole thing was a wake-up call for me. I realized I don't want to live with my life slammed in fast forward anymore."

That much, at any rate, was true. The lure of the sea always had surpassed his love of the law. Besides, he no longer loved the law. He had come too close to understanding how it failed to protect people like him, people whose rage was directed at the perpetrators of lies and deceit.

MacLean didn't give a shit how his decisions had impacted Benedict's life; he hadn't cared the night he failed to sign with the firm and he hadn't cared when he'd signed with the firm's competitor. He probably hadn't thought twice about what he'd led Benedict to believe about that dinner on the night of May 23.

And Thacker. Christ, Thacker had acted like Benedict's supporter, but in the end he'd stabbed him in the back. The security guard and Calloway hadn't done anything personally to Benedict. But they'd been in the wrong place at the wrong time. *They had been in his way.*

It all came back to *shit happens.* You deal with it, hope for the best, and go on.

Anita swung her right leg onto the deck and slid off the railing. "I'm going to get some paper and a pen. We need to make a list."

"Good idea."

He caught her hand as she started past him, and she gazed down at him, eyes roaming his face, as if seeking something. Then a smile touched her mouth, just the corners, a quick, young smile, and she touched two fingers to his mouth. "Be right back."

(3)

Charlie parked the van in a mango grove just up the street from Benedict's house. She opened the drawer under the seat, brought out her weapon, and tucked it into the waistband of her jeans at the back. Her windbreaker covered it.

"You armed, Logan?"

"I haven't touched a weapon since the day I got shot."

"Meaning what? That you won't carry one now?"

"Meaning I don't own one."

She reached into the glove compartment for Jess's gun and two spare clips. "Be my guest." She handed them to him. He snapped the clip in with the ease of a pro.

They headed on foot through the grove, night sounds rising and falling around them. "I just want you to know that I appreciate what you said to me when we were back at the center," Logan said.

Charlie glanced at him, his long, graying hair loose now, sort of wild, the wind blowing it around. "It's not every day I get to tell someone to fuck off, Logan."

He laughed. "Hell, I deserved it."

"What do you think those other sketches are about?"

"This is going to sound nuts," Logan said, "but maybe the dementia or the Alzheimer's gives her access to information in a way that's beyond our capacity to understand."

"That's a switch in attitude for a reluctant pioneer," she said with a laugh.

"A what?"

"That's what Leo considers you. A pioneer. The reluctant part was my contribution."

"I guess I'll take that as a compliment."

They emerged on Benedict's street and moved quickly into the cul-de-sac where his home was located. In the starlight, the house seemed surreal, tucked back behind an electronic gate and a fence. The encroaching thunderheads from the east, great threatening shapes in the moonlight, seemed to be headed directly at the house. An optical illusion, she thought, but the metaphor didn't escape her.

A light or several lights were on somewhere, offering enough illumination to make out a few details. The house looked like the kind of place where a successful lawyer would live. Trees spread across the half-acre of property, a jungle gym loomed off to the side, lush landscaping swept down the slight incline from the front porch, colorful flowers billowed over the sides of the gracefully twisting driveway. It didn't qualify as an estate, but it seemed damn close.

Logan stood at the gate for a few moments, staring at the house. "No one's in there," he said. "The air feels empty. There're no lights in the windows, just the glow of night-lights."

"I'm still going in. I need to see the rooms where this bastard lives." *Maybe that's how he felt about me.*

She scaled the gate, and moments later Logan dropped to the ground beside her. They ran up the driveway, through the trees, and stopped when they spied the black Mercedes in front of the house. "Someone's home," she whispered.

"The place is empty. I'm sure of it. Trust me on this one, Calloway."

But suppose you're wrong?

No, he wasn't wrong. She, too, felt the emptiness of the house, the way it seemed to wait for its family's return. "You coming?" she whispered.

"I'll stay here and see what I can pick up from the car. When the others arrive, I'll whistle and you get out of the house. I'll keep them out here as long as I can. Your boss will go ballistic if he knows you went inside before he did."

"Thanks."

She took off into the trees and shrubs at the side of the house. At the back, a dock jutted out into the canal. An empty dock. A *sailboat, just like Lily drew.* Had Benedict gone sailing for the weekend, a good hubby and father who had taken his wife and son with him?

She opened the screened porch door and entered the pool area. Fancy deck, very pricey, very classy. A cat, curled up on the patio table, woke up, hissed, and darted through a cat door in the sliding glass door. If the Benedicts were like other cat owners, she thought, then a neighbor might be coming in to feed the animal and change the litter while they were gone for the weekend. That meant a spare key might be hidden somewhere out here.

Charlie went over to a clay pot that held shoots of bamboo, tilted the pot toward her, and felt under it. Sure enough, the key lay there, and it got her into the poolside bathroom.

As she breathed the air that Frank Benedict had breathed, walked across the floors where he had walked, and ran her hands over surfaces that he had touched, images flashed through her with brilliant intensity, in vivid detail, a mind swell that connected one bit of information with another. She felt circuits in her brain overloading and knew that a dark tide was rising and would sweep her away just as it had swept Logan away in the past.

She suddenly stopped and folded her arms across her chest. *Breathe. Ground yourself.* She doubled over at the waist, allowing blood to rush into her head.

Shit happens. Don't get in my way.

Had that been her or a genuine impression?

Was it the bottom line? Was Frank Benedict a shit-happens kind of guy?

She felt better when she straightened up again. Not great, not even like herself, but able to think, to function. Charlie turned and looked at the various items stuck to the refrigerator. The boy's artwork. A monthly calendar for June. A schedule for a creative writing class that would start next week. And a typed list of names and phone numbers entitled *Important Numbers.*

Charlie ran her finger down the list of names. *Bruce, Steve, Lisa, Aunt Bobbie, Grandpa Randall.* Charlie grabbed the sheet from the fridge door and ran over to the phone. She punched out the number, an area code around Daytona Beach. On the fifth ring, a man answered, an old man with a raspy, dignified voice who sounded irked at the late-night call.

"Mr. Randall, please."

"This is *Dr.* Randall."

She noted the correction. "Dr. Randall, my name's Charlotte Calloway. I'm with the FBI. It's imperative that I get in touch with your daughter. Do you have any idea how I might contact her? She's not at home."

"The FBI? What's going on? How did you get this number?"

"Sir, I have reason to believe your daughter may be in danger."
Or she may be an accomplice. "Do you know how I can get in touch with her?"

"In danger how? What're you talking about?"

"I'm talking about her husband. He's the suspect in a murder investigation and—"

"Jesus," he whispered.

"Who is it, Grandpa?" A child's voice.

"It's for me, Joey. Go get your grandmother for me, will you?"

"Sure."

Then: "Agent Calloway, I'd like your badge number again, please."

She reeled it off. "Sir, please, if you know where your daughter is . . ."

"They went sailing for the weekend somewhere up around Sebastian. The Indian River. They were going to anchor off one of the islands up there. What murder investigation, Agent Calloway?"

"I'm not at liberty to say, sir. Is their son with you?"

"Yes, he is."

"Under no conditions should you allow Mr. Benedict to take the boy."

"That no-good son of a bitch won't find us here. You have a pencil, Agent Calloway? I'll give you my cell phone number. Please call me as soon as you know anything."

Charlie jotted it down on a napkin. "Does your daughter have a phone with her? Is there any way I can get in touch with her?"

"She has a phone, but I haven't been able to get through to her. She probably turned it off."

"What kind of boat are they on?"

"A sloop. One mast. It's forty-feet long, with a blue hull. It's called *Someday*."

"Thanks, Dr. Randall. Thanks very much. I'll be in touch."

Charlie slammed down the phone and ran out the back door just in time to hear Logan's long, shrill whistle.

22

•

Meltdown

(1)

Anita felt as if some unbearable weight had suddenly lifted from her shoulders. *Living the dream:* that was how she and Frank had talked about it in the early days of their marriage. Someday, they would live the dream, thus the name of the boat. Now, suddenly, *someday* lay only a week in the future.

Her parents wouldn't like it, she thought, glancing slowly around the crowded, dimly lit cabin. They would think she was nuts, selling everything, taking off like she was a college student headed to Europe for the first time. And what about Joey? What about Joey's education? What about Joey's childhood? Yes, she could expect those kinds of arguments. But she was no longer a kid; she was a woman pushing forty who had lived too long the way her parents thought she should live. The idea of becoming nomadic, of sailing off into one of those Key West sunsets appealed to her in the deepest way.

They would have to make a few changes here in the cabin, that much was immediately apparent to her. It was one thing to sail for a week in such cramped quarters; it was another entirely to live on board for a year. They would need a larger stove, a large fridge, a larger shower, more storage area. But these details could be worked out in Panama or the British Virgins, where sailors proliferated and cheap labor could be found.

She made her way through the galley, past the table, and through the doorway to the bunk area at the bow of the boat. The lower, larger bunk was where she and Frank usually slept, with Joey on the narrower upper bunk. But if they were going to live on board, she and Frank would need more privacy. Joey could use the conversion bunk in the galley, where the table and booths folded into each other. The door between them would need a new lock, she thought, and wrote that on her notepad.

She jotted down a few more items, her mind already light-years ahead, anticipating needs like fresh water and extra gas for the engine and freeze-dried foods for when they ran low on fresh fruits and vegetables. Joey's picky eating habits would be a problem initially, but if he got hungry enough, he would learn to eat freeze-dried foods and fish that they caught. He would learn things on this trip that he would never forget. He would stash away memories that would be with him for the rest of his life, that would shape the rest of his life.

And sooner or later on this trip, she thought, she and Frank would be able to place the events of the past weeks completely behind them. They would be able to do it because "for better or for worse" meant exactly that, and too many people were too willing to cut and run when "worse" entered the equation. Several days ago she'd been ready to cut and run.

Twenty years from now she would look back on this time, and on tonight in particular, as a major turning point in their lives as a couple and as individuals. She would be fifty-eight years old then, ensconced on some wonderful plantation in Costa Rica, with horses in the barn and dogs and cats in the yard. Joey would be married by then, perhaps with a family of his own, his children close by. Maybe she and Frank would even have other children, she was still young enough, and what better way to start fresh?

Lost in her fantasy, Anita tripped over Frank's bag on the floor. The stuff he'd tossed on top of it slid off, car keys and clothes, his marine bag and his wallet. She stooped to pick everything up, a reminder that living in a tiny cabin would require major adjustments in terms of personal space.

They would be living practically on top of each other when they weren't topside. Frank and Joey would have to understand right from the start that she wouldn't be constantly picking up after them, playing maid and wife and supermom. After all, this trip would be as much her trip as it was theirs; the boys, she thought, would have to realign their thinking about her, that much was apparent.

She shoved Frank's clothes back into his bag, zipped his keys into the side compartment, shoved the marine bag under the bunk, and picked up his wallet. It lay open, credit cards spilling out, Joey's most recent school picture bent at a corner, bills poking out. Anita straightened everything and found another picture stuck to the back of Joey's.

Humidity, she thought, and knew that would be a problem too. Humidity on a sailboat wasn't like humidity on dry land. It was a fact of life, something you couldn't escape, and you either adjusted to it or made other arrangements. Maybe they could install a small window AC unit, something that at the very least would keep their sleeping quarters comfortable at night. There was nothing she hated more than damp sheets when she tried to sleep.

She pulled the photos apart and, thinking the second photo was Joey's older school picture, looked at it. For long, breathless moments, her brain refused to define what she was looking at, refused to make the connection between content and meaning.

Anita knuckled her eyes, looked again.

It came to her piecemeal. A pregnant woman, belly showing. A pretty woman hamming for a camera. A woman in the full throes of pregnancy, so comfortable with who and what she was at that moment that she had lifted her shirt and exposed her very large belly to the camera. A woman laughing. A woman whose face she recognized.

Charlie Calloway.

The air seemed to rush out of her lungs, out of the cabin. It was as if she suddenly found herself in a vacuum, the vacuum of outer space, of inner space, the vacuum of incomprehension. She clawed through everything in the wallet now, tearing out bills, shaking loose credit cards, and found several newspaper articles that had been copied in a reduced format. *Hit & Run. Security guard. $1,000,000 reward.* These words sprang out at her, seized her, and she literally saw red.

She scooped everything up, her hands shaking, her heart hammering, and ran into the galley, where the light was brighter. She dropped everything on the table, smoothed out the newspaper articles, put the photo down.

You were fucking her, the Calloway woman. That's what this whole thing was about. He was involved with her and something went wrong. Maybe she threatened to tell Anita, maybe the Calloway woman had ended the relationship. However it went down, Frank had tried to kill her.

Premeditated murder.

Murder one.

And the baby, my God, whose baby was it?

Anita backed away from the table, a sob clawing its way up her throat, her fist pressed to her mouth. *You tried to kill her and then came running home and lied to me and made me an accomplice.* "Bastard. You bastard."

And the sun tea. He had definitely drugged her. He had drugged her and gone back to the U-Haul place and he had killed the security guard. *Sweet Christ, he's crazy, I've been living with a lunatic. He made love to me, a madman made love to me.*

Bile flooded her throat and she ran into the head and vomited. *Got to get out of here.*

Her mind raced, seeking an excuse to go to shore, an excuse Frank would believe. Supplies, she thought. They needed supplies. She needed something from the car. No, no. Not at this hour of the night. He wouldn't buy it.

She went over to the sink and rinsed out her mouth. *Think, dammit, think.* Anita raised her head and looked at herself in the tarnished mirror, her hair wild and frizzy from the wind and the salt, her eyes haunted with the truth. That photo loomed in her mind, Charlie Calloway, laughing, her hands on her big belly.

You fucked her. Got her pregnant.

She would get him drunk, wait until he fell asleep, then escape in the dinghy. It sounded good, but Anita knew she wouldn't be able to act normally. She couldn't go topside and sit across from him and say *More wine, hon?*

She couldn't pull it off.

Cell phone.

Of course. She'd brought her cell phone. She would call 911.

The marine patrol. The Coast Guard. Her father. Someone. Dear God, who? Who could get here fast enough? And what should she do until they got here?

Hide. She would have to hide.

She hurried out of the head and into the cabin. She squatted in front of her bag, unzipped it, dug out her cell phone. She turned it on and saw that the battery was nearly spent. The charger, where had she put the charger? No, that wouldn't work unless the generator was on. If she turned it on, Frank would come below to find out why she'd turned it on.

Maybe the phone had enough juice in it for one call.

Make it the right call, Anita. You'll get only one chance.

Then it had to be 911. The numbers for the Coast Guard and the marine patrol were posted topside, next to the captain's chair.

"Anita?" Frank called. "You okay down there?"

"I'm in the head," she called back, and ran into the bathroom and shut the door, praying Frank wouldn't come down here.

(2)

They poured into and out of Frank Benedict's home, six cops in full riot gear who weren't taking chances even though Logan had told them no one was home. Then the garage door went up and Mitch marched out and came over to Logan and Charlie.

"There are cages of spiders in the attic," he said. "And computer equipment that links him to the break-in at the U-Haul company. And a license plate. We ran it. It belongs to the missing Beamer. Now all we need is Benedict."

"We told you he wasn't here," Charlie said, then her cell phone rang and she excused herself and walked out of hearing range.

"So what now?" Logan asked him.

"We stake out the place, wait for him to get back here."

"Good, then you won't mind if I split."

Mitch laughed. "I don't mind if I never see your mug again, Logan."

The urge to sink his fist once more into Mitch's mouth flashed through him and died. "It's mutual," he replied, and walked away, down through the trees past Charlie.

Charlie caught up with him. "That was Leo. He's got a seaplane. It's coming in just up the street, at a park on the intracoastal."

"A seaplane? For what?"

"I know where Benedict is."

(3)

Anita, near panic now, leaned against the bathroom door, her eyes on the ceiling, following the sounds of Frank's movements topside. He was probably cleaning up the grill. That would give her a little more time. *Please stay up there.*

She punched out 911 for the fourth time. Her first three tries hadn't gone through, either because the battery was too low or she was out of range. But 911 had to work wherever you were, she thought, and punched the digits again.

She looked at the cell phone window. *Roaming . . .*

Anita pressed the phone to her ear, praying it would ring.

I loved you too much, Frank.

Tears leaked out of her eyes.

One ring.

She squeezed her eyes shut. *C'mon, c'mon, go through. Someone pick up.*

Static burst in her ear, but she thought she heard a faint voice saying, *The nature of your emergency, please.*

"My name's Anita Benedict," she whispered. "I'm on a boat in the Indian River, off—"

The phone went dead.

She pressed back against the door, the phone clutched to her chest, panic galloping through her now.

I'll go topside, act like myself, and when his back is turned, I'll knock him out and escape in the dinghy. Four miles lay between her and the mainland. The dinghy didn't move very fast, he might come to before she got out of sight. No, her best bet would be to say she needed another swim and dive overboard and not stop swimming until she reached the island. It lay only three hundred yards away.

Even if Frank swam after her, she probably would have enough of a head start to reach it before he did. And once she was on land, she would hide. She could climb a tree or burrow under the brush, something. Anything.

Get out now, fast, while you still can.

She grabbed a T-shirt from the hook on the back of the door and reached into the hamper for a pair of shorts. She pulled the clothes on over her bathing suit, then realized her clothes would tip Frank off if she suddenly announced she was going swimming again.

She tore off the shirt and shorts and glanced around for something she could use as a weapon just in case he figured it out before she hit the water.

Towel rack, yes, that would do just fine. Solid wood. Not too thick, but heavy enough to knock him out if she hit him in the head.

Anita popped it out of the wall, flushed the toilet so that Frank would hear it and know she was on her way back up. When she didn't appear, he would call for her. She would be hidden in the galley, near the stairs, so that she could slam the towel rack over his head as he came down into the cabin to look for her. This would save her from the charade she wasn't sure she could pull off convincingly, the charade called *Hon, I'm going for another swim.*

She wished she hadn't turned on a light in the cabin. But the shadows near the stairs would hide her.

It would work. It had to work.

You got her pregnant and maybe she promised you that she would leave her husband, promised it right up until the very end, then changed her mind and dumped you. You tried to kill her and lied to me, lied . . .

Anita crept into the narrow hall, the floorboards creaking. She heard water lapping at the sides of the boat, heard the wind whistling around the portholes, and she tightened her grip on the towel rack and stepped into the galley.

Frank stood with his back to her, stood there at the galley table, where she'd left the newspaper clippings and the photo of Charlie Calloway. He turned when he heard the floorboards creak, turned and looked at her with homicidal eyes. But when he spoke, his voice was menacingly soft.

"Jesus, Anita. You should've left it all alone. You shouldn't have gone snooping around in my things. You—"

"You were screwing her. Screwing that woman. You got her pregnant and she dumped you and then you tried to kill her and you lied to me and convinced me to help you get rid of the car." She kept moving toward him, very slowly, her arm stiff at her side, the towel rack hidden by her leg. "You lied to me, Frank. You lied to me about everything. You drugged my tea and you killed the security guard. You—"

He exploded with laughter. "Fucking Calloway? When did I have time to do that? Huh? In my sleep? Where the hell did you get that idea?"

His laughter threw her; she hadn't expected it. "Then how'd you get that picture, Frank?"

His expression went utterly blank. She could almost hear something misfiring deep inside his brain. Then blood rushed into his face and in a low, savage voice, he said, *"Don't you dare question me in that tone of voice, bitch."*

And he came toward her, fists clenched, his eyes impaling her, piercing her, commanding her. For a split second, fear nearly overpowered her. But she saw him screwing the Calloway woman and thought of all those lies, and her arm swung up with brutal swiftness and she struck him in the face with the towel rack.

His hands flew to his face. Blood poured out of his chin or his mouth or both, she couldn't tell for sure. He stumbled back and fell into the table, and Anita sprang for the stairs. But she wasn't fast enough. He tackled her at the waist, and they both crashed to the galley floor and rolled.

Anita kicked and clawed and writhed to free herself. But Frank outweighed her, he was stronger. He punched her in the face and stars burst in her eyes. He punched her in the ribs and she heard them cracking and splintering. He kept shouting at her, shouting that she was a stupid bitch and that he knew she'd been planning all along to turn him in for the reward.

Something snapped inside her, a clean, swift sound, like that of a roof collapsing beneath the aggregate weight of debris that had never been cleared away. Floodgates opened, adrenaline poured through her, and in a sudden burst of strength and speed she jerked her leg free and sank her knee into his balls.

She knew that he made a sound, but couldn't tell what it was, not a shriek or a scream, nothing that simple. This seemed to tear from the very depths of him, from the darkest core of his heart. Then he slipped to one side, clutching himself, and Anita scrambled to her feet, her face and mouth bleeding, pain burning through her side. She couldn't get past him to the stairs, so she spun and ran toward the cabin, her body burning with pain, every breath, every step, an agony.

Anita slammed the door, threw the lock, and looked frantically around for something to push against the door. The dresser, if she could slide the dresser in front of the door . . .

(4)

Wells unloaded a canvas bag with an assortment of weapons in it and tossed a high-powered rifle to Logan. "I hope you still remember how to use that, Logan," he shouted over the noise of the seaplane's engines.

Logan ignored the remark. He assembled the scope and loaded the rifle. Wells and Charlie did the same. "Okay, guys," the pilot said. "Can anyone give me an exact location for this boat? Is it in the river? On the ocean? I need a location."

Charlie, seated next to Logan, studied a map of Indian River County that clearly showed the river, the inlet, the channels to the ocean. Strung through all the blue were dozens of small islands. "Somewhere around Sebastian," she replied.

"The sketches," Logan reminded her.

"Right here." She reached into her bulging bag and pulled out the sketches Lily had made. The puzzling sketches.

Logan took the sketches and reached into his pocket for the abandoned hermit-crab shell. He rubbed it with his thumb, putting himself into the frame of mind he was in on the beach. He conjured Lily's particular feeling tones, wrapped them around himself, then looked at the sketches again, through her eyes.

He felt, suddenly, what he should have felt when he'd been touching the old woman, that her brain had been scrambled and pieces of herself lay strewn across some vast inner landscape. It was as if the core of her personality had been uprooted from time, so that only an eternal now existed for her. But within this now, through her drawing, she was able to bridge the gaps to the past—and to the future.

The mechanics of whatever had been at work seemed to be equal parts of magic and mystery to Logan. But he couldn't deny what he felt just then, that Lily Lincoln's mental condition had somehow enabled her to glimpse future events that seemed to pertain to the man responsible for injuring the dog who had become her friend.

And suddenly, the sketches made sense to him. They were like the mosaic of the woman's mind, pieces of the truth tossed here, there. By turning each sketch around so that his perspective changed, he began to understand what he was seeing.

The sailboat wasn't just a sailboat; it was the scene of an unspeakable act. The rectangular shape off to the right wasn't another boat; it looked like some sort of shop, maybe a bait and tackle place. Behind the sailboat lay an island, where the tree branches braided together in such a way that they seemed to form words, but not words in any language that he knew.

Logan kept turning the paper this way and that. "Do you have a mirror on you, Charlie?"

"A mirror? For what? What're you looking for in these anyway, Logan?"

"I may be wrong. But give me a mirror and let's see."

As she fished around in her bag, the pilot said, "Hey, about that location."

"We're working on it," Wells told him. "Give us a few minutes."

"Okay, but we're approaching Fort Pierce now. Then Vero. Then Sebastian."

Charlie handed Logan an open compact and he held it up to the sketch. The words *Mott's Isle* appeared in the mirror. "My God," Charlie breathed. "How'd you know?"

"I didn't."

Wells, studying the map, let out a whoop of glee. "I found it! Mott's Isle. Looks like it'd disappear in a high tide."

"Is there any way you can cut the engines before you land?" Logan asked the pilot.

"If I'm low enough," the pilot replied. "But then you'd be swimming to the boat and your weapons would get wet."

Wells suddenly snapped his fingers. "Wait a minute. We've got an inflatable raft. If we land on the far side of the island, they'll hear us but they won't see us. We cut across the island on foot, inflate the raft, and one of us paddles it toward the sloop with the weapons inside it, while the other two swim along behind it. It's late, they're probably asleep, they won't be expecting us. Even if they're awake and see someone out paddling, so what? They're not going to think anything of it."

Charlie didn't know whether it would work. She needed to see the sloop first. But she wanted one thing clearly understood. "I board the boat first."

She looked at Wells, at Logan, just daring them to argue. Neither of them did.

23

———•———

Fire

(1)

Bitch, bitch, bitch.

Benedict pressed a dish towel with ice wrapped in it against his chin, trying to stop the bleeding. His jaw had begun to swell. He ached all over. But he was sure he'd done more damage to her. He knew he'd broken a couple of ribs and some bones in her cheek as well. It was nothing compared to what he would do to her when he got his hands on her.

He pressed his ear to the door, listening. At first he heard nothing. Then she gasped or sobbed, he couldn't tell which, and he heard something scraping across the floor. A barricade, he thought. She figured that by barricading herself in the bunk area, she would be safe until—when? Daylight? and then what did she think she would do? Yell for help? Yell to whom? Passing boaters? He would get her out long before then.

He went into the head and combed through the medical supplies for a butterfly bandage. He slapped on some antibiotic ointment first, fixed the bandage to his chin, and taped a piece of gauze over it, putting pressure on it so the bleeding would stop. Then he went back into the galley and listened at the door again.

No sounds.

He banged his fist against the door. "You've trapped yourself in there, Anita. And I can outwait you. I've got the food and water."

Silence.

"Okay, bitch. Have it your way. I'll break down the goddamn door."

He backed away from the door, making sure he stepped on the floorboards that creaked. Almost immediately, he heard her moving more things around in the bunk area, trying to fortify the door against his imminent attack. That would keep her busy long enough for him to head topside.

Benedict stopped briefly in the galley for a roll of electrical tape and a pair of scissors. Then he went topside and crawled onto the roof of the cabin so she wouldn't see his feet through the portholes. None of the portholes was open, and he intended to make sure she couldn't open them. He cut a dozen strips of tape and proceeded to seal the portholes shut. He worked quickly in the event that she was brain-addled enough to think she could make a break for it through her barricade before he got below again.

He caught sight of her briefly just before he taped the last porthole shut, a dark shape flattened against a wall, as if she hoped to make herself invisible. Then he slapped the last piece of tape over the glass and went below again.

Rags, a broomstick, more tape. He worked fast, worked as if he'd been preparing for this moment for most of his adult life. His nimble fingers wrapped and taped, wrapped and taped. And when the mop head looked plump and meaty, he saturated the rags in charcoal lighter and went over to the stove for the box of kitchen matches. Smoke the bitch out, he thought, and went over to the door.

"Last chance, Anita. You coming out?"

Silence.

"Suit yourself, bitch."

He turned on the small counter fan and aimed it at the cabin door. Then he lit a match and held the mop head over the sink as he brought the match to the rags. It exploded into flame, burning hot and fast, thick black plumes of smoke snaking away from it.

Grinning, Benedict waited until the flames had diminished to a hot glow, then went over to the door and swung the torch, creating more smoke. Tendrils licked at the wood and slithered through the crack under the door.

He heard Anita coughing.

"Ready to come out yet, bitch?" he shouted.

She pounded on the porthole windows.

Benedict lit another match, touched it to what remained of his torch, and the little fan blew more smoke under the door.

He hurriedly made another torch, a larger, plumper torch that burned hotter and brighter and belched more smoke. He shouted again, shouted and laughed and challenged her to come out, then two distinct sounds cut him off: the shattering of glass and the distant drone of an engine.

The glass worried him more than the engine. If she'd broken something in the bunk area, she might use it as a weapon. Or, worse, maybe she'd found a way to bust the porthole glass, which meant she would claw a hole in the tape so she could get some air. If she got air, she might last longer in there and he would be forced to break down his eight-hundred-dollar door. And he really didn't want to do that. He wanted her to roast, to fry, he wanted to see her fly out of the bunk area with flames riding her spine and eating up her hair.

He grabbed the bucket of rags and the charcoal lighter fluid and swept up the box of kitchen matches. He went topside and started taping the rags to the tape that already covered the portholes. He didn't stop long enough to check each porthole for slices or holes in the tape.

When he was finished, he saturated each little nest of rags with the lighter fluid and lit a match to it. *Burn, bitch, burn.*

And just in case she figured she would somehow escape in the dinghy, he untied it and shoved it away from the sloop.

(2)

Thick, putrid-smelling smoke began to fill the bunk area now, pouring in through the portholes. Anita had thought about making a break for it through the door, but knew he would be inside the cabin again before she'd dismantled her barricade.

No way out.

She would just soak a blanket down with the bottle of water she kept in the storage slot next to her bed, then flatten out on the floor and seize her first opportunity. If she didn't fry first.

Coughing and nearly blind from the smoke, her ribs screaming with pain, Anita finished tearing apart a pillowcase with her teeth and fashioned a bandanna to cover her mouth and nose. It didn't help much, but it might buy her a few minutes.

She jerked a blanket off Joey's bunk and poured the water over it, trying to distribute it evenly. But there wasn't enough water. Frantic now and unable to breathe much longer, her oxygen-deprived brain spat up one final option. The hatch into the dark, dank hull.

Anita draped the blanket around her shoulders and stumbled over to the storage closet in the far wall. She threw the door open, and a box of supplies tumbled off the shelf to her feet. She'd forgotten that she'd packed a few things in there while preparing for the trip.

Unfortunately, she hadn't thought to pack anything immediately useful like a gun. Or a knife. Or even a can of pepper spray. But the four bottles of water would be sufficient to soak down the blanket and the flashlight and beef jerky would definitely come in handy.

Minutes later she yanked open the trapdoor of the hatch and turned on the flashlight. With the wet, heavy blanket around her shoulders and a small bottle of water tucked in the pockets of her shorts, she started down the ladder into the abyss under the galley and the cabin.

(3)

The sight of the flames seized him, seduced him. For moments Benedict stood there, staring into them, understanding for the first time that the flames lived and breathed, that they were as alive as he was, possessed of an elemental power that would eat the bitch alive.

Suddenly, the wind fanned the flames, lifted them, and a tongue of fire leaped into the bucket of rags that he'd left on the roof of the cabin. They burst into fire, burning so hotly that the plastic bucket began to melt, then to burn.

Before Benedict moved, the stream of fire rolled down onto one of the lawn chairs. He flew toward the metal bait bucket on the other side of the sloop, leaned way over, and scooped up water. He hauled it toward the stern, where the portholes were, and hurled it on the flames. They sputtered and spat and hissed, but now the lawn chair went up.

Blankets, he thought, he needed blankets to smother the flames. He dropped the metal bucket and ran past the burning lawn chair. A seaplane suddenly swept into his view, coming in low over the island to the west. Benedict waved his arms and shouted for help, then raced down into the cabin for blankets.

(4)

Frank Benedict's phantom image danced in Charlie's eyes, Benedict on the burning sloop, Benedict. Screw the plan. She was out of here. "Land the plane!" she shouted. "Land it now!"

The pilot banked steeply to the left and came around again, altitude dropping steadily. Sixty feet, forty, twenty. Charlie left her rifle on the floor, knowing the water would render it useless, and leaped through the open door of the seaplane.

She struck the water feetfirst and sank fast and furiously. Fortunately, the river ran deep there and she never touched bottom. Already, her arms and legs propelled her toward the surface, and she broke into the air about twenty feet from the sloop.

She scrambled up the ladder, heaved her body over the side, rolled to the door of the cabin, leaped up, and stood to one side. She heard him now, heard the man who had killed her husband and son raving like some escaped mental patient.

Charlie positioned herself at the side of the door. She had a vague awareness that the seaplane had landed, of heat at her back. Then waves of madness and rage crashed over her, washed through her, and nearly suffocated her. She could feel him completely, as if she were snuggling down into his bones, sensing him in the same way a spider senses a minute vibration in its web when a gnat gets caught in it.

She drew a knife from her belt, a hunting knife that had belonged to Jess's father.

C'mon, Benedict. Come through that goddamn door.

And he did. He came barreling up those stairs, a blanket draped around his neck like some sort of medieval mantle. He waved a torch above his head and shouted that the bitch could burn, he didn't care, the bitch could burn.

This one's for Jess, Charlie thought, and kicked her right leg swiftly, powerfully, and caught him in the side.

Benedict staggered to the left and fell back against the doorjamb. The blanket slipped away from him, then he lost his balance and tumbled back down the stairs into the cabin. Charlie grabbed onto the ledge along the upper part of the door and swung through the opening, the knife still in her hand.

She took in everything with a sweeping glance—the heap of smoldering blankets, the torch burning against the floor, the large wooden keg sitting on a table in the corner, and the closed door to the sleeping area, the middle of it crushed and splintered like a human skull, ready to collapse inward. But no Benedict.

Charlie came slowly down the stairs, heart hammering, a wall of sweat flashing across her back. The blankets kept smoldering. A finger of fire licked at a braided rug.

Fire. Rug. The old lady had seen this.

Bureau regulations required her to identify herself, to demand that Benedict come out with his arms raised and all that other horseshit. But she hadn't come for the bureau. She'd come for Jess and Matthew and the future they would never have. She'd come for herself.

"Hey, Benedict!" she shouted. "There was a witness to your atrocity. And we have the equipment from the U-Haul company. And the plate for the Beamer. That's three murders, pal."

Her bare feet touched the last step.

Her grip on the knife tightened.

The blankets hissed as they started to burn. Smoke curled toward her and her eyes began to water. She coughed and covered her nose and mouth with cupped hands. She willed her new sense to open the hell up, to show her where he was hiding, but nothing came to mind except an image of herself dying down there from smoke inhalation.

So sit down and meditate on it.

Charlie knew that if she backed off now, she would never forgive herself. So she suddenly dived to the right of the burning blankets, where the torch lay, and scooped it up. *"I'm going to torch your fucking boat, Benedict!"*

And she touched the torch to the curtains that hung over the windows by the stove.

They went up, burning fast and furiously.

"There go the curtains," she shouted. "Next I do sheets, dish towels, whatever is in these cabinets." And she yanked open the storage doors above the stove and thrust the torch inside. "I've got nothing to lose, Benedict. You already killed everything I loved."

She smelled her hair singeing. The room blurred. Instinct reared up and seized her rage, and suddenly she wanted only to get out of the cabin, to let the bastard bake. She backpedaled, then heard something, a noise unconnected to the fire.

Charlie whipped to her left, and he exploded from the shadowed corner where he'd hidden and flew toward her through the smoke, a human torpedo that she perceived in some weird slow motion. She thrust the knife upward, knew that she'd missed, then dived too late. His arms clamped around her legs, and they crashed to the floor, bodies pressed together like lovers, and rolled toward the burning rug and blankets.

She no longer held the knife. But she smelled him then, smelled him in a way that she had never smelled another living thing, smelled him from the inside out, his fury and rage, his crimes and deceptions, the cluttered darkness of his heart. And when he grabbed her hair and slammed her head to the floor, she sank her teeth into his arm and tasted all the things she had just smelled.

He bellowed and she heard the rage. He reared back and she saw it permanently carved into his face. He drew his fist back, she saw it happening, saw that fist in the smoke, and she writhed and lashed out with her nails and clawed at his eyes, and at that moment she touched the rage, the fury, the darkness. His fist slammed into the floor next to her head. Everything inside her coalesced into a single focused thrust to survive. She groped for the burning rug and seized it and flung it at him, at his head, in his face.

He fell away from her and Charlie rolled and pushed up on her hands and tried to crawl through the smoke. She heard Benedict shrieking somewhere in the smoke. She could barely breathe. Her ears rang. Her hands felt burned, her lungs were scorched. She knew she had only seconds before she passed out.

Someone shouted, Wells or Logan, she couldn't tell which, and couldn't make out the words. Gunshots exploded through the cabin, something burst just above her head, and she felt water. It spurted from the wooden keg and poured over her and ran across the floor. The flames hissed and spat and smoke rose in thick, crippling clouds.

The water soaked her clothes, her hair, her skin. It soothed her where she hurt and she thrust her face into it and opened her mouth and seemed to breathe it in like a fish. It revived her enough so that she stumbled to her feet and lurched like a drunk along the wall, her eyes stinging with tears, one hand pressed to her mouth and nose.

She heard sounds but could no longer distinguish what was human and what was other. The floor in front of her suddenly blew upward, and something clambered out, something with wild, pale hair. It lumbered toward the writhing pyre in the heart of the smoke, the pyre that was Benedict, burning alive.

Anita Benedict threw herself onto her husband, beating him with a blanket, trying to put out the fire. Charlie reeled after her, fell on her, grabbed her around the neck and pulled. Anita somehow broke Charlie's hold and scrambled onto Benedict's smoking legs and leaned into his burned face and screamed, *"Fire's too easy, you son of a bitch!"*

Then she sank the hunting knife into Frank Benedict's throat.

After that, everything happened so fast that Charlie couldn't grasp the sequence of events. It was as if she'd come unglued in time and stumbled into a universe where none of the physical laws applied. She felt a rush of wind. She heard shouting. She saw Wells and Logan. She flew like a bird. Then there was nothing.

(5)

Logan felt it building, sensed it coming, and grabbed the back of Wells's shirt, pulling him away from the door. An instant later Charlie burst out of the smoke and the flames, her voice echoing across the quiet lagoon. *"She's gonna blow!"*

Logan shoved Wells over the side of the boat, then threw himself into the water and dived deep and swam like hell. His belly scraped bottom, muck drifted up around him. He kicked off his shoes.

The water muted the noise of the explosion, the propane tank on the stove going up like the end of the world. Logan felt it as it blew apart the sloop. Pieces of flaming wood struck the water and sank. He clung to the bottom, his fingers embedded so deeply into the muck that he would always feel the shit under his nails. The decaying algae. The disgusting softness.

His toes sank into the stuff and he pushed off, using the bottom for leverage, and propelled himself away, away.

Logan's head broke the surface about thirty feet from shore. He didn't know whether it was the mainland's shore or some other shore. He didn't care. He rolled over and lifted up on his elbows, the shells and rocks cutting into his skin. Only the sloop's mast remained above water, oil and gas and debris burning around it.

He crawled onto the shore and collapsed. He stared up into the belly of the star-strewn sky, grateful that he was alive. That he hadn't been injured. That the events of three and a half years ago would not be repeated, at least not for him.

When he felt a little stronger, he rocked back onto his heels, pressed his hands to his thighs, and got up. Wells lay a few feet away, sprawled against the sand. Logan made sure he was still alive, then dropped to his knees and shook him until he came to. "You're not dying on me, Leo, so forget it," he said. "We've got movies to see."

Then he moved down the beach to the next shape.

He guessed this was Anita Benedict. He shoved his hands under her and rolled her over. She groaned in agony, her badly burned arms like tissue paper in his hands. Most of her hair had been burned away, just a few tufts poking out here and there. Her face looked as if she had stuck her head in the oven while it was on broil.

She began to gag and Logan rolled her gently onto her side with one hand and lifted her head with the other. It came to him then, came when he least expected it with such force and clarity that he knew she had released it and that it had flowed directly from her into him.

The car, the quarries, the nightmare she'd lived since the night of the accident, the knife she sank into her husband's throat.

She vomited, her body heaving violently, and then she went still. She died in his arms, a charred stranger with memories that lingered until he took his hands away from her and laid her in the sand.

As he crawled down the beach, it began to sprinkle, a friendly summer rain. And when he found Charlie, her mouth was open to it. To the light rain.

She lay on her back on the beach, near a cluster of palmetto bushes, her arms flung out at her sides. She breathed, he could hear it, hear her breath, and her eyes were open. He knew without looking, without touching her, that her hands were badly burned. She didn't speak, but her eyes followed him as he scooped the cool sand over her hands, burying them in the stuff.

Then he lay down beside her, his arm around her waist, and held her body against his own. He shut his eyes and willed his strength, meager as it was, into her. Her fingers closed around his arm and her mouth moved against his ear, and she whispered, "So we'll go to a movie, okay? Your first in four years."

And he laughed and heard sirens closing in fast from every direction and felt water washing over his feet. "Calloway?"

"Still here, Logan. The rain feels good against my hands."

"The old lady was right about the sailboat. About the fire."

"And you were right about everything else."

Her head rolled onto his arm and his fingers stroked her hair. Logan opened his eyes to the soft, glorious rain.

Lily breaks off thin stalks of red flowers and sticks them in the rich black soil that fills the clay pot on the ground beside her. The flowers will root and then she'll give it to . . . well, someone, she has misplaced the person's name.

"Mom? You've got company."

Lily glances around to see her daughter coming across the yard with a slender woman who looks familiar and a dog she definitely knows. "Henry," she calls, and he races toward her, galloping like a magnificent horse, and she throws her arms around him.

"Mom, do you remember Charlie? Charlie Calloway?"

Vague memories stir inside her, secrets that she can't quite seize. "Hi," she says, rising, brushing off her hands.

"It's good to see you again, Mrs. Lincoln."

Lily holds out her hand, then notices that the woman's hands are bandaged. She stares at the bandages, certain she has seen this picture before. "Fire," she says softly.

Charlie and Chrissy look at each other. "See what I mean?" Chrissy says, and Charlie simply nods and sets a cage on the ground.

"About two months ago, I mated Paz. I mean, Henry. Now he's a father." She crouches and opens the cage door.

A pup the same caramel color as Henry pokes his head out and

Lily's heart melts. She reaches inside and helps him all the way out and the pup covers her face with kisses and she laughs and Henry barks.

"He's mine?" Lily exclaims.

"If you want him," Charlie says. "He's the pick of the litter."

And suddenly it comes to her, the sailboat, the fire, the bad man. She goes over to this woman and puts her arms around her, hugging her close. "It's going to be okay now," she says. "You and the pioneer have a lot of work to do, okay?"

She steps back and the woman, astonished, stammers, "I can't thank you enough for everything."

But Lily has already forgotten her. She's on the ground with the pup, with Henry's son, wondering what she'll name him. When she looks up again, Chrissy stands there, hands on her hips. "Doris will be by at noon, Mom. Just wait till she sees this pup."

Lily smiles and sits back on the ground with the pup, content in the knowledge that sometimes in life all the best things come to pass.